C000148249

For Lynwen
With all good wishes

Peter Powell
May '98

WOODREEF

Roscoe Howells

First Impression—1997

ISBN 1 85902 465 3

© Roscoe Howells

Roscoe Howells has asserted his right under the Copyright, Designs and Patents Act, 1988, to be identified as Author of this work.

All rights reserved. No part of this book may be reproduced, stored in a retrieval system, or transmitted in any form or by any means, electronic, electrostatic, magnetic tape, mechanical, photocopying, recording or otherwise, without permission in writing from the Publishers, Gomer Press, Llandysul, Ceredigion.

*Printed in Wales
at Gomer Press, Llandysul, Ceredigion.*

To the memory of those
who had to seek their fortunes overseas
but whose hearts forever yearned for Home.

Pembrokeshire words which appear in this novel

a: he, it
afeart: afraid, frightened
aim: to try, endeavour
all-a-both: both, two together
apple-bird: the bullfinch
balls: small oval lumps of culm mixed with clay and water and
  kneaded by hand in the shape of balls for use as fuel
bitty: small
bloody warriors: wallflowers
bring: to take
budram: gruel consisting of oat-meal steeped in water
burgage: a small field near the house
cabal: row among several people
clegged: constipated
clicksy: giving oneself airs
clom: clay mixed with straw
cluck: of a hen; broody, ready to sit
cockalorum: a rod or wand used by charmers or faith healers
cocklolly: the shearwater
cocklynave: the night cry of the shearwater
court: an enclosure in front of a house, forecourt
croggans: Welsh people who visited the sea-shore in summer
crut: a boy, lad
cuckoo's shoes: dog violets
culm: the slack of anthracite; fuel made of a mixture of this and
  clay
cutty: small
decline: tuberculosis
dog's lugs: foxgloves
drabbit: an imprecation, 'Confound it!'
dram: an open truck on rails used in collieries
drill: furrow or row for seed or potatoes
droppers: fuchsias

dull: half-witted, idiotic
dullery: foolery
dulling: a fool
fair does: fair play
filty fine: very smart, overdressed, showy
firing: fuel
for all, f'rall: in spite of
fox: a single fine day during poor weather
frit: a small person or thing
gambo: a cart with side poles instead of a box
gantling: gantry
greet: friendly, on good terms
gwain: going
hall: the family room in a farmhouse
hisht: be quiet
hollin': shouting, making a great outcry
howsomever: however
hun: term of endearment, abbreviation of 'honey'
indeed-in-double-deed: emphasising an assertion
lake: a stream, brook
main: very much, greatly
mewk: a small sound
middling: moderate, fair
mind: remember
mine: iron ore
molly-hawn: slut, prostitute
molly lamb: pet lamb
nice-gutted: fussy about food
noy: wooden container for salting meat
patches: where iron-ore was dug from the cliffs
peace: to pacify, quieten
piss-a-bed: dandelion
pobbles: pebbles
pollers: people who picked iron ore
pompren: a wooden footbridge
punt: a small rowing boat

rals: *up in the rals*-in a great passion
rammas: a long, rambling story
rappers: foxgloves
rottle-dull: empty-headed, addle-pated
scarly: boisterous, windy
sea-pyat: the oyster catcher
servant, sir: a common form of greeting from a social inferior
skew: settle
slatch: inferior coal or coal dust
sleever: a liquid measure for beer – about ¾ pint
slype: to come or go secretly
so: as
spiddacks: long wooden thatching pegs
stuggy: thick-set, sturdy
stum: smother, bank up the fire at night with culm or balls
summer blossoms: primroses
tack: person, tool or device
taler: the man who tells the tale before the wedding and keeps count of the wedding presents, the best man
tallet: hay-loft over stable; the unceilinged loft of a cottage
thicky: this one, that one
trapsing: trudging, plodding along
tub: cask
wash-in-the-tide: bathe
winch: a deep well from which water is drawn by a windlass
wopple: a lather of sweat
worrit: to worry

PROLOGUE

I, Matt Rodda, am going Home. It was a promise I made to Mother before she died, and I need a holiday.

Father and Mother were still small children when their parents brought them out here to New Zealand. Some of our family had come long before that, and several of the family had gone to Canada.

We have had no word from those in Canada since before the war, and have even lost touch with the family in Wales. To Mother that was a cause for sadness, because she was a great one for family. Nowadays it seems to be fashionable for everybody to be tracing their ancestry, so I laughed and said, all right, I'd be in the fashion.

Mother always encouraged me to write down as much as we knew of the family's story. To the outsider it might sound far-fetched, because some of the Roddas had the second sight, and Mother was one of them. She had a premonition that I would find my true destiny only if I went home to Woodreef, where the first Matt Rodda found his destiny nearly three centuries ago.

Life seems to be all television these days and nobody wants to listen to the old family stories any more. When I was a boy we would sit round the fire of an evening and listen to the same stories over and over and over again. Some of them went back to the time of the first Queen Elizabeth, and even to the Normans who were there before the Tudors. Mother said to write them all down, otherwise everything would be forgotten. Maybe over the years they could have been embellished here and there, but I could only tell them as they have come down to me.

'Young' Matt, Father's great-grandfather, was born before the French Revolution. He had some good schooling and a long head on him, as they used to say, and in a big notebook he recorded something of what he knew and had been told. He was known, even when very old, as 'Young' Matt, because his great-grandfather had been a Matt Rodda, who had arrived at Woodreef before the first Jacobite Rebellion, and had been known as 'Old' Matt. He, too, had written of happenings in his days. There were also some old letters, so, with Mother's marvellous memory, it has been possible to make a record of what happened over the years. Occasionally I would be going through old great-gramfer Matt's books or some of the letters, and it would jog Mother's memory and she would repeat conversations word-for-word from years and years before she was born.

From a special part of Wales they came, known for hundreds of years as Little England Beyond Wales, which Grandma reckoned annoyed some people. Travellers in olden days had called it Little England Beyond Wales because it was so different. The people didn't speak any Welsh at all, only English. It was not ordinary English, though, and we had been brought up to know the old words, and to use them amongst ourselves.

The place from which they came was called Woodreef. Since time out of mind it had never been known by any other name. There was no knowing what it really meant, but somebody once said that it was part English and part Welsh. The wood was obvious, but the reef could have been a corruption of the Welsh word *rhef*, meaning fat or thick, because the woodland thereabouts had been dense, or rich, or thick, in days long gone by. Maybe Welsh speaking people had once lived there, but who would know after all this time?

Sometimes Mother and Father would tease each other by saying they were from two different counties, but we knew that was daft, because they had shown us the place on the map, tucked away in the far corner of Wales in the south-west. One of them would say it was Pembrokeshire, and the other would say Carmarthenshire, but the Carmarthenshire bit was right down in the corner of the county and was Pembrokeshire in everything but name. There was also a map, hundreds of years old, by a man named George Owen, and it had Latin names, and old spellings, which showed this little corner as being in Penbrok as the spelling was at one time.

True, Woodreef was in Carmarthenshire on the bigger, more recent map, but Mother said that didn't count, and Father always finished up by laughing and admitting he knew it to be true, because Gramfer said that all the people round Marros were exactly the same in their speech and their customs as the folk the other side of the stream in Earwear in Pembrokeshire where Mother's people had always been.

Grandma, who had been born and brought up when Queen Victoria was still on the throne, lived to a good old age, and had a great fund of stories of long ago. It was marvellous to hear Gramfer and her talking of the old home and the people, and such a shame that Father and Mother were never able to go back to see their birth-place.

I wrote to a newspaper in Pembrokeshire asking if readers knew anything of the Pembrokeshire Roddas, but there was no response. There was, however, an interesting item in the issue which they sent to me with my letter in it, about a man who had been using his metal-detector and found two silver buttons. Apparently they had the same markings as two silver buttons which we had in our family. We had heard the story of them times without number, so I wrote to the man and have arranged to call on him.

I sent a letter once, addressed to the 'present occupier' at Woodreef, but never had a reply. I shall know the place when I see it, though, because we have the beautiful picture which was painted in springtime long, long ago. A lovely old stone-built house it is, with a chimney rising to a round tower. Grandma said many of the chimneys were like that, and the artist showed all the lovely daffodils, and the snowdrops and primroses, and the furze on the bank just coming into bloom.

There was one small field in the picture with a mass of small daffodils, but I know they are not still there. In later years there was a great fashion for them and they became known as the Tenby daffodil. Tenby is a place near Woodreef and there were fields and fields of the little daffodils in that area, and the bulbs were all dug up and sold. People have always been willing to do anything for money, but times were hard, I suppose, and they would have been glad of any bit of extra, no matter where it came from.

Later in the year, Grandma said, the cabbage rose tree growing by the front door would be a mass of big, heavy-scented pink blossom. There is a glimpse of the river in the picture as well, which Gramfer and Grandma always called a lake, which no doubt sounds funny, but unless it was a big river, they said it was always called a lake. Well, this wasn't a big river, but it was more than a stream, and there were trout there, as well as sewin coming up from where the lake ran into the sea by the New Inn at Earwear.

Before Mother died she read through most of what I have written and put me right on a few points, and jogged my memory about stories Grandma and Gramfer had told me when I was a boy.

There was much which I had to omit, and I have said hardly anything about their old country customs, their superstitions, or their old-fashioned cures in times of sickness, with their wonderful herbal medicines and ointments. Then there were the other times of the outbreaks of awful fevers, which no medicines could cure, and which wiped out whole families.

There were the seasonal practices in their farming, such as the children picking the stones in the hayfields before 'locking up' as they used to call it, the camaraderie at haymaking time, helping back from one farm to another, the women taking the drink and the food out to the men, and the meal round the kitchen table when the day's work was done. And with mention of customs, there was that friendly business of a man without any land of his own having a drill of potatoes in a farmer's field and, in return, helping when it came haymaking and harvest, and time for the farmer to lift his own potatoes.

How much I could have written about their pastimes and the children's games, all the dogs and cats, and the horses and other animals, which were for ever a part of their lives.

Then there were the weddings and the funerals, and the customs which went with them. There was the pig-killing, the breaking-in of young horses, and the tradition of the blacksmith

14

shop where boys with warts used to go to soak their hands in the water in which the blacksmith used to dip the red-hot iron horse-shoes when he was shaping them.

Nor have I said much about the chapel, the singing and the prayers, and the way people would discuss the sermon as they walked home, and how some of them were very devout and would not do certain jobs on Sunday, and were very strict and narrow about games of cards and dances and one thing and another.

I started writing about some of these things in places, but had to leave it out, otherwise there would have been no end to it. Much of it about the long line of ancestors way back over the years would be difficult for outsiders to follow, wondering who was who for much of the time. Even the younger ones of the family may not be able to follow it. But that will not matter. It is the story which is important.

Now, at forty years of age, for the first time in my life I am going Home, and I will fill in some of the gaps here and there by talking to local people who will know much more than I do.

Mother said to start at Woodreef because she was convinced that from there I would be able to trace the Canadian Roddas. She spoke to me of one or two other premonitions as well, but I would not dream of repeating them here because people would laugh at me.

I have arranged to hire a car when I arrive, and then I shall drive towards the west, where the golden sun sinks in the hills, just as in the song which Mother used to sing. A lovely voice she had, and the song was called, 'My Little Grey Home In The West.'

And I shall keep on driving until I reach Home.

CHAPTER 1

1710 - 1715

1

It was only by chance that the first Matt Rodda came to Earwear. And that was best part of three hundred years ago. Maybe if the export trade in cloth and wool, and leather from the tanners, had not died, he would never have thrown in his lot in the other sort of Trade with the crew running for the Gentlemen. So that was chance, too.

All up along the coast from his native Cornwall he had worked in the traders since he had gone to sea as a boy. Right up to Gower, and north to Aberaeron, he knew every bluff and bay, and every creek running inland from the great waterway of Milford Haven. Much of it had been legitimate trade, but the wars with the Frenchmen were dragging on, and there was a heavy duty on brandy, tobacco and silks. So the Trade in all these, and occasionally salt, was there for the taking, and the chance was too good to miss. There was good money to be made in handling the contraband, and excitement to go with it.

Little enough did he remember about the place where he had been born and spent his early boyhood. His father had been lost at sea, and his mother had died young. Her sister, Etta, had cared for him for a time, and Parson Tregellis had taken an interest in him and taught him to read and write, and he was well spoken. But that was by no means all. Parson Tregellis had also taught Matt something about the Trade, because the vicarage cellar was never without an adequate supply of brandy on which no duty had ever been paid.

Matt had a long head on him, too, as the saying was, and he had always been big enough to take care of himself, even against older boys. Then Etta had picked up with a drunken sailor, and

Matt had gone to sea. Once aboard the *Cornish Princess* it had come as no surprise to him to learn that Parson Tregellis had a part share in her, which was maybe why the skipper, Hezekiah Trevanion, had accepted him so readily.

Bearded and broad-shouldered, Trevanion was a striking figure. That had been Matt's first impression, and it had been strengthened when he had noticed the anchor tattoed on the back of Trevanion's right hand. On the little finger of his left hand was a twisted gold ring, with a snake's head which had a ruby for its eye. Right from the start, he had treated Matt well enough, which was by no means the case with many lads he knew who had gone aboard ship.

Matt, for his part, was interested to learn from the skipper's stories of voyages to far-off lands, and Trevanion had encouraged him to read and broaden his mind in the same way as Parson Tregellis had always done, and the years of his youth had hurried by. He was twenty now, but still with no real home, and he often wondered if he would ever have a chance to settle down. Then, on that first run into Earwear, in the year 1710, he met Mona.

He had been working with the Gentlemen for nearly two years, and had heard about the Trade at Earwear but, for the most part, the *Cornish Princess*, a hundred ton schooner, had been working the creeks and small harbours round the far west of the rugged Pembrokeshire coast, and up towards Cardigan. On more than one occasion they had sailed into Carmarthen Bay with legitimate cargoes, and all the way up the Towy river to the great commercial and administrative centre of Carmarthen itself. They had done much good Trade, too, at Manorbier, round the coast from Caldey, and even at Tenby across the bay from Earwear. But the beach at Earwear, by all account, was no place for any sort of boat if there was a sea running, especially from the sou'west, and it was from there that the worst of the weather came. So it was hardly worth the risk.

On this trip, late of an autumn afternoon, they were bound for Solva in the north of the county with a cargo which included silk and brandy. They had rounded Worm's Head, and the *Cornish Princess* was beating up across Carmarthen Bay from Gower, under a moderate off-shore breeze from the north east, when they were hailed by a small fishing boat working out of Laugharne. The danger was clear. Some Jacobite messenger was believed to have taken ship from France and was being watched for at St Ann's Head off Milford. The militia were out in strength, and it could be bad business for any boat involved in the Trade making for Solva.

'Howsomever,' said Eli Canavan, who came aboard the *Cornish Princess*, 'there be a Gentleman at Earwear as be willin' to do a deal for all. If so be thou's 'oud fancy it I'll bring thee in there.'

Of stuggy build, Eli Canavan was. Although Matt, at over six feet, topped him by several inches, there was yet an air of quiet strength about him, with his dark Celtic features and unflinching brown eyes, whereas Matt, more of the Saxon colouring, was fair-haired and blue-eyed.

Matt had always found it somewhat difficult to communicate once they found themselves further up in the Welsh-speaking areas anywhere north of about Solva. Now, not for the first time, he recognised, as Eli spoke, how alike the speech was all round this coast to their own way of speaking, and how many of the words, too, he had so often heard being used on the Gower coast. In fact Trevanion had once told him that his own family had gone down to Cornwall from these parts and had later married into the Trevanions. It was his mother, he said, who had married a Trevanion, and she had retained her broad Pembrokeshire accent to the end of her days. There had to be a common bond somewhere with settlers who had come from overseas in years gone by.

2

Darkness had long since fallen, and a pale moon was rising above the far-off Towy Estuary, when the *Cornish Princess* hove to under Eli's guidance in the shadows below the high cliff of Dolman.

In later years Matt was to give thanks many a time for having met up with Eli. There was nothing about the coast of Carmarthen Bay he did not know, all the way down from the treacherous Cefn Sidan sands to Ginst Point off the Laugharne Estuary, and beyond the great stretch of Pendine sands past Gilman Point and Ragwen, westwards to Marros, Teague's Dingle and Telpyn, to the Blackhorn caves running inland from the great rock known as Black Hall off Earwear. Laugharne may have been his cradle, but the whole of Carmarthen Bay was his oyster. Even more important, he knew the people, and the ones who could be trusted. That was to say, as far as anybody in life could be trusted. Over the years Matt was to learn that the people of Laugharne were a close-knit crowd, but he found Eli Canavan to be loyal right to the end.

A dim light had already beamed fitfully three times to show that the coast was clear, and they were near enough in-shore to hear the waves lapping the beach. It was not long before a punt pulled alongside with a cloaked figure in the sternsheets, a rope ladder was lowered for him, and he came aboard with assured dexterity. Trevanion took him below deck and nodded for Eli to go with them.

It struck Matt afterwards that Eli's confederates, whoever they were, must have had every confidence in his ability to carry out his mission, because shadowy figures, who had been waiting in readiness, were soon swarming aboard and off-loading bales and tubs into small boats, which appeared from nowhere out of the shadows, and disappeared as quickly along the rocky coastline to the east. Then, as the moon rose higher, making a swath across the water, Matt saw the dim outline of several cobs and ponies on the beach, as a small flock of sea-pyats bleeped their evident disapproval of this nocturnal disturbance.

In the midst of these well-drilled operations, Eli Canavan went off in the punt with the cloaked figure, and Hezekiah Trevanion called Matt to the rail from which vantage point he was keeping a keen eye on all that was going on.

'We've done a middlin' good deal,' Hezekiah said, as he took his pipe from his mouth and spat over the side. 'That was the

Squire's man. And fair does, a didn't try to screw me down too tight just because a knowed we had to get shut of this lot an' couldn't run in nowhere else. By all account there's good business to be done here. But the landin' can be main scarly on times.'

'Who's the Squire?' Matt said.

'Squire Elliot. A's strong for the Old Faith, but this Eli Canavan reckons a's square to deal with. Canavan seems to know what a's about an' a says we can run plenty o' stuff in up along to'rds Laugharne an' still do business down here with the Squire.'

Trevanion clearly had some idea in his head, but it took Matt by surprise when he said, 'I'll tell thee what I'd like thee to do. Thou's for ever be on about settlin' down, so how would it be to have a spell ashore here to see what the chances be like for all?'

'What you got in mind, Cap'n?' Matt asked.

'There be a good head on thee. Canavan knows a man who could have a place for thee. Lives up along the valley at a farm called Woodreef. A's strong in the Trade an' lookin' for business. The trouble be, this be no place much for landin'. Canavan reckons that we could land up along his way and the Woodreef man could do good trade with this Squire Elliot. 'Twould be main helpful for us if thou could'st get thy snout in the trough for all.'

'How long for?'

'Till the spring maybe. We got a couple o' good runs on afore that, but come the spring an' I reckons by then thou could'st have a fair sort o' notion as to how the wind be blowin' round here.'

It had never been truly in Matt's heart to go to sea. Had it not been for the way things had turned out with Etta, he would have been happy enough to stay ashore. The country life had ever been in his blood, and never had he yearned for the home he had left, such as it was and for what little he could remember of it, more than when they were sailing close inshore, and he could see cattle and sheep grazing, and folks working in the fields of the coastal areas.

The night's work accomplished, the *Cornish Princess* had been made ready for sailing by the time a blood-red sun was coming up over the twin humps of Gower Peninsula on the south-east horizon. Two men had gone ashore for casks of fresh water, and Eli Canavan had sent a character to Hezekiah Trevanion with a wether in prime condition, just fit for slaughter. Long before the schooner had weighed anchor and was running before an off-shore wind towards Caldey, Matt Rodda was sitting down at a scrubbed oak table to a hearty breakfast of ham and eggs, bread thick cut, and a mug of steaming coffee, at the New Inn.

3

Peat was burning with a red glow in the wide, open fireplace, and hams, encased in muslin, hung from the smoke-blackened beams where the brass and copper utensils sparkled. Sam Rawles, a weather-beaten character of cheerful visage, was by no means unfriendly, but Matt soon understood that he was one of those who deemed it wiser to keep a still tongue in the presence of strangers. And to Sam Rawles, as yet, this 'man from off', who had just come ashore, was an unknown quantity.

Of any of last night's cargo to come ashore, there was never a sign, although it had been common knowledge to the crew of the *Cornish Princess* that it was to the cellars of this hostelry that the pannier-laden cobs and ponies had brought much of it. It was to be some little time before Matt was to become privy to the secret of the underground tunnel which led from the Inn to Squire Elliot's mansion at Earwear.

Nothing further or more definite had been said about the place called Woodreef but, such was the apparently far-reaching influence of Eli Canavan, it was not entirely surprising to Matt when Sam Rawles came in to say that the lad from Woodreef was outside. And Matt discovered that the lad also had a pony and gig, which had come for the specific purpose of conveying the 'man from off' to his new home, along with whatever possessions he might have.

Apart from the money he had saved with the bank at Truro, he had a few golden pieces and some silver pounds hidden in his seaman's chest. He also had two canvas kit bags with such spare clothes as he owned. As Matt came out, Nipper Jim tugged his forelock and said, 'Servant, sir.'

He could have been no more than ten or eleven years of age, but he handled Kit, the grey roan Welsh pony, with practised ease as he sat with his feet on the dashboard of the gig. To his surprise, the 'man from off' said he would walk.

'I've been at sea so long, Nipper,' Matt said, 'it's a nice change to feel the good, firm land under my feet.'

'Ha'st thou been at sea long, then?'

'Since I was not much older than you are now.'

'In the Trade with the Gentlemen is it?'

'I've been doing a bit with them, but I been all over before that. How about you?'

'Been at Woodreef since I can remember. Never had no father nor mother. But I be good with the hosses. Gaffer says he never seen the likes of it. Gaffer been good to me.'

'Who d'you call Gaffer?'

'Mister Barlow.'

'Is he in the Trade?'

Nipper Jim gave Matt what might have been described as an old-fashioned look. 'You be a man from off,' he said, 'an' what they says in the Trade is them as asks no questions isn't told no lies. An' Miss Mona alus says to me not to tell no lies. So if thou doesn't ask me no questions then I can't be tellin' no lies can I?'

Matt smiled, 'Well done, Nipper,' he said. 'Well done. And who's Miss Mona?'

'Gaffer's daughter. She been good to me as well. Learned me to read and write, but not much. I likes the hosses best.'

At this point, as they passed beneath a high, overhanging rock, the track narrowed, Matt dropped back behind the cart, and conversation for the time being had to cease. Nothing loath, he was able to take in more of his surroundings as the road led inland from the rear of the New Inn, through a richly wooded valley.

23

Down the bed of this valley a small river was rushing, muddied from recent autumn rain. Matt was to learn before long that it was referred to, as were all such streams, as a lake. He needed no-one to tell him, however, that it would be rich in sewin and trout.

The trees, oak and beech, elm and sycamore, ash, and areas of alder down near the river, were a riot of autumn colours, copper and russets and burnished gold, nuts were dropping from the hazels, and red squirrels were busy in the tracery overhead. Along the way a few cottagers eyed him speculatively, but nodded or raised a hand in cheerful greeting.

Eventually, there was a fork in the track and they began to climb the side of a precipitous slope. The woodland towered above them on their right and, in places, whenever a gap opened between the trees to their left, Matt looked down on the magic of the valley below. The stout little pony was pushing hard against the collar hereabouts, and Nipper Jim jumped down to walk alongside her with his hand on the bridle.

And so they came at last to Woodreef.

4

Matt was never to forget that day. It was autumn, with heather a riot of colour, and a great stillness heavy on the air.

But it was not for any of this that Matt would remember this day. Breath-taking and strangely peaceful though the loveliness of it all was, what else could it do but pale into insignificance beside that memory which must ever remain in his heart and in his mind for all time? For it was on this day that he first set eyes on Mona and, as he looked into her grey blue eyes, he knew that never again would he want to go to sea, even though he could not know then that this place would mean home to him for the rest of his life.

Almost unnoticed, Nipper had unloaded Matt's few belongings and gone off to the stable to unharness Kit.

Matt had seen but little of women during his years at sea, and he had never gone with those of the crew who sought the company and services of the slatternly molly-hawns and young dolly-mops in some of the ports where the *Cornish Princess* had been a regular caller. And now they seemed a world away from this lovely vision of purity in a simple blue gown that showed the blossoming of her slender figure from girlhood into young womanhood. Her light brown hair had been drawn up and swept back from her rounded forehead. A smile seemed to be for ever playing on her rosy lips. Her chin was firm, and her cheeks were dimpled. She looked him straight in the eye as they met by the courtyard gate, and then, sensing the intensity of his gaze, she coloured slightly and gave a slight curtsy.

Matt knew his manners better than to offer her his hand, but then she gave her own hand to him in a firm handshake, and said, 'You'll be the man from off Eli told us to expect.'

'My name's Matthew,' Matt said. 'Matt everybody calls me. Matt Rodda. And you'll be Miss Mona.'

'Mona Barlow. Father's away to Earwear this morning, but he shouldn't be long.'

'Busy in the Trade, no doubt, after last night's doings I suppose.'

'I shouldn't wonder,' Mona laughed, and her laughter was bright and carefree. 'But come you in and have something to eat.'

'No indeed, thank you, Miss. Nothing to eat. Sam Rawles has just fed me like a prize fighting cock.'

'Well, bring your things in anyway. There's a room ready for you.'

'And how much do you know about the Trade?'

'You'd better talk to Father about that. What's your interest in the Trade?'

'That's why I'm here, isn't it?'

'Well, talk to Father, then.'

'You're as close as Nipper Jim, I see.'

'And you won't get much out of him, either.'

'Yes, I've found that out already.'

'What else have you found out?'

Matt sensed a note of apprehension in her manner.

'I've heard it said that some of you are strong in the Old Faith round here.'

A troubled, yet defiant look, came over the girl's face as she frowned slightly. 'Would that be so bad, would you say?'

'Not all that bad,' Matt said. 'But dangerous in these times maybe.'

'We'd die for the Faith if we had to.'

She went quiet for some moments before looking earnestly at Matt and saying, 'You don't look like the sort of man to betray us.'

Matt gave her a warm smile. 'I like to think I wouldn't betray anybody. But thank you for the compliment even so, Miss.'

Mona, too, smiled again, and said, 'In that case, never mind about the Miss. My name's Mona.'

And from that moment their friendship was to grow, and to blossom into love, although it was to be another five years before they married.

5

For Matt Rodda, Woodreef meant a new world and a new life. Much though he had known in his boyhood of things of the countryside, this was different. Life here seemed to be a world on its own.

The years of his youth spent at sea had made him self-sufficient and well able to take care of himself, but here there was much which was new to him.

Seth Barlow had made him welcome right from the start. A bluff character in late middle age, he had, Matt soon learned, married later in life than most men, and Mona had been the only child of a brief marriage. Her mother, a girl from Earwear, had died young when Mona was born, so that Mona was now mistress of the household. All this Matt could easily accept and understand. There were, however, so many undertones.

Hezekiah Trevanion had indeed spoken truth when he said that some of them were strong in the Old Faith. It was an elderly priest who had given Mona such schooling as she had and, as he became accepted and trusted, Matt began to learn more of the effort she and her father would make to get to Mass at Earwear. It was there that one of Squire Elliot's forbears had long ago built his own private chapel. There was a priest-hole for a hiding place for the priest, and there was the tunnel of which Matt had known nothing when they had landed their cargo on the night when he had first come this way.

It was no small consideration in these times, as he had learned from old Parson Tregellis, to admit to Roman Catholic sympathies, let alone to practise in the Faith. Yet, some there were in Wales who so hated the new form of religion which had been foisted on them by the English oppressors that, rather than accept it, they became Dissenters. But some, dwindling sadly in numbers now, stuck faithfully to the beliefs which had been handed down to them. Squire Elliot was one of them.

Matt was not sure of Gaffer Barlow, but he noticed that Mona's father always went secretly with her to Mass at Earwear. In due course, Matt was to learn from Mona that her father had been true to her mother's memory in the promise he had made to her on her death-bed to bring their little girl up in the Faith. Later, when Matt accompanied them when they went to the Anglican church at Marros, which they had to do sometimes rather than arouse suspicion or invoke fines for non-attendance, he would notice her lips moving silently as, with eyes closed, she surreptitiously fingered the beads of her rosary throughout the Vicar's sermon. She treasured her rosary, too, because it had belonged to the mother she had never known, and had been blessed by a priest who had suffered much and had eventually died for the Faith.

Whatever hardships and privations were known to those on the land at this time, they reckoned in the valley of Woodreef that there were many who were faring far worse. The tunnel, which enabled Mona and her father to attend Mass secretly at Earwear, was also an important link for those in the Trade with the

Gentlemen. More important still, perhaps, was the fact that Gaffer Barlow, and Squire Elliot, too, for that matter, were prepared to share some of the fruits of their illegally gotten gains. Maybe, Matt thought, it was sheer good-heartedness, or maybe it was the price to be paid for loyalty and connivance. If so, it was a price worth paying.

Miserable though the pittance was which came from the land itself, there were other activities from which the valley hummed with life. The most immediately useful to Matt was the wool and cloth mill at Earwear, and Tucking Mill, close downstream below Woodreef itself. In all of the cottages, too, the women were carding wool and busy at their spinning wheels, and the cloth which they wove went to Tucking Mill for the fulling and dying to finish it. Twice a year the finished product went to the buyers who came to the big fairs at Laugharne.

The family at Tucking Mill were the Kerseys, direct descendants of the Flemish weavers, who had come over seven centuries before, not long after the Norman Conquest, and had practised the skills of their trade ever since. Here, Matt was to buy a length of best kerseymere for the making of a pair of knee breeches and a three-quarter length coat for best. He bought a length of heavier tweed as well, for everyday wear, and there was a tailor in the valley to make the garments.

There was a cobbler, too, so it was not long before he was able to discard his more habitual ganzy and seaman's boots for footwear made from leather which had also been produced, if not in the valley, then near enough to it beyond the coast road, at the tan pits which were in the dingle running down to the beach at Telpyn. There was lime to be had for the tan pits from the kiln at the Mead, just beyond Earwear.

Even though there was no longer any export trade in the products of the tannery and the woollen mill, they were still busy producing to supply the local need. One of the basic necessities for the treatment of the skins from the tanning pits was a supply of pigeon dung, and there was a mediaeval dovecot at Woodreef where pigeons were kept for the purpose, as well as for producing young birds for the oven occasionally. The dovecot had been built in the years after the Normans came, and Gaffer Barlow could relate details of his family way back to those far-off days. The valley was rich in the trees which produced the bark for the tanners, as it was with the alder and sycamore trees from which the clogs were made, and so busy were several of the valley dwellers in the making of clogs in their cottage homes, that one part was known as Clog Valley. The clog-making, like the weaving, was a skill which had been brought over by the Flemish settlers. Clogs were cheaper to buy than leather, and harder wearing.

For firing, too, they were well provided. Apart from a sufficiency of wood for burning, they were more fortunate than the folks of some areas because there was a fine moor of peat at Earwear, and Squire Elliot was generous in allowing the cottagers to avail themselves of it. For the rest they had to drive coal dust from the field pits, and slime from the beach at Earwear where there had been a vast forest a few thousand years ago. Although most of the trees had now decayed to become slime, when the autumn gales churned up the sand there were still tree stumps, and even bunches of decaying nuts, sometimes to be seen clearly. On one occasion Matt dug up the great antlers of some long extinct species.

6

Before Matt had begun picking up his knowledge of these matters, however, a little here, a little there, and become more and more part of the life of the valley, news had come of an event that was to change the whole course of his life.

The original intention had been for Matt to spend the winter months as far as possible making contacts in this area, which was not too familiar to Hezekiah Trevanion, firstly for legitimate business up the estuary of the great Towy river to the important and busy port of Carmarthen, as a cover for the considerably more remunerative Trade in the running of contraband further along the wild and lonely coast to the west. The contacts for this clandestine trade would also need to be made, but far more discreetly, for it was known only too well that almost everywhere in the world there would be a Judas. The strength of the excise presence would need to be assessed, the revenue men identified, and the facts ascertained as to those amongst them who could be bought. Hezekiah Trevanion was a great believer in the well-worn maxim that every man had his price.

It had soon become evident to Matt that, in all of these contacts and enquiries, Eli Canavan would figure prominently.

'It isn't what thee knows, fellah', Eli said at one of their early meetings. 'It's who thee knows.'

Well, Matt knew Eli for a start, and his instinct told him that the relationship would most probably be to his advantage.

Spring had come early in the benign climate, and the snowdrops covering the banks of the river in great drifts were already being overtaken by the profusion of golden daffodils. The charcoal burning of winter had finished, and the few itinerant burners had moved on, for the sap was rising in the trees, and the workers were making a start on the urgent work for that short season of but a few months during which it was possible to strip the bark needed by the tanners. Then Eli Canavan brought the news that the *Cornish Princess* had fallen foul of the revenue men at last.

Word had come by way of a ship putting in to Laugharne, and it was not a happy story. Whilst Hezekiah Trevanion had always understood that every man had his price, it came hard for him when he was to discover that the old maxim applied equally to a member of his own crew.

It was always easy to be wise after the event, but it had not come entirely as a surprise to Matt, who remembered well the ageing, shifty-eyed sea-dog who had bragged that when he was young he had been with Tom Salkeld, the murderous pirate who had taken the island of Lundy and set up his well-defended base in that stronghold commanding the Bristol Channel. Matt was inclined to doubt it, if only over a question of age, but now, it turned out, he had bitten the hand that had fed him. There had been a fight, and one of Trevanion's crew had been taken. Even so, there was still a lack of witnesses who would dare to testify. A magistrate with more than a passing personal interest in the trade had contrived to intervene, and the eventual result had been nothing more serious than an end to the freebooting activities of that particular vessel, because Parson Tregellis was one of those who deemed it wise to sell his share, and the *Cornish Princess* fell into other hands.

Shortly afterwards, Eli Canavan was able to report that Hezekiah Trevanion had called it a day himself and, with the money he had put by, together with his own share from the sale of his beloved ship, had swallowed the anchor and set himself up in a snug little inn, appropriately enough called 'The Ship Aground', at the head of an inlet on the Cornish coast. Old habits, it seemed, died hard. He had the contacts, and there was still good money to be made.

So it was that Matt Rodda came to Woodreef, not merely for the winter, as intended, but for the rest of his long life.

7

Had it not been for the Trade, with the active support of Squire Elliot, times would have been desperate indeed for those who sought to wrest a meagre living from the land. There was a little to be made, too, from driving coal from the many field pits to the boats which came in to the beach at Wisemansbridge beyond Earwear. It meant neglecting the land, but at least it put a crust in the children's mouths. For those without the few extra pence which came from such sources, it was poverty and hardship beyond description.

A few years after Matt's arrival a school was opened at Earwear in a house provided by Squire Elliot, and endowed by a relation of his, Sir John Philipps. The 'Good' Sir John, he was known as.

Anything that Squire Elliot did was likely to find favour with Mona, and she had certainly been pleased to hear of this particular idea.

'It's a terrible shame for country children to have no chance to learn anything in life,' she said.

Matt had been well taught by Parson Tregellis, and he agreed with her. Even so, he loved to tease her sometimes.

'And what good d'you reckon it'll do 'em?' he said.

'Well, I told you, didn't I? It's to do with the Society for Promoting Christian Knowledge.'

Matt laughed and said, 'I suppose they could do worse than try to improve some of these savages. What'll they teach 'em?'

'For goodness sake, Matt! If they can learn to read, at least they might have a chance to understand something about the Scriptures. And they can get a bit of a grasp of the basics of things that will be useful to them.'

'Such as what?'

'Such as farming for the boys, and seamanship. And maybe domestic service for the girls.'

Matt became serious. 'The only trouble is,' he said, 'the poor souls will probably find they'll have to be working on the land most of the time. Or worse still, down the pits.'

Mona knew it to be true. Full of compassion, she said, 'Well, the Squire's doing his best. And nobody can do better than that.'

It seemed to Matt that the Elliots had always been strong in the Faith and doing their bit for God. A couple of hundred years earlier an ancestor of Squire Elliot had built the church at the top of the hill, and had then added a chantry for the singing of Masses for his own soul, and for the souls of any of his family who might subsequently be buried there.

'But that awful old King Henry stole the church from us,' Mona would say. 'He was the one. Stole the churches from us. All the churches. Including our church, where Mother's ancestors had worshipped for years. And then he put a stop to the singing of Masses, and so nobody was buried in the chantry after all.'

But the road up to the church was still known as Chantry Lane, and by the wayside there were cottages where there were folk who remained true to the Faith and to the Squire.

Although Hezekiah Trevanion had ceased to operate in the Trade, there remained plenty of others who, like their fathers before them, had worked the territory for generations. The coast from Earwear all the way up to the Laugharne Estuary was by no means ideal for such operations. There were no sheltered creeks and bays, so there was a much higher risk from the elements, exposed as the open beaches were to sou'west winds and high running seas. But the few scattered farmsteads and cottages were remote and lonely, and there was such a length of coast involved that the revenue men had a well-nigh impossible task on their hands. And Earwear still had its share of the Trade, even though those involved had not earned the same unenviable reputation as some of the folk, the wreckers intent on plunder, over towards Pendine, who used false lights to lure ships to their doom on the inhospitable coast.

By the time news came of Hezekiah Trevanion's enforced exit from the Trade, the relationship between Matt and Mona had already begun to deepen, and her father had found Matt not only a capable and ready ally, whose strength was of great benefit in the handling of tubs and bales, but one with rather more learning than many, and with a good head for figures. So it was that he became accepted without question as part of the household. The servants deferred to him, and to Nipper Jim he was a hero who had sailed the seas and 'been all over'. The three maid servants slept together in a loft above the big kitchen, and Nipper Jim and the two men servants of the farm in the loft over the stable. From the beginning, Matt had been given the little bedroom at the back, overlooking the wild acres of heather and gorse running up beyond the hovel known as the Caban, towards Crunwear and the quarries below Llanteague.

Matt was interested in the Caban, and how it had come by its name. To him, a cabin had only ever meant something on a ship. It was Mona, as so often happened in those early days, who was the one he asked, and who told him the meaning of the name, and the custom whereby the Caban had come to be built.

'It comes from the Welsh,' she said.

'Do you speak Welsh, then?'

'Of course I don't. But I know a bit of history.'

'So how d'you explain a name like that?'

'Very easy,' Mona said. 'From the Welsh, *Caban-unnos*, or *Tŷ-unnos*. They reckon it means house in a night. 'Twas a custom going back to the time of the great Welsh lawgiver, Hywel Dda. If a house could be built in a night and the fire was alight by morning, and smoke going up the chimney, then it belonged to whoever had built it, along with the bit of land that went with it. So when anybody wanted to build a house like that, they had the materials ready and the neighbours would all pitch in and do the job overnight.'

Matt found it hard to believe. 'How could anybody build a house in a night?' he said.

Mona laughed, 'Oh, of course, it couldn't be much of a house, being built in a short time like that.'

'Well, what did they build it of, then?'

'Just clom walls, mixed with straw or brambles, and a bit of rush on the roof for thatch. And it didn't even matter if there wasn't a chimney, as long as there was a hole in the roof with smoke going up through it.'

She smiled her sad little smile then, and said, 'But at least it was somewhere for the poor souls to live. And it could always be improved on later, and the rush thatch on the roof strengthened.'

It was perhaps Matt's interest in the character who lived at the Caban which had prompted his question, as much as any interest he might have professed in the name itself, but when he came to know the house with its low doorway he thought it something of a contradiction to find the furniture to be of such a solid and substantial nature. There was a kitchen table made of oak, an arm chair, too, and three kitchen chairs, all of oak. There was a solid kitchen dresser with beautiful dishes and plates of delft, which Matt was subsequently to learn had come from one of the many shipwrecks along Marros beach. There was a skew, which also served to partition off the sleeping area, and in which there was a cupboard bed, as well as a rough-hewn bed of oak boards covered by a patchwork quilt. The roofing timbers, too, were rough-hewn. And the dresser, the skew and the cupboard, like the table and the chairs, were all made from oak grown in the valley and fashioned by valley craftsmen. An iron oven was alongside the ball fire in the iron grate. The fire, burning night and day, would be sorely needed to keep out at least some of the damp from the miserable hovel.

Will Squint Eye, who lived there, was a relation of Eli Canavan, but that was nothing to go by because, as far as Matt could make out, nearly everybody was related to everybody else somewhere or other along the line. And they were not always all that greet. Will Squint seemed to be genuine enough, but you could never be too careful.

'You don't need to worry about Will,' Mona said. 'He's the salt of the earth.'

Then, during the running of a small cargo of brandy tubs, Matt became privy to the secret of the tunnel from New Inn to the mansion at Earwear. It was on the same occasion that he was eventually to meet Squire Elliot's man, Henry Philbert.

The door to the entrance of the tunnel at the New Inn end was in the cellar, cunningly concealed behind an old oak high-backed skew. Beautifully arched, and fashioned of dressed stone, the tunnel was surprisingly dry for the whole of its length of maybe half-a-mile to the roomy cellars below the mansion. By the flickering light of the lanterns Matt cast his eyes about the cellars and reckoned that, even if Squire Elliot and his friends never took delivery of another drop of brandy or fine French wine, they would need to have a powerful thirst for many a long day to drink their way through the stock the Squire had already laid by. Will Squint was one of the trusted company, and it was then Matt knew for sure that Mona's assessment of him, even if it was no more than woman's instinct, must be right.

By this time, too, Will Squint would seem to have been

35

satisfied that he could trust Matt, because it was on the occasion of the running of this particular cargo that he told Matt of the building of the tunnel a hundred years previously.

'How come you know so much about it, Will?' Matt asked him.

'My gramfer,' Will said.

'Your gramfer?'

'Why, aye, boy. A worked on it hisself. And 'tis still only them as uses it as knows all that much about it.'

'How d'you make that out?'

'Well 'tisn't the sort of thing to go shoutin' about all over the place is it?'

'Didn't everybody know when it was being dug?'

'Not like that.'

'No?'

'Why, no, fellah! There was a mortal lot of tunnels bein' dug at that time. There was a couple bein' dug down at Crickdam when they was diggin' the mine out at the Patches.'

'The mine?'

'Th'iron mine. Th'iron ore as they calls it. There was coal there as well. An' then there was another tunnel bein' dug for the coal into the bank above the mansion down at Rhydlancoed, an' a couple more as I don't know nothin' much about f'rall.'

'So what did they say this tunnel was bein' dug for?'

Will Squint chuckled. 'That was just it by all account. The ones workin' on it was all in the Trade with th'owld Squire, an' nobody else never asked no questions. With tunnels bein' dug all over the place one more didn't make no difference like that.'

At the darkest recess of the far cellar under the mansion, there was a loose flagstone, which gave access to steps leading up to the chapel. Looking round as if to ensure that there was no-one else within earshot, Will lowered his voice and said, 'I knows I can tell thee because Miss Mona trusts thee. What only a very few of us knows is that the Trade isn't all as the tunnel is used for.'

'The Old Faith, you mean?'

'That's it,' Will said. 'There's a good many of us secret Catholics

36

as been glad to be able to come and go over the years along this owld tunnel.'

Lowering the flagstone back into place, Will said, 'I won't show thee now with thicky Philbert about, but halfway up the steps is a panel where the priest's hidey-hole is let into the wall of the mansion itself.'

Henry Philbert, Matt gathered, was often present when a cargo was delivered through the tunnel, and it had soon become clear that he was very much the trusted agent of the Squire, who apparently spent some of his time at his other residence at Boulston, near the County town of Haverfordwest. Until the meeting when Will Squint initiated him into the secrets of the tunnel, Matt had only ever seen Henry Philbert that momentous night when he had come aboard the *Cornish Princess*, when Hezekiah Trevanion had put in during an emergency to land his cargo at the Blackhorn caves, and then the agent had been merely a shadowy and heavily cloaked figure. Even so, he had exuded an air of authority and efficiency.

Dark haired and brown eyed, he was a comparatively young man of medium height and pleasant demeanour. His suit of broadcloth was well cut, but he was not overdressed. Nor could his manner in any way be faulted, and yet Matt's instinct told him somehow that the manner could be no more than a facade and altogether too charming. It spoke volumes for Matt that Will Squint had been wary of saying anything within Philbert's hearing. Matt suspected this still further when Mona told him that Philbert would not always be at the Mass.

'There are many times,' she said, 'when he should and could be at the Mass, and he is not there.'

To Mona, that was manifestly a serious sin, and Matt had already learned enough of her Faith and her goodness to know better than to tease her on that score.

8

In the summer time, five years after the *Cornish Princess* had paid her one brief visit to that remote part of the coast, Matt and Mona were married.

Even when they had declared their love and were talking of marriage, Mona did not seem to mind that Matt was not of the one True Faith. She loved him, he was a good man, and that was all that mattered to her. Time was when the Law said that, for the marriage to be valid, it was necessary to have the parson. But for years recusants had not bothered, and the Law ignored them. To Catholics, Mona said, marriage was a private and personal commitment. Even so, it was a source of great joy to her that the priest came to Woodreef for the ceremony in the hall, to bless them and to say Mass. That part was in Latin and Matt did not understand it, but it had so obviously been a source of great happiness to Mona that, such was the depth of his love for her, it gave him great happiness, too.

As time went by, Matt felt that he was beginning to understand something of her Faith. Once when he had gone by the underground passage to collect a small keg of brandy, Mona had gone with him to see the priest for confession. Afterwards, Matt crept up to the little private chapel to look for her. Oblivious to all else, she was kneeling, fingering the beads of her beloved rosary, and gazing up rapturously at the beautiful little stained glass window with its picture of the Crucifixion, and Mary, the Mother of Jesus, weeping at the foot of the Cross.

Father Pascal, a small, bright-eyed Frenchman, by no means in the first flush of youth, had been at Earwear mansion for some years, studying so it was said, but living quietly, teaching, and saying Mass regularly for the Faithful. It made life no easier for him that there was now a strong undercurrent of feeling running against the Catholics. Their every move was watched by some, and no doubt duly reported on.

Much of the trouble locally sprang from the nearness and

accessibility of the coastal area to Catholic Ireland, to say nothing of the presence of Irish Catholics who had settled in the area. About twenty years ago Catholic King James II had drafted many Irish soldiers into his army, and some of them who had come over stayed on.

It was one such, by the name of O'Fagan, who had built a tŷ-unnos in the richly wooded valley which ran down to the wild and lonely beach on the Marros side of Telpyn. One of his mates had referred to him as 'a broth of a boy.' Be that as it may, he was only ever known as Teague, because Teague was the local name for an Irishman and, as time went by, the name Teague's Dingle, came into being, because that was where Teague lived. How he lived was anybody's guess. If pressed, he would probably have said, the best he could.

At the time of the drafting in of the Irish soldiers there had been a rebellion in the West Country, led by the King's own half-brother, the Duke of Monmouth. Catholics tried to say that Monmouth was illegitimate, but people in Pembrokeshire knew better, because his mother was a Pembrokeshire girl by the name of Lucy Walters, from down Haverfordwest way, who had been married to his father, Charles II, before ever he became King. When the rebellion failed, Monmouth had been executed. However much that may have suited some of the Catholics, there were people in Pembrokeshire who were none too pleased. As far as they were concerned, he had been executed by his own Catholic half-brother. James II had been overthrown eventually, and then died, but now this young son of his, James Edward, another Catholic, had set himself up as Pretender to the throne and was on the Continent, where some of the French were for ever willing to stir up strife.

The coastal traders had brought many stories of doings in the West Country at the time when the Pretender's father, before he had been overthrown, had sent Judge Jeffreys there to preside at what they called the Bloody Assizes following that failed rebellion. It was said that Jeffreys had had more than three hundred

Protestants put to death, and sent eight hundred, some of them women and children, to slavery in the Colonies, and many of them were known to have been innocent. So the likelihood of another Catholic coming to the throne was cause for consternation. And with all the traffic between the Pembrokeshire coast and Ireland, and with news of the Jacobite rising in Scotland, any Catholics had to be suspect.

It was not long after Matt and Mona had married, of a night in autumn, when a full moon was casting shadows through the woodland, and the household had long since gone to their mattresses, that Matt was awakened by pressure from Mona's hand.

'Listen,' she said.

There was a brief silence, and then Matt heard quite distinctly a tapping at the bedroom window which he recognized as being unmistakably that of Nipper Jim. Matt was puzzled, because there had been no word of any boat being expected. And there was, too, a disturbing note of urgency about it.

Pulling on his breeches, Matt went quietly down to draw the bolts of the heavy door to admit a clearly agitated Nipper Jim, a youth now, still small, but with the compact and wiry frame of the born ostler, and the wisdom of ages in his face.

'Mister Matt,' he gasped, 'for God's sake come quick. Will Squint have sent me. The sodjers is down at Earwear, and they've come to take the Father away.'

'How d'you know?'

'Will Squint's cousin come up from Earwear, and Will said for God's sake for you to come for you'd know what to do.'

'Where's Father Pascal now?'

'A be in the hidey-hole, but the mansion is surrounded because the sodjers knows a be in there an' they said they'll only have to wait.'

'And where's Will Squint?'

'Will be away to Earwear to the tunnel, an' a said for me to take horse if it be right with you an' ride for Laugharne to find Eli Canavan.'

Matt thought for but a few moments before he said, 'Take one of the big cobs, then, Nipper. Take Shanco. If you have to bring Eli back with you, Shanco'll be stronger than a pony for all.'

As though having anticipated the emergency, Mona was fully dressed when she came down minutes later.

Matt told her briefly the tidings Nipper Jim had brought and said, 'Better wake your father. Tell him what's happened, and go back to bed.'

He took her in his arms then, kissed her, and said, 'There's no need to be afeart. Just tell your father. He'll know what to do.'

The first leaves of autumn were falling as Matt hurried down the track for the New Inn. He thought it could have been foolhardy to carry a lantern, but the moon pierced the tracery of whatever leaves remained on the trees with sufficient light for the way to be clear to someone so familiar with it. He slowed in his walk after he had passed under the high rock and then stopped. For a while he stood and waited. Then he heard an owl hoot twice from somewhere in the direction of the Inn, and he hooted twice in return.

Terrifying though it had been at the time, in later years Matt would laugh about the events of that evening, and the story was to pass into legend to become a treasured part of folklore.

It was one of the men from Earwear Moor, up Chantry Lane, who came silently up to him in the dark to engage in low-voiced and urgent conversation.

Nathan, one of the innumerable Squint clan, reckoned they had everything under control, as long as Matt could take care of the matter from there on.

'The friggin' sodjers be swarmin',' he said. 'They be watchin' everybody as go into the New Inn and everybody as come out. But don't thee be worrit about 'em an' their owld capers. Just thee be sure to come tomorra evenin'. Cousin Will be all fixed with the Father from there on.'

Soldiers had indeed surrounded the mansion, and they knew enough of the layout to be watching the New Inn. Even if they were stopping nobody from going in, certain sure it was they would keep careful watch on everybody coming out. Nathan Squint did not need to be any sort of fortune teller to know that.

'How has it all happened, Nathan?' Matt said.

'That friggin' Henry Philbert. We alus knowed a was a bad bugger. But a can reckon to mind his back from now on, for two men'll meet afore two muntains.'

Well, even if Philbert had turned his coat and betrayed them, the cause was still far from having been lost. Philbert could be dealt with another day. For the moment, the little French priest had to be their main concern.

Nathan Squint of Chantry Lane slyped away into the shadows, Matt waited patiently for a while, and then went into the Inn. The turf fire had been made up, but the company was strangely subdued. Perhaps it was because there were two strangers amongst the regulars who were fewer in number than usual. Even they would understand that there would be no idle chatter in front of strangers. Matt called for a sleever of ale, and Sam Rawles gave him no more than the faintest flicker of a wink. Matt spoke to him cheerfully of the weather, and inconsequentially of one thing and another for a short while. Then he drank up his ale and left for home, exchanging a civil greeting with the strangers as he went. Not far up the lane he moved into the dark shadow of the high rock and waited. Nobody was following him. Somewhat disappointed, he went on his way up to Woodreef, whistling cheerfully, just in case. It looked as if the strangers knew that Will Squint was somewhere along the tunnel.

At first light the next morning a slight and bent figure, clad in rough woolcloth and leather chaps, wearing a heavy woollen bonnet, and carrying a sack on his back, came out from the low door under the archway from the cellar of Earwear mansion into the garden, to make his slow, trudging way across to the Moor and up Chantry Lane. His working day had evidently begun early, and he was of no interest to the two soldiers lounging by the entrance gate. As far as they were concerned the vital point was the New Inn for, sooner or later, according to their

42

information, the priest would have to come out there from the cellar and their mission would have been completed.

Later in the day, as the sun was sinking in a ball of fire in the west, Matt Rodda came down the lane from Woodreef with a pony in the shafts of the small gambo. He crossed the lake at New Inn and travelled along the coastal track above the beach in front of the mansion at Earwear. Then he turned up Chantry Lane. As the light was fading, he returned, with the bent figure clad in rough woolcloth and leather chaps, and wearing a heavy woollen bonnet, sitting alongside him on the front of the gambo. His sack was behind him.

When they reached Woodreef, Eli Canavan was waiting, and he urged Father Pascal to hurry, because the boat taking him back to France would be sailing with the tide from Laugharne before daylight. The next night Eli Canavan returned to Woodreef with Will Squint's clothes of rough woollen cloth, leather chaps, and heavy woollen bonnet. He carried, too, a small, finely wrought crucifix, which the priest had sent for Matt and Mona with his prayers and blessing.

It was a couple of nights later when Will Squint turned up at the Caban wearing a priest's old cassock, but nobody ever suggested he might be able to say Mass for them.

Much as Henry Philbert knew, it was fortunate that he had never known the exact secret of the priest-hole, and report had it that the authorities were not best pleased with him when they recalled that he had said he had the man they wanted under his hand and all they had to do was take him. Thus denied his 'thirty pieces of silver', he had no future with the Whig faction, and had a greater sense of self preservation than to wait for the return of Squire Elliot.

Will Squint was mortified that he could play no part in bringing Philbert to account, but Mona pacified him.

'Do not trouble yourself, Will,' she said, in her gentle way. "Vengeance is mine," saith the Lord. "I shall repay."

Years later word came that Philbert had gone to the Colonies, but no more was heard of him. And nobody was ever to bring word as to whether or not the Lord had repaid.

CHAPTER 2

1720 - 1820

1

Matt and Mona had married at the time of the Jacobite rising.
Five years later, in 1720, Seth Rodda was born. There had been
two children before that, both girls. The first had been still-born,
the second died after two days. Granny Hudson came down the
valley from the cottage at Greyrock, with her herbs and simples,
and Seth lived. But Granny Hudson said there would be no more
children, and Granny Hudson was right.

Gaffer Barlow had died the year before the grandson who had
been named for him was born, but the boy had his gramfer's
colouring and, as he grew, everybody said that he was a real
throwback to the old man, although the young Seth showed
every sign of developing with his father's fine physique. He had
all the devil-may-care bravado of the old man, and the same
disregard for any laws that did not suit him. Coupled with his
father's strength and build, it began to look as if this younger Seth
might well develop into one to cause trouble.

All things considered, it was perhaps not too surprising that
there was a tendency for Seth to be spoiled. On the odd occasion
when Matt tried to correct him, Mona, with her gentle nature,
would tend to say, 'He's all right, Matt. Don't be too hard on
him.' Sometimes she would say, ''Tis more important to set him a
good example than to keep on at him.'

The trouble was, as Matt constantly tried to point out to her,
Seth was only too quick to understand, because Mona would say
it in front of him. Once, when he was older, and had been
particularly fractious, Matt took his leather belt to him and gave
him the hiding he felt he deserved, but that upset Mona so much
that he could see there was no future in that either, for not for

45

anything in the world would he risk spoiling their marriage. Plead with Mona as he would, Matt could not seem to get her to understand, and it saddened him, because it was the only serious friction that ever really entered into their life together.

The first signs of what might lie ahead came, before Seth was even into his teens, one summer when the travelling charcoal burners came to Greyrock. Their work was hard, and their ways were rough, which was scarcely surprising, having to live the way they did.

When they came they either built new huts or repaired some of those still standing from the year before. The huts were made of poles driven into the ground in a circle, tied together at the top and covered in turves. It was a crude, nomadic type of dwelling for essentially gypsy type people, with nothing on the face of it, apart from the novelty, to attract a boy with the comfort of a good home. If those who came to Greyrock were no rougher than many, there was certainly one boy amongst them, by the name of Josh Essex, who was usually up to no good, and he was the one who seemed to have such a strong influence on Seth.

Most of the children of the woodland and the valley were glad enough to crawl to their straw mattresses after a day toiling from light to dark, sometimes in the fields, or herding the pigs for the pannagers in the woods in the cold, wet weather. Some went down the valley and beyond Earwear as far as the Patches at Crickdam to pick the iron ore. Whatever work they had to do, it was hard for them in times when food was difficult to come by, as was the money to try to buy it. For a boy to stay out all night on top of all that was beyond understanding.

Seth, however, even after a hard day's work, no matter how much Matt and Mona tried to discourage him, did indeed begin to stay out at night on the pretext that he was helping with the all-night watching of the kilns. Matt had his doubts, but Mona was all too ready to accept the story. As she said, and Matt could not dispute it, the charcoal burners had been coming to the valley ever since anybody could remember. It was a well-organised and recognised business for supplying, amongst other

46

purposes, the needs of the iron industry, and during the season there was a steady train of pannier-laden ponies and donkeys carrying the charcoal away from the valley.

The cordwood for burning had been cut and stacked during the previous autumn and winter. Mostly it was of the more slender species of tree, together with the lop and top of the bigger timber which had been sold for better prices, and a careful system of coppicing ensured that there was an adequate supply, year in and year out.

It was a time-consuming business tending the heaps as the charcoal burned. Once the wood had been stacked and covered with turves, a constant watch had to be kept in case the wood flared up and burned right through. Then more turves would have to be added, and sometimes water might also be needed in an emergency during the coaling process. However near the stream the charcoal platform was, the water still had to be carried. So there was indeed plenty to do, and Seth had a plausible excuse for helping his friend, Josh Essex.

That was all right at first, and nobody was troubled unduly by the poaching of rabbits, except the gentry, because it was reckoned that even the wandering people had to live. If they were willing to take the risk of being caught by the gentry's bailiffs and transported to the Colonies, or even caught in the cruel and vicious man traps, with the chance of being crippled for life, then that was their own look-out. But then the poultry started to disappear, and it was not always the work of the fox.

A year or two later came the sheep-stealing, and that carried the death penalty. Whether Seth Rodda was mixed up in it nobody knew for sure, but it caused Matt and Mona many sleepless nights, especially when another of the charcoal burners, young Brad Essex, who was no more than fourteen or fifteen, and a half-brother to Josh, was caught and hanged in Carmarthen, which the magistrates said should teach everybody a lesson.

However much Seth, as an only child, had been over-indulged, it became clear as he grew older that it was now too late to do very much to influence him for the better, no matter what sort of example might be set for him. Matt and Mona tried to make him understand that the smuggling was one thing, but the risk of the death penalty was different altogether. When people stole sheep it was from those they knew, and to whom they might be known. With the smuggling, they were robbing nobody but the Government what they lost in duty. Walpole, the Prime Minister, was said to have some big scheme to put a stop to the smuggling by appointing more revenue men to check at the warehouses, but it never came to anything, and Squire Elliot's deliveries never found their way to the warehouses anyway. Seth had more than one stand-up fight with the revenue men, but he was never caught, and the Earwear men involved in the Trade prospered to a certain extent.

They needed to prosper, too, because times were hard beyond belief. Corn was scarce, prices were high, and Seth was twenty when there were corn riots in many places. In May of that year he had gone by boat, quite legitimately as it happened, along with Josh Essex, to help with a cargo of coal from the beach at Wisemansbridge to Pembroke town. Whilst he was there the colliers came to the quay and broke open the hatches of a vessel due to sail for Bristol with a cargo of corn. Some of the corn they carried off to the market and demanded to be allowed to buy it at their own price, at the same time threatening to set fire to the town if their demands were refused.

The magistrates came then to read the Riot Act, which had been passed at the time of the Jacobite troubles a few years before Seth was born. But that did not trouble Seth, and he was a willing helper. Unlike a few of the colliers, he not only evaded arrest, but managed to carry a sack of corn home with him. Josh Essex was one of those arrested, but the public outcry was such that they all had to be released and, when Josh eventually managed to make his way back to their camp by Greyrock, Seth made sure that he had his share of the corn.

For a year or two following this escapade, Matt and Mona, having pleaded with Seth for so long to mend his ways, at last began to entertain some fond hopes that he might be showing signs of leading a slightly less wild life. The hanging of young Brad Essex had given Seth cause to ponder and, reckless though he was, he had enough sense to know that the trip to Pembroke might well have ended more unfortunately for him.

In some ways Matt almost regretted that they no longer had the stocks outside Marros Church. Since coming to Woodreef he had heard some grim stories altogether from Will Squint and a few others whose families in years gone by had suffered indignities in the stocks at the hands of the gentry. But the stocks had been smashed one night and had never been replaced. Matt felt that a spell in the stocks might bring even Seth to his senses and maybe save him from a worse fate. Having voiced these thoughts, however, he did not pursue the argument because Mona seemed to be so horrified. It was obviously too reminiscent for her of the time when Matt had taken his belt to a much younger Seth.

It was not only the escapade at Pembroke, nor the hanging of young Brad Essex, that disturbed Matt and Mona on Seth's account. For some time the authorities had been trying to discourage thieves by burning them in the hand and by public whippings. Now, however, it had been decided that, since there was a shortage of servants in the Colonies, it would be just as well to send the miscreants out there to get them out of the way. Too many country folk were being transported for the flimsiest of reasons, and at least Seth seemed to be developing enough sense at last to have no great desire to add to their numbers.

If he needed a chance to keep out of the way whilst any enquiries were still being made into the riots at Pembroke, it came by virtue of a providential and most timely offer from Will Squint to go with him in the summer on his annual cattle droving trip.

It was one of life's ironies that even those who had cattle could rarely afford to eat meat. They needed to realise every penny they could in order to pay the rent and to live. Eli Canavan, riding his own pony these days and apparently prospering, came

49

to Marros Fair to buy some of the Black cattle that were on offer, and Will Squint went with him to drive them to Laugharne, where they were shod. From there they would ford the river at St Clears and then the cattle could be driven to Carmarthen and on to Llandilo, Llandovery and Brecon, being joined by other herds as they went, and maybe changing hands three or four times along the way before eventually reaching the fattening grounds of the Midlands or East Anglia. Will Squint had his contacts, and would usually engage with the buyers each time to stay on with the cattle to the end of the journey. At a time when farm wages were a shilling a day in the winter, it was useful beyond words to be able to earn three shillings a day for droving in the summer.

Mona had made sure that Seth was well shod, and had knitted knee-length woollen stockings for him to protect his leggings during some of the rough and wet going with which, Will Squint had told her, they would have to contend in some of the more hilly areas. Hywel Dda went with them, too.

Matt it was who had named this noble-hearted corgi, after the great mediaeval Welsh lawgiver who had referred to this breed of the cow-shed when he had codified the Ancient Laws of Wales more than eight centuries previously. But Will Squint, who had little knowledge of Welsh history, and even less familiarity with the Welsh tongue, found it easier to call him Dai. Rich fawn in colour he was, with a striking white chest, and his alert brown eyes seemed to say that he had taken in every word that was said to him. For weeks before the great annual droving he showed quite clearly, by his excited anticipation, that he knew what season of the year it was.

Like Hywel Dda, Seth also enjoyed the excitement and, although he only went for one season, it gave him ideas, not always for the good, for later in life. With many hundreds of cattle on the move, bellowing and trumpeting their dust-clouded advent as they advanced in great herds, and with some of the drovers being mounted on their hardy mountain ponies, the way ahead was well-prepared to supply the needs of the drovers at the various hostelries and alehouses. Seth soon recognised the great camaraderie which existed, and also the wisdom of many people travelling together in such a lawless age, before there was any well-established banking system. As a result, many well-to-do travellers, carrying considerable sums of money, availed themselves of the opportunity to join the great caravan.

Almost two months after they had set off, Hywel Dda returned on his own. Mona became anxious, but Matt laughed and said that Will Squint and Seth could be expected within the week. And so, in due course, they did indeed return, safe and sound, without having been robbed along the way of the money they carried, some of which was for Eli Canavan. They brought, too, much news as to what was happening in the outside world, including the information that more and more people were seeking their fortunes overseas in the Colonies.

To some extent, following Seth's useful and perfectly legitimate trip with Will Squint, Matt and Mona hoped that he might settle to a steadier life-style, and indeed, for two whole summer seasons after that he went to work at the Patches at Crickdam digging the iron ore. He had worked in the winter, too, when there was work to be had in the woods cutting timber ready for the charcoal burners in the summer season, and there was a demand for pit props as well, with coal being increasingly used for firing. Most of those on the timber worked on the land in the summer, but Seth showed little inclination for this and, as soon as the season started, he would be away to the Patches.

The work was hard, but there were girls working there as pollers, picking over the mine, as the iron ore was called. Rough types some of them were, who gave as good as they got, but their company and badinage suited Seth. There was one girl even more forward than the others, and he had his fun and games with her, and some wild nights and torrid sessions in the fern. There was much he had learned from some of the younger drovers on that memorable expedition.

Then, on a Day for the King, when Seth Rodda was in his early twenties, he met Hannah Skeel.

Diwrnod i'r brenin the Welsh called this holiday, this Day for the

51

King. Not that there were many about the place who spoke Welsh, but there were a few, and the term had become accepted. The Day for the King had been brought in about two hundred years previously, way back in Tudor times they reckoned, when, for six days during the year, farmers had to go with a horse and cart, and labourers had to give of their labour, to work on the roads to keep them in repair. The trouble was that nowadays there was hardly anybody to oversee the work to make sure that it was done, so that it had become no more than a day off. And it was on this day at Marros Fair that Seth met raven-haired, dark-eyed Hannah from along Pendine way.

They were married a year later, when Seth was twenty-five, and Matt was able to use his influence with Squire Elliot's bailiff to get them the cottage on the corner at the top of the steep lane which led out from Woodreef Valley to the all-important road that ran along the coast through Earwear and Marros, to Laugharne and St Clears.

2

Matt and Mona could have been forgiven for thinking that, with the right partner, Seth might have settled down and kept out of trouble. In a number of ways folk reckoned that he and Hannah had a better chance than many. Two small fields, facing south, went with the cottage, and there was a useful stable with a tallet, so they could keep a cow, in addition to a cob and a pony, for there was a bull at the farm up at Clyngwyn where anybody in the valley could take a cow which needed servicing. Beyond the stable, at the bottom of the garden, there was also a stone pigscot, so a pig could be kept as well.

Matt and Mona, however, having been disappointed so often, had feared the worst, and it was not long before their worst fears were realised. What they did not know about Hannah's family, Eli Canavan was able to tell them. A wild lot they were and, as

Eli said, nothing was too hot or heavy for them. Wrecking was only a part of it. They were also prominent amongst those who showed false lights to lure helpless mariners to their deaths on a merciless shore, and Hannah was as hard-bitten and ruthless as any of the men of her family. Ever mindful of his own youthful years spent at sea, and with his inherent decency, Matt drew the line at this barbaric practice.

There had been no talk of having a priest when Seth and Hannah were married, because there had been no regular priest at Earwear since Father Pascal had gone, and Seth had shown little inclination to respond to Mona's entreaties for him even to learn his rosary and say it. Now there was news of another Jacobean rising in far-away Scotland, this time led by the Young Pretender, and Catholics were very much under suspicion.

It was, however, to everybody's advantage that Hannah was well-known to many in the Trade. Their cottage was ideally placed for the leaving of messages, and the stabling, with its tallet, was ideally suitable for the storing of goods which needed to be kept from the sight of prying eyes. Where the lane from the cottage came out onto the coast road, it was flat for a few hundred yards between the top of the hill coming up from Earwear, before starting to rise steeply again as it went on towards Marros. At the other side of the road, at the point where the lane joined it, another lane led down the valley towards the sea to the beach below Telpyn.

Near the point itself there was a cleft in the face of the rock known as the Chimney. A natural step formation climbed right to the top of the cliff to the fields above and, should they so wish, those using it from the Marros side need never show themselves to unfriendly eyes keeping watch down by the Blackhorn caves towards Earwear.

It was in this valley running down to the beach that the tanning pits were. Like the tanner in the Bible, who also had a house by the sea, the tanner's name was Simon, and he had been so named because his forebears had all been tanners and named Simon. Many of the finished hides were carted down the lane by

Hannah's cottage for the cottagers who worked at their trade in Clog Valley, and nothing was easier than for Simon Grigg to hear the word from Hannah, or to leave word with her in passing. So much a part of the operations was she that the trysting place soon became known as Hannah's Plain. And it was but a short, sharp climb from there up to the bluff of Dolman Head, where lights from far out to sea could be observed, and answering lights returned.

The Trade still flourished and, under Hannah's wild and passionate influence, Seth Rodda was soon to become the reckless hell-raiser of which he had shown every sign as a mere boy. No longer did he go in search of work at the Patches in the summertime, or seek work in the woods in winter. There were easier pickings to be had on the highway, as he had observed when he had gone as a drover with Will Squint, and he began to gravitate eastwards more frequently in the direction of the notorious Three Lords Inn on the road leading overland from Marros to Laugharne, a haunt of highwaymen, where more than one traveller had been hocussed and done away with.

Plead with Seth though she might, it was not long before Mona was making excuses for his wild behaviour and blaming it on Hannah. Wild influence though Hannah undoubtedly was, Matt knew in his heart that they were a pair well-matched.

Surprisingly, perhaps, it was to be some time before there was to be any sign of children but, as old Granny Hudson was wont to say, 'Grass wunnat grow on the highway.' And there was no knowing how free Hannah had been with her favours before she settled down with Seth. They had been married for six years before Josh was born, named after Seth's boyhood mate, and Josh was two years old when his baby sister, Delilah, arrived.

Saddened as she was by Seth's wild and ungodly life, it was small comfort to Mona that the parsons were also having an unprofitable time. Unwilling to accept the new religion which had been foisted on them by the English King, the Methodists, inspired by John Wesley, were doing their best to persuade and save people from so many of the evils which were bred by the people's poverty. Nor was there any lack of raw material on which to work, even if their labours bore little fruit. At Pwll, a secluded valley inland from the church at Marros, there was a cockpit, and here Seth was a regular spectator. He had no cocks to enter in the fights, and did not make himself prominent, but he observed those who gambled and won. Local winners were of little interest to him, but those who came from further afield and had to return eastwards by the lonely road to St Clears were lucky indeed if they were not waylaid and relieved of their winnings and any other valuables they may have been foolish enough to have about their persons.

Then, in 1756, when Seth was thirty-six, war with the French broke out again, and there was money to be made once more. Demand for charcoal for the iron smelting had been slow for some time but, with the nation at war, there had come a great demand for timber for ship-building. The purchasing agent was a young man by the name of Gervaise Gideon. Where he came from nobody knew, but Eli Canavan, an old man now, made it his business to find out, and he duly reported to Nipper Jim that Gideon was a relation of Henry Philbert.

As a horseman, Nipper Jim was inclined to say, 'Show me what they're bred from, an' I'll tell thee what to expect,' and he passed on the word to Matt and Mona about Gervaise Gideon that there was bad blood there. But Gervaise Gideon, like Henry Philbert before him, was smooth, and Seth would not hear of such a thing or heed their warnings. Smartly attired in his velveteen breeches, high buckskin boots, and his frock coat with silver buttons, he cut quite a dash, and Seth could not help but be impressed. He took him to the cockfighting, and vouched for him amongst the company at the Three Lords Inn. In due course he even initiated him into the secrets of the Gentlemen in the Trade, but fortunately, as it turned out, not into the secrets of the underground tunnel to the mansion at Earwear.

Seth was forty, and Josh and Delilah were not yet ten years of age, when Gervaise Gideon, reputedly for the standard reward of forty pounds, betrayed Seth to the authorities. The militia came to the cottage without warning late on a bright moonlight night, and they were waiting for Seth as he came down the lane, whistling happily in his usual carefree way, to be caught like a rat in a trap. In some ways he was fortunate not to be whipped in public like a common rogue or vagrant, which might not have been too bad, all things considered, and some would have said he was lucky not to be hanged. But he was sentenced to transportation for life and sold into slavery in the Colonies.

It was difficult to know with children how things festered in their minds, but Josh was old enough to follow most of the talk of Gideon's evil which had deprived him of his father.

Within the year, Mona had died of a broken heart, and Matt would probably never have smiled again had it not been for young Josh.

In the autumn it was that Mona died, when the valley was bathed in the light of the harvest moon, fifty years after Matt had come ashore that never-to-be-forgotten autumn, not knowing that he would never again go to sea, but spend the rest of his life with the beautiful girl with whom he had fallen in love in that spell-binding moment when he first set eyes on her. Age had not dimmed her beauty for Matt. To him she would ever be the same bright-eyed girl of happy laughter.

If she had oft'times been over-indulgent with their only child, it was but running true to her gentle nature. However much it might have disturbed Matt on odd occasions over the years, it was not in his heart to think of such things now that they were both gone. For forty-five years he and Mona had been married and had never spent a night apart. Almost daily would he hear the sound of the latch on the door of her dairy, and the sound of her clogs on the cobbles of the court outside. As the weeks of emptiness dragged wearily by, and he began at last to sleep fitfully in the long, dark nights, he would sometimes wake from dozing and stretch out his hand to her on the feather mattress of the old double bed, only to realise yet again that his lovely young Mona was no longer there. Then he would bury his face in the lonely pillow and sob, and try to pray and to put his trust in the Lord, as Mona had ever urged him to do. And he would hear her dear voice again as she used to quote from the Psalms.

Young Josh, too, felt his Grandma's death keenly and asked Matt to take him through the rosary and explain things as Mona had done as he sat upon her knee, and as she had done when Josh's father had been the same age. But Matt had long since understood that Mona had ploughed a lone and infertile furrow with Seth in that respect, and admitted to himself with a sense of sorrow and regret that he had never interested himself as much as he might have done in their son's religious improvement. So he put her rosary and the crucifix away, wrapped reverently and carefully in a piece of velvet from Mona's sewing box.

Sometimes Matt would write in his big notebook of his loneliness, or of the happenings of the day, and sometimes write down memories of his happy life with Mona, and of how young Josh had come to live with them at Woodreef.

The pair of them were now to become firm companions, and Josh proved to be an apt pupil. At the big spring tides Matt would take the boy down to the beach at Earwear, way out to low water where the fat, full mussels were to be found on the rocks amidst the remains of where, thousands of years ago, the forest had been. In the river, when the sewin were running, he taught him how to take these choice fish by stealth and by lamplight under cover of darkness. Then, whilst Josh was still little more than a boy, they had the excitement of the great bull seal, and that was something else which was sufficiently unusual for Matt to record some of the details of the story in his big notebook.

For whatever reason, Matt had found himself developing a close affinity with O'Fagan over at Teague's Dingle, and it was no surprise of a cold day in autumn when O'Fagan came to Woodreef in some excitement.

'God save all here,' he said as he came in. It was his customary greeting. He was bringing the great news, he said, that there was a fine bull seal sleeping under the foot of the cliff down on the beach below Teague's Dingle, and the tide was far out.

''Tis a fine specimen he is to be sure,' said O'Fagan. 'A fine specimen he is. So will ye be after comin' wid me to turn him into some good meat for the winter?'

'Faith, Teague,' Matt said, 'have you ever killed one?'

'And have I ever been after killin' wun,' O'Fagan said. 'Holy Mary, Mother of God, and how else would ye be after thinkin' that we ever had a bit of meat inside of us over there across the water, and wasn't me owld man after comin' from the Kerry country and the islands where the great big selchies was.'

Matt had done a bit of it when he was a lad long ago in his Cornish youth, and he told O'Fagan something of those days.

'But that was a long time ago,' he said. 'My old bones are none so active now as in those days.'

'Ah, sure, me good man, and what matter is there in that at all? Ye can give me a hand to cut him up. And won't it be great it will be for the little fellah here to be after learnin' all about it so?'

So they went then, the three of them together, Josh all agog with boyish excitement, and Matt took his old seaman's knife and a sharpening steel with him. As they went down by Teague's cottage O'Fagan collected a strong ash staff, fashioned like a club at one end.

Once when telling Josh something of his own boyhood, Matt had told how the men, when they went hunting the seals, would kill them by a blow to the nose. Josh had always heard it said that this was the only way to kill a badger, but that was something he would never do. He liked the old badgers and there was no point in killing them because it was not as if you could eat them. At least, he had never heard tell of anybody eating badger meat, but

Matt had told him many a time that the old timers reckoned that seal meat was as good as pork any day. And the chance of a bit extra to eat in these hard times was too good to miss.

Sleeping at the foot of the cliff the great seal was, just as O'Fagan had said, and O'Fagan's description of the size of him had been no exaggeration either.

'By God!' Matt said as he gazed at him in awe. 'He must be six hundredweight if he's an ounce.'

At the sound of voices, the great bull seal opened his eyes and raised his head before making a kind of wind-driven noise that seemed to be half-growl and half-roar. Then, flinging the pebbles in all directions behind him with his flippers as he came, he charged down the beach.

O'Fagan stood his ground as the seal came at him and, with one mighty swing of his cudgel, struck with unerring accuracy at the bewhiskered snout. It was a paralysing blow, and one more, to be on the safe side, finished the job.

After that the real work began as Matt prepared to skin the great seal before cutting it up. But first of all he sent Josh home to fetch the horse-and-cart and to tell a couple of the cottagers to come with him. Some there were who expressed doubts about the fare on offer, but nobody was too nice-gutted to refuse something for nothing in such hungry days. The pig-killing season had not yet started and the noys were hurriedly cleaned and prepared for salting the meat. For those who had never tasted seal meat there was an agreeable surprise, and they held themselves to be in Teague O'Fagan's debt for a long time to come. For good measure, Matt had the skin made into a nice, warm coat.

During that winter O'Fagan came to Woodreef more frequently than usual. Often, during the long winter nights, the killing of the great bull seal prompted him to tell them tales and legends handed down in his own family 'across the water', as he always called it, of the hunting of the seals in years gone by, and Josh absorbed the stories avidly.

O'Fagan had a pleasing tenor voice, too, and once he sang a

quaint old ballad with a line in it which said, 'I am a man upo' the land, I am a selchie in the sea.'

One of the stories he told was how, not long after he came to Teague's Dingle, he had killed a seal cow with a most beautiful skin. It had the usual dappled grey markings, but the white was a distinctive silver. It was far too beautiful to be made into an ordinary old coat, O'Fagan said, so he had kept it until somebody might come along who would really appreciate its value. And then he told of a legend that after the seal cow had been killed she would be wandering the earth in human form, and that was the meaning of the old ballad. It was not such a story as Josh had heard before, but it all made good listening during the long, dark evenings of winter.

Then, for whatever the reason, Teague O'Fagan packed up his few belongings on his ass-and-cart and moved on. But before he went he gave Josh the beautiful silver seal skin.

'I have the feelin' in me old bones, so,' said he. 'And if the feelin' isn't after bein' in me old bones, then 'tis in me moind it is sure enough. But 'tis round here it belongs so it does, and the feelin' is after bein' wid me that 'tis yourself is the wan to have it, so 'tis.'

The night that Josh fetched the skin from Teague's in late summer was following days when a great storm had been blowing. Now, the wind had abated, but the pebbles could still be heard as they were rolled up and down the beach far below by the ocean's surge. Then, an unearthly and demonic scream rent the silence of the night.

'Mary, Mother of God!' said O'Fagan and crossed himself, ''Tis the spirit it is.'

Josh burst out laughing and said, 'What spirit, Teague?'

''Tis the cry of a soul in torment, so it is.'

'What art thee talkin' about, Teague? 'Tis only a cocklynave as they calls it round here. 'Tis the night cry of the cocklollies. Shearwaters. Gramfer Matt's told me about 'em many a time. They nests on the islands, but that would be one blowed off course and they calls to their mates to find 'em in the dark.'

The scream sounded again, but this time further out to sea.

O'Fagan crossed himself once more and said, 'Tis a soul in torment, Josh, so it is. The spirit of some poor soul lost at sea and roamin' the deep eternally in search of a restin' place. May the souls of the faithful departed through the mercy of God rest in peace. And may perpetual light shine on 'em.'

O'Fagan stared out into the darkness as yet again he crossed himself. Thinking of what Grandma Mona's great faith and beliefs had meant to her, and maybe out of deference to her memory, Josh did not laugh again, but he chuckled to himself on the way home.

Much as he had heard from O'Fagan about the silver seal skin, he had still not expected to handle something of such smooth and delicate loveliness, so he took it home to Woodreef and stored it away carefully in the bottom drawer of the oak tallboy, and there it was to remain until boyhood had blossomed into youth.

Before that happened, however, old Gypsy Peg came to Woodreef Valley to camp for the season, to weave her baskets of willow, and to make her clothes' pegs. The previous season she had spent in Teague's Dingle. Her son, Zephania, came with her, leading their pony in the shafts of their flat-bottomed cart, and with a lurcher on a piece of string trotting along beneath at the rear.

4

Some folk looked askance at the gypsy woman and gave her a wide berth, as Matt described it in his sailorman fashion, but no harm was there with her, and if Zephania snared a rabbit now and again, and landed enough trout and the occasional sewin to keep themselves fed, it was no more than they needed to live from one day to the next. For the most part she was welcome with the women of the cottages.

From the great Hearne family they came, and there were those in the valley who had a special affection for them, which was rooted in a legendary happening some years previously, when

Peg's husband, the sherengro of their much bigger camp in days gone by, had been alive. He had gone with one or two others to call at the farm of the Wentlows up Crunwear way ostensibly to beg for food. Not surprisingly to those who knew them, because the Wentlows were a despised and ill-tempered family, the request for food had not only been refused, but refused in a brusque and uncouth manner.

'Well,' Will Squint had laughed, when a wandering vagabond had told him the story later, 'there's more ways of killin' a pig than stuffin' the bugger with swill or barley meal f'rall.'

Nothing deterred by the Wentlows' refusal, Peg's old man had scattered, in the area where the Wentlows' young pig was feeding, a handful of poison distilled from some herb or other known only to the gypsy people. No more surprising than the Wentlows' original refusal was the fact that their young pig took bad and died that night. First thing the next morning, young Zephania had been sent to say that the rumour was that the Wentlows' pig had died and, if that was true, would the Wentlows like the gypsy folks' sherengro to come with the others to carry the carcass away.

Safe within the woodland, the gypsies set about disembowelling the carcass and thoroughly cleansing the innards of all traces of the poison, and that night there was a feast of roast pork such as they had not enjoyed for many a long day. In the course of time the story passed into the folklore of the valley, and many were the jibes and catcalls the Wentlows had to endure down through the passing years.

It was one warm evening as the light was fading, and Josh was walking through the wood with young Billy Squint, who was working at Woodreef, and where he slept in the tallet above the stable, that they came on Peg's camp.

'Kushto bokt, prale,' said Billy. It was the first intimation that Josh had that Billy had any knowledge of the strange language of the gypsy folk. But his Romany greeting was returned amiably and they were invited to join them round the wood fire above which a blackened tin of coffee was steaming.

Peg gazed long into Josh's eyes and then said in a low, clear voice, 'You are one with the second sight, my gorgeous. Sit you by the yag, tiny tawny, and let Old Peg look into it and pen you what is to come.'

She and Zephania spoke strange words together then, and there were but few words Josh was able to comprehend. There were such words as *tivara* and *dooria* and *apah*, which, Billy told him afterwards all meant water, or the ocean. But there had also been the word *mára*, which meant death, and Gypsy Peg had used that word more than once.

Then she used the word *truppo* which apparently meant body and, immediately afterwards, started talking about the *broch-mór* and the *morlo*. And Billy said they meant the same thing and were Welsh as far as he knew, because *morlo* was the Welsh for seal, *broch* was the Welsh for badger and *mór* the Welsh for sea. And old Will had once told him that some of the croggans he had known used to talk about the seals as sea badgers.

What Peg had been saying, Billy said later, was that death would come to Teague's Dingle because of what O'Fagan had done in killing the great seal, so maybe she had spoken to the superstitious Irishman of these things the previous year and that was why he had moved on.

They drank coffee together then in silence and there was a great peace upon the valley.

For some time no word was spoken and then, at length, the old gypsy woman broke the spell. 'You must excuse us for speaking in the Romano jib', she said in her low, strangely musical voice, 'for there are some things it is better you should not know. But you will know them when they happen because you will remember what old Peg has told you.'

She lapsed into silence again then as she gazed intently into the fire.

'Some day, my gorgeo rye,' she said after a while, 'you will know great happiness and much sorrow. You will meet a rawnie and you will love her, but she will not be for you.'

63

A spark crackled from the flames, and Peg said, 'I see a carver in the fire, too. A cheat, my gorgeous.'

Then there was another long pause and silence before the gypsy woman said, 'I see harko. And I see the plastamengros. But they will not come in your time. They will come in the time of the one who comes after you. And the one who comes after you will not be troubled by the plastamengros. I see a body and a high cliff.' Another short pause, and she said, 'I see a drowning, too, which is not drowning, and it is not sad, and there will be much you will never understand until the great ship comes, because some of it is not clear to me. But the great ship will come for you, and then you will know such happiness as no mortal could ever know. And it is because you have the second sight that you will know this to be true. It is not given to many folk to know such happiness.'

Often, long after Gypsy Peg and Zephania had moved on, and other folk had moved into Teague's, Josh thought about the old gypsy's strange predictions, which he did not even try to understand. Then, gradually, he forgot about them, and as a young man went with his Gramfer Matt when the old man was involved in running the brandy and tobacco, the salt, and the silks and the fine wines. Eventually, he was initiated into the secrets of the underground tunnel.

It was a source of never-ending frustration to the parish constables that, even when they received what seemed to be sound information from their various informants, they were never able to arrest the culprits, because the goods would be landed at the Blackhorn caves, just inside the boundary of one county, where their jurisdiction ended, and then be reputed to have turned up at Earwear, just inside the boundary of the adjoining county, where their writ did not run. The parish constables could be forgiven for knowing nothing of the secrets of the underground tunnel which made the transition possible, and Josh wondered whether that was what old Gypsy Peg had meant when she said that the plastamengros would not trouble him.

Josh, by this time, had made his home permanently at Woodreef with his Gramfer Matt, but called on his mother whenever he was passing Hannah's. He was fond of Delilah, but had an idea that this young sister of his could well be going the same way as their mother. His own nocturnal peccadillos with his Gramfer Matt, apart from the poaching, were generally confined to the more respectable participation in the Trade.

It was of an afternoon in early autumn, when the trees were turning to gold and copper, that Josh walked to Teague's Dingle. Towering above the beach was a headland known as Top Castle, steeped in mysticism, where many centuries ago, long before the coming of the Romans, the early Celtic invaders had built their fortifications to repel any further invasion from the sea. Word was awaited of a small cargo of brandy, and Top Castle was a fine vantage point from which to survey the great sweep of Carmarthen Bay. Across from Monkstone to Tenby's north beach and harbour, the church spire, St Catherine's Island, St Margaret's Island, and way out to Caldey on the skyline, the view was clear. No sign was there of any likely looking vessel as yet, however, so Josh went on down to the beach where he and Gramfer Matt had gone with O'Fagan a few years ago to kill the great bull seal.

He had time on his hands, so he thought he would walk further along to where the sunken forest was. It was part of the same great forest which lay buried at Earwear, and the autumn storms now and again turned up something of interest. Along the great length of wild and lonely beach, too, where the high tide had left its flotsam and seawrack, there was no knowing what might be found. The beach and the sea had been in his blood from the time he had gone with his Gramfer Matt to the beach at Earwear, when he could do little more than toddle, long, long before he had ever begun to serve his apprenticeship in the Trade. And so often had he listened to Gramfer Matt's tales of his own boyhood aboard ship that he thought it was maybe small wonder he felt such an affinity with the sea. Gypsy Peg had spoken of a big ship that would come to meet him and he half-wondered whether his own future would be on the high seas rather than on the land.

He was startled out of his reverie by the sight of a lone figure in the near distance coming slowly in his direction. It was clearly the figure of a woman and, as she approached, Josh saw that she was a girl of somewhere near his own age, not yet twenty, and his pulse quickened. Her gown was simple, and her feet were bare. Her shoulder-length, golden hair was perhaps her most striking feature, but there was a depth of feeling and something of sadness in her gentle brown eyes which stirred him deeply, and her voice, when she spoke, had the lilting music of a soft, deep-ocean swell lifting and lowering seaweed on the deep-sea rocks.

'You seem surprised to see me,' she said, and Josh felt the colour come to his cheeks as he realised that he was staring at her.

He said, 'Forgive me for starin' at thee, Miss, but we hardly ever sees anybody down here we don't know. Where's't thee come from?'

'Oh, here and there, I suppose.'

'So, what brings thee here?'

She smiled her sad smile then and said, 'Will you promise not to laugh if I tell you?'

'How should I laugh?'

'You might think it sounds strange. I'm interested in the seals.'

'There's nothin' strange about that. But we don't see many of 'em here like that.'

'But you see some occasionally, I suppose?'

Perhaps it was her gentleness, or maybe it was his instinct, but Josh said nothing about the killing of the bull seal. He only said, 'Aye, sometimes. About this time of year.'

'Indeed. This is when they have to come to land to breed. It is when they are at their most vulnerable if people want to kill them.'

She gazed out to sea, then suddenly said, 'Did you ever hear about the silver seal skin?'

'The silver seal skin? What about the silver seal skin?'

'The story goes that it was a young seal cow that was killed round here not so long ago. Did you ever hear about such a skin?'

'What's thy interest in it?'

'My interest is simple. And you'll say typical woman no doubt. I'd love to have it for a coat.'

'I'll give'n to thee then,' Josh said spontaneously. 'Drop dead, now. If I never muv from here alive again, I'll give'n to thee.'

'What d'you mean, you'll give it to me?' There was eagerness in her every gesture. 'D'you have it? How d'you come by it? Was it you killed her?'

'Oh, no! The man who killed her gave'n me?'

'Where's it now? Tell me.'

'I've got'n home, in the drawer. I always thought 'twas so beautiful 'twould be a shame to make'n into a coat, but if thou's'd like'n thou ca'st have'n.'

Her lovely brown eyes filled with tears as she said, 'You cannot possibly know what this means to me.'

'Ar't thou all that keen to have a seal skin coat, then?'

'More than you'll ever know or could ever understand.'

'Come home with me now, then, an' I'll give'n to thee.'

Rather shyly the girl said, 'Oh, no, I couldn't do that.'

'How not?'

'It wouldn't be right.'

'Wou's't thee tell me thy name, then?'

'Tomorrow,' she said. 'Come at the same time tomorrow and bring the silver seal skin with you. Can you do that?'

'Why, aye, I can do that.'

'Very well. And thank you so much. It's a great kindness you'll be doing me. And perhaps tomorrow I'll tell you my name.'

Little did Josh sleep that night as he tossed and turned and thought of the beautiful girl. There was never a doubt or question in his mind but that he loved her. Could this be the rawnie, the beautiful young girl of old Gypsy Peg's prophecy? What was it she had said? Something about, 'You will know great happiness and much sorrow. You will meet a rawnie and you will love her, but she will not be for you.' Those were her words. He had never met such a beautiful girl as this, and he was sure, sure, sure beyond words or any shadow of doubt that he loved her.

The hours dragged by until he awaited her coming on the beach the next day. When she came his heart was beating until he seemed to hear the thump of it above the sound of the waves, and, as she took the silver seal skin from him without a word and buried her face in it, the tears of pure happiness rolled down her cheeks and she whispered at last, 'Oh, dear, dear man! You have made me so happy. But I cannot talk to you now. One day I shall come back, but I don't know when or how. Come tomorrow at the same time and I'll tell you who I am.'

No word could Josh find to break the magic of the spell as he watched her walk away, and his eyes followed her every step until her figure was no more than a blurred speck in the distance.

His wait until the next afternoon was even more wearisome as he walked the beach in anguished longing. He had never known time to be so leaden-footed. A small party of sea pyats bleeped their busy call and hurried to and fro, their orange beaks exploring the wet sand for food. Off-shore a lone cormorant dived for fish, and curlew swept wide beyond the water's edge with their haunting call. The sun sank on the western horizon and the light began to fade. The autumn storms had passed, and the sea was a mirror of diamonds from which the sinking sun danced with a myriad lights that turned to red and died to purple. And then, slowly and surely, a seal swam into his ken. For a while she floated, snout upward, and gazed towards him. Then she rose out of the water and seemed to wave a flipper. As she dived to be hidden from his sight for ever, he saw that, although she had the usual dappled grey markings, the white was a most beautiful and distinctive silver, and the terrible truth dawned upon him.

For a long time he sat on the rocks thinking of the stories Teague O'Fagan had told him and how he had laughed to himself about them. What were the words in the old ballad he had sung about the seals? 'I am a man upo' the land, I am a selchie in the sea.' That was it. But how could a seal become a person when the skin was stripped from her? And how could she become a seal again if she recovered her skin?

The seals, O'Fagan had said, loved music. Josh wondered whether he could learn the music and the song of the seals and be able to call her back to him.

The shades of night had long since fallen and he was shivering. Of a sudden there was an unearthly and demonic scream from out of the darkness far out to sea as though somebody was being pursued by all the fiends of hell. He knew well what the sound was, but he shivered again and felt strangely disturbed.

The Psalm in the Bible said to ponder on your bed and be still. Far into the night he lay sleepless and pondered. Was this perhaps the silver, the *harko,* of old Peg's gazing into the fire, or had she meant something else altogether? She had talked much in her strange language of the *broch-môr* and the *morlo*. She said he had the second sight, or some such nonsense, and he tried not to be disturbed by such talk.

But not for a long time could he bring himself to talk about his experience. He would mention no word of it to anybody. Not even to Gramfer Matt.

6

Hannah had been but thirty-five years of age when Seth was taken from her. She had no more children, but many a man to share her bed, whilst her involvement with the highway continued unabated. More than once, dressed as a man, she rode with confederates but, for the most part, was a bearer of messages, an organiser, and a receiver. Delilah, as she grew to young womanhood, was to learn easily from her tempestuous mother, and she took her first serious lover when she was fifteen.

Times, however, even amongst the gentry, had brought about financial casualties. Squire Elliot had died, heavily in debt, and eventually some of his lands had to be sold. The mansion at

Earwear was neglected and fell into decay, and that was not the worst of it. With the loss of the old Squire, there was the double loss of the reliable outlet for so much of the contraband which for years had passed along the old tunnel.

Then many things happened at the same time. The news on everyone's lips was of the great Captain Cook's voyages to the New World, and it was of great interest locally because a young man by the name of John Martin, from the nearby parish of Ludchurch, was known to be sailing with him. But of more immediate interest in the valley was the fact that Gervaise Gideon had acquired the Caban.

Will Squint had died and, just when it seemed that his old clom cottage would fall into an even worse state of disrepair, Gervaise Gideon came along and set the builders to work. Stone was brought from the quarry on Crunwear Mountain to strengthen the clom walls, the thatch roof was stripped and replaced with stone slates, and a tallet was added above the living room. Outside, a new stable was built for a pair of horses. Speculation as to whether Gideon intended to live there himself was soon laid to rest when it was realised that the comfortable new dwelling was to be used for the installation of a young doxy by the name of Leah Rhys, until recently a lady's maid of some class at the mansion of Rhydlancoed beyond Earwear.

Of a striking and rather superior type of beauty she was, and it was understandable that Gervaise Gideon should have been susceptible to her charms, as it was equally understandable that she should have had her young head turned and been deceived by his smooth-tongued flattery. Knowing his duplicity, it was no doubt also inevitable that, when she was found to be with child, he should have abandoned her. Nor was it entirely surprising when she disappeared shortly afterwards and the word came a week or two later that her poor, rock-mangled body had been washed up on the beach below Teague's Dingle beyond Telpyn Point.

Delilah had just passed her eighteenth birthday at the time, and with the wild, dark beauty of her mother, and the seductive wiles she had long since acquired, it was not difficult for her, once life had again settled into its routine, to cast her eye towards Gervaise Gideon. It was as he cantered his horse along Hannah's Plain that he first had serious word with her. Reining to a halt and doffing his hat in a bold flourish, his easy talk quickly led towards what promised to be their first assignation at the now unoccupied Caban.

For all her wild ways, Josh still had his brotherly affection for her, and hatred for their father's betrayal had smouldered within both of them since childhood. Josh was more than ready to fall in with Delilah's plan for dealing with his betrayer.

Will Squint had referred to Gideon on one occasion as 'The celebrated linen-lifter', and said, 'Toff or not, he don't mind if she's a dozen letters short reciting the alphabet as long as she's a good looker.' The chances were that Delilah had never learned her alphabet in the first place, but she was certainly a good looker and, whether she knew her alphabet or not, she knew one or two things besides. One thing she knew was that Gideon had been to bed with her mother more than once, so it would not be wise, she said, to ride down past Hannah's cottage. Far better, for the first time at any rate, for him to come up the track along the valley through New Inn forest. It would be a longer way, she said demurely, but far more discreet. And she urged him to come by moonlight. Which is what the eager Gervaise Gideon did, riding his horse beneath the dappled shadows of the overhead leaves on a warm summer night. It was much darker than a mere dappled shadow as he came under the high, overhanging rock, however, and he scarcely knew what had happened as a noose dropped neatly over his shoulders from the darkness above to be pulled tight and pinion his arms. Nor did he see anything of his assailants as Josh and his companions, unspeaking, dragged him from his startled horse and tied his ankles. Then they stripped off his clothes and plastered him in tar and goose-feathers.

Josh cut the silver buttons from Gideon's coat and, as he turned them over in his hands, he remembered old Gypsy Peg talking about the *carver*, the cheat. And Gideon had turned out to be a

71

right *carver* if anybody had. Josh remembered, too, that she had talked about *harko*. Billy had not known what that word meant, but later on Josh came to know that it meant silver. So here was the silver all right, if that was what she had meant, if not in fact the silver seal skin, and very handsome buttons they were, too, and obviously worth a lump of money. The letters G.G. were embossed on them, and they were surrounded by the intricate pattern of a crown and a sword.

Josh thought it looked like a fair haul in one way and another, but reckoned it might be too risky to keep Gideon's clothes. These and his buckskin boots he threw into the lake. His fellow conspirators were rewarded with Gideon's gold watch and the well-filled purse he had on him. His horse went with them, too, and that changed hands at the Three Lords Inn later the same night, never to be seen in the area again.

If there really was anything in Gypsy Peg's predictions, it was comforting indeed to know that there would be no trouble from the *plastamengros*.

7

Not for some years was there to be any further word of the doings of Gervaise Gideon, except that he was known to be somewhere up-country beyond Carmarthen, and that he still had contacts at the Three Lords Inn. It seemed that he had better sense than to venture anywhere near Woodreef, and Hannah was doing good business by her tried and trusted methods, if not on anything like the same scale as of old. Delilah continued as her apt pupil.

Josh, however, had now become a fixture at Woodreef and much more a man of the land for, truth to tell, farming was seeing better times. As his old Gramfer Matt had said to him on one occasion, 'A dying pig will kick.' The poor would always fight back. They had been talking about the terrible poverty which the countryside had known for so long, when those who worked on the land had been so despondent and depressed, glad enough to eat potatoes on the many occasions when no corn was available to make bread.

'I can mind the time,' Matt said, 'when folk would grow a few potatoes in the garden and give 'em to neighbours as a special gift for a bit of a special treat like. Then of course the time come when they was our staple diet, along with bread and cheese, and budram made from oat-meal. That was all we had.'

But now, farming people were looking for ways in which to improve their lot, how to conserve more food to winter their stock, and how to grow better crops. Even the King was known as 'Farmer George.'

The only trouble was that the gentry also showed themselves to be ready and willing to take advantage of the new prosperity, and they enclosed even more of the land over which since time out of mind commoners had had the rights to graze their few animals freely. The gentry and their agents tried to justify what they were doing, but one of those with a great sympathy for the poorer people replied with a rhyme which became popular,

> *'It is a Sin in Man or Woman*
> *To steal a goose from off a Common,*
> *But who can plead that Man's excuse*
> *Who steals a Common from a Goose?'*

Not only did the commoners lose their grazing, but they lost their previous sources of turf and furze for firing as well. The young shoots of the furze were also of great use for fodder. There was a need, too, for something to replace the loss of their livelihood for labouring people. With the onslaught on the woodland for timber for ship-building during the war with the French, and the continued demand for timber for pit props, charcoal burning had withered and almost died. The tan pits offered little reward, because life had become increasingly difficult for the clog-makers.

For generation after generation, there had been craftsmen in the cottages of the valley who lived by the trees of the forest. From the day he had arrived at Woodreef, Matt Rodda had loved the splendour of the majestic beech trees and, on the smooth grey surface of one particularly noble specimen, he had carved a heart with an arrow through it, and with his and Mona's initials intertwined. And the carving grew with the years until the day when the timber merchants, in search of quality wood for the furniture makers, came to cut the tree down.

There had indeed been an abundance of timber for every need. The old saying had always been 'heart of oak for durability, willow for lightness in weight, and ash for toughness'. All of these had been there in plenty, as well as alder for the clog-makers. And then there was the sycamore. Not only did the clog-makers value it highly, but it served so well for the making of rollers for the mangles and for the rollers used by the cloth-makers. Dairy and household utensils, platters, bread-boards, rolling pins and butter pats were all fashioned from the wood of this most useful tree, to say nothing of the whistles which every child learned early in life how to fashion. But now the timber merchants were paying good money for it, and the forests fell before the woodman's axe in great swathes. And with oak trees no longer there to provide acorns for the pigs, the pannagers had to turn elsewhere to try to earn their daily bread. Some found work on the farms but, not surprisingly, more and more of the poor people had to turn to the parish for relief, and so became an added burden for the farming community who had to find the money to support them.

At the Caban, however, there was some evidence for the belief that the Lord did indeed work in mysterious ways. Thanks to the carnal desires and intentions of Gervaise Gideon, apparently departed and with none to mourn his going, the Caban was now a modest house. Where the Squint clan had previously had such a close connection with the folk at Woodreef, Will Canavan, a grandson of old Eli who had been so involved at the time when Matt Rodda had come ashore, had now come down from his native Laugharne to settle. There was a burgage by the house and one other small field, and he managed somehow with a day here and a day there.

Increasingly, however, some of the younger and more enterprising amongst the cottagers, encouraged in some cases by news brought back by the drovers, set sail for the Colonies. Others, without wanting to go that far, set off for the coal mines and iron works of the Welsh valleys. Some of them went on a seasonal basis to earn money for their families during the winter, and then came back to work on the land through hay-time and harvest. Eventually, they did not come back but put down roots, whilst some went even further afield to be swallowed up in the ever increasing populations of the great industrial centres of England.

On one occasion two young men from Earwear, younger than Josh, ventured only as far as Tenby to see whether there would be any possibility of going to sea in one of the fishing boats. They went to sea all right, but only because they were taken by one of the Press Gangs who were in the habit of showing up from time to time to take the unwilling away by force to serve in the Royal Navy in miserable conditions and for miserable money. On another occasion, one such Gang landed on the beach at Pendine and made a quick foray inland to take away some men who were working at the hay.

It was no time for honest men and women to be living too close to the shore. The pirate, Paul Jones, made several visits to the coast and was known to have called to take on water at Caldey, the island across the bay. The honest inhabitants of that island, so it was generally understood, had always been more than ready to do business dealings with the pirate fraternity. Hannah certainly seemed to know what was going on most of the time, but nobody would have made the mistake of calling her an honest woman. Even so, she seemed to be content for her son, Josh, to go his comparatively honest way with his gramfer in search of an honest living from the land. But to do that was not always easy. It was not only the vagaries of the weather with which they had to contend, for there began at about this time a new fashion for hunting the fox.

There was still a bounty being offered for the killing of foxes and badgers, and the custom was to hang the heads on the ancient cross in the churchyard at Marros, where the heads of wolves had once been hung. There were no wolves these days, but Gramfer Matt had an old story of the last wolf that had been killed there. Old Gaffer Seth Barlow, when he was a boy, had talked to an old man who, in his youth, had been there in Teague's Dingle when the last wolf in the parish had been killed. That had been just before the death of Good Queen Bess, and some folk reckoned it had been the last wolf to be killed anywhere in Wales. At one time, Gaffer Barlow had said, the people had been known to shut themselves in the Church to protect themselves from packs of marauding wolves. At that time wolves had been hunted with hounds. Once the wolves had all been killed, there had begun the sport of using hounds to hunt foxes instead. It never seemed to be very satisfactory to follow the hounds on foot, however, so then they began to follow on horseback.

Teague's Dingle was still a renowned place for foxes and badgers and many other animals. The bounty for a wild cat was sixpence, for a dog fox it was a shilling, and for a vixen sixpence. Josh always reckoned that if they wanted to get rid of the foxes it would be better to pay more for the vixens, because they were the ones that did the breeding. He had a great interest in the wild creatures, and studied their ways, and it was this which made him sad that a bounty of sixpence was paid on a badger. He thought the poor old badger was misjudged. Certainly he would never kill one himself, and eventually he made a pet of a cub which had been abandoned when its mother had been killed. Billy Brock, as Josh called him, became quite well-known in the precincts of Woodreef for a year or two, and was a friendly character much loved by children.

Sometimes Josh questioned himself as to his own motives in saving Billy Brock and rearing him and making such a pet of

76

him. Certainly he could not have put his feelings into words, nor had he spoken to anybody of his strange encounter on Marros beach and the experience with the beautiful girl and the silver seal skin. Gypsy Peg had spoken of the *broch môr* had she not? And Billy Squint said that the term meant sea badger, and that was what some of the croggans called the seals. He still thought about that beautiful girl sometimes, and dreamed about her now and again, but he believed he had recovered from that brief love affair, if love affair it could be called. Calf love was what the older people called such affairs of the heart.

He had never forgotten his feeling of utter helplessness as the seal had seemed to wave to him before disappearing and leaving him standing, lonely, bewildered, and sad beyond words, on the deserted beach, when he had been left with the conviction that it was the girl herself. He was not so sure now, and wondered what fanciful idea it could have been. No wonder he felt he could not tell anybody such a fool of a story. But perhaps it was that awful loss which could have prepared him now for the loss of Billy Brock when the foxhounds came to Woodreef Valley and killed him.

Josh did not blame the huntsmen, and it would not have done him any good to complain, any more than it would have done him or anybody else any good to complain when the gentry came that way foxhunting and broke down the new hedges and scattered the cattle and sheep. They did not come down that valley anyway as often as they came to Teague's Dingle, because there were more foxes over that way. But they came far more often to hunt the otters, which abounded in New Inn lake, rich as it was in fish. Josh was delighted for them to kill as many otters as they could. All the better for the sewin and the trout. The gentry's bailiffs could patrol the river as much as they liked, but Josh and the cottagers would still take their share.

8

Ben Knox, a clog-maker, with a couple of cows and a sturdy Welsh cob, came to the small-holding known as Furlongs, the other side of the valley from Woodreef, when Josh was twenty-five years of age. Ben Knox was a widower, but he had two daughters. And the name of the older daughter was Phoebe. Unlike his father, Josh, apart from his crazy and passing infatuation with the beautiful girl on Marros beach, had been little interested in women until he set eyes on Phoebe. And then he knew it was the real thing, as the saying was.

It was one morning in May, quick with life and the song of the birds, and full of the rich promise of growing things that, as in the story in the Bible of Rebecca meeting Isaac at the well, Phoebe came to draw water from the well as Josh was walking by and, rather shyly, he offered to carry her heavy wooden bucket for her. They were married that same year when heavy dews were on the grass, mists rose in the gathering gloom, and the autumn leaves were turning to pale gold and burnished copper, and they made their home at Woodreef. Young Martha was still at Furlongs and old enough to keep house for her father.

By the time Josh and Phoebe married, Delilah had found herself to be with child by one of the highwaymen of the Three Lords' connection and had left home, but whether they ever married nobody knew, nor for many years was there to be any word of a child. It was hard to believe that either of them could have sought or found honest employment, because it was not easy to move to another parish, since every parish had to support its own paupers, and so many of the people were a charge on the parish, drawing Poor Law relief. Everywhere there was evidence of the poverty, as poor, miserable vagrants roamed the roads in search of food and shelter, no longer able to cut turf for firing from the formerly open land which had now been enclosed. As often as not a cruel whipping was the only reward for their begging. But Delilah and her man, wherever they had gone, could be relied on to rob their way through life until they came to whatever violent end might be waiting for them.

Seth Rodda had not been born until shortly after the death of his maternal gramfer, Mona's father, Seth Barlow, after whom he had been named. But now, in turn, although he was never to see him, Seth Rodda's own grandson, the baby Matt Rodda, arrived in time to be nursed by his great grandfather, old Gramfer Matt Rodda, after whom the baby was named. For more than a year, the child was to be a great delight to him. Then old Gramfer Matt Rodda died in his ninety-first year, a whole seven decades, a man's lifetime according to the Bible, after he had come ashore on that momentous night from Hezekiah Trevanion's *Cornish Princess*. Two days after the old man died, baby Matt crawled out, unseen, and somehow found his way down to the lake. His lifeless little body was pulled from the water when it was found downstream at first light the following morning, and he was buried with the old man in the same grave.

Old Gypsy Peg had foretold a drowning, but she had got it all wrong when she had said there would be no sorrow. Josh was heartbroken at the double blow, because he had made his home with his Gramfer Matt at Woodreef from early in his life and truly loved the old man, but a year later, another boy arrived. Phoebe said, 'The Lord gave, and the Lord hath taken back. Blessed be the name of the Lord.' So the new baby was also named Matt and, as the years went by and tales were told of 'Old' Matt, so it was to become more and more the custom for folks to refer to 'Young' Matt. In the ten years that followed his birth, two more boys and two girls were to be born.

9

Matt was no more than five or six when Phoebe was spring cleaning and turned out the drawer in which Grandma Mona's rosary and crucifix were kept. To Matt's stream of questions as to what they were, his mother said it was only a lot of old foolery and take no notice of it. Josh, however, tried to explain as best he could according to what he had learned at Mona's knee, and at least was able to repeat the words of the Hail Mary and the bit about 'pray for us now and at the hour of our death.'

Matt sensed his mother's disapproval, but that night as he slept there came to him a sort of vision of a lady in blue standing by the foot of his bed with a beautiful glowing light all round her. Although she had not spoken he had the feeling that everything was very peaceful, and that she would always be there and take care of him. Vague though it all was, it was somehow comforting and, as he grew older, the conviction grew stronger, and he began to think that it must have been the Mother of Jesus to whom the Catholics referred as Our Lady.

Whether Matt was something of a favourite because he replaced the one who had died nobody seemed to know, but he was one of the lucky ones and was able to go to the little school at Earwear which had been started in the time of Squire Elliot, and he proved himself to be a fair scholar.

Good though he was at his books, and work though he had to when there was work to be done in the fields, he still found time to go to the beach, and Josh was ever pleased to go with him. It was in their blood and part of their way of life, especially after storms, when there was every chance that the sea might throw up some form of bounty.

It was as he came from school at Earwear of an afternoon one harvest time, when he was about twelve years old, that he had a strange experience. Near the sandy common at Earwear there was a cottage, built originally as a *tŷ-unnos* on a rocky piece of ground, and it was there that his friend, Fred Billy Shifty lived. What his real name was Matt didn't know, but his father became known as Billy Shifty because he once said that ever since he could remember he seemed to have been shifting from one place to another. Fred Billy Shifty had not been to school that day and Matt went to see where he was.

Beyond the house, a stretch of sand dunes ran down to the

seashore and, before he could reach the house, Matt saw to his puzzlement, that the sea was in far higher than he had expected it to be and was already running far up towards the dunes. He could not understand it because, not only had it gone high tide, but the sea was not rough and there was no great strength of wind behind it. And then, as he stood there he realised that the tide was fast approaching the house and the place where he stood. Rooted to the spot, but not in the least frightened, he had indeed a strange feeling of well-being as the sea came inexorably on to engulf the house and the place where he stood. Still the water rose until it was far above him, yet he still breathed freely and had a strange feeling that death must be something like this and that there was no need to fear it.

Then he saw the great ship. Whence it came or whither it went he could not say, but it was a fine ship and the sight of it gave him a feeling of such joy as he had never known and could never have explained.

Phoebe smiled when he told her of it, but she said, 'I knows 'tis a nice'l story, hun, but don't thee go fillin' thy head with too much owld dullery like that. It say in the Bible to beware of them visions as they calls 'em.'

'But 'tisn't dullery, Mam. I seen it all happen and the big ship. Indeed I did. Indeed, indeed-in-double-deed.'

'Hisht now, hun. I've told thee afore. Don't thee say things like indeed. There be no need for that. The Lord said, "Let thy communication be yea, yea, or nay, nay, because whatsoever be more than them cometh of evil." If thou says thou seen it, then thou seen it.'

'Well, I seen it then.'

'Very good then, hun. Now get thy bit o' grub down an' go an' see if there's anythin' thou ca'st do to help thy father.'

There was an entirely different reaction, however, when Matt told his father. They had always been close and had a good understanding. When Matt found him, Josh was sharpening a bundle of spiddacks ready to thatch a rick of straw for the winter.

'Don't thee think no more about it now, fellah,' he said. 'Go thee to bed for tonight, an' maybe tomorrow I'll tell thee somethin' as I've often wondered about tellin' thee, an' I can see now as the time have come f'rall.'

Following this Josh began to tell his son, a little now and a little again, something of his own boyhood, of the strange prophesying of Old Peg, and of the even stranger episode of the silver seal skin which had followed. Many a time he had talked to the boy of his old Gramfer Matt and, from a very early age, he had come to understand how much his father had loved the old man.

However dire the poverty of the time, Phoebe, who was a great believer in doing the best you could in life, said there was never any excuse for not being as respectable as possible, and she said this when she decided to smarten up Josh's best coat by sewing on the four silver buttons which she found in the drawer of the Welsh dresser when she was spring cleaning.

Silver buttons or not though, Josh said, they could never be any consolation for the loss of the tunnel. True, it had not been of as much use as in the days of old Squire Elliot, but it had served its turn on the odd occasion. But now, the dire news was that the underground tunnel to Earwear mansion was to be no more, and there was consternation beyond words amongst those still involved in the Trade.

The Estate, the people were told, had been bought by Captain James Ackland. Apparently he was a gentleman all right, but not a Gentleman in the sense of being interested in the Trade such as old Squire Elliot had been. This new Squire was interested in improving everything. The mansion was greatly altered, a new drive and entrance came into being, much work involving new walling was done on Chantry Lane, and great stones were used for pitchings on the beach as a bulwark against the sea. All this, Josh admitted, was good for those who were so desperately in need of the work, but the closing of the tunnel was a grievous blow.

Times had been hard, food scarce, and corn prices high. Great was the unrest, bitter was the feeling throughout the land, and the magistrates had been quick to call in the military to quell the corn riots. There was trouble over in Ireland, and then an invasion at Fishguard in the north of the County to which Captain Ackland was called away. So the wars with France had started again, and Napoleon became a hated name.

With the wars there had come a renewed demand for timber for ship-building, and the meagre livelihood of those who still depended on the woodland crafts was threatened even further. It was small wonder that the smuggling Trade had continued to have no shortage of willing participants, and Hannah her share of involvement, but it was doubtful whether she would have valued any of the bank-notes, which had recently been introduced, as she would the gold and jewellery.

Now, however, with the closing of the tunnel, the Trade, as Josh had been brought up to know it, as had generations before him, had been crippled. From now on any involvement would be more over towards Pendine, and that lot had everything carved up for themselves, and there would be no welcome for anybody from down Earwear way.

Phoebe had been amused when Josh told her how he had come by the silver buttons, but it was something which was never talked about in front of the younger children, even after Josh had told Matt. Perhaps that was just as well, because there was word now that, with the renewed demand for timber for ship-building, Gervaise Gideon was once again in the area.

What dealings, if any, he had with Hannah at this time nobody knew for sure. Whilst Josh had continued to enjoy his share in what was left of the Trade, not since he had made his home with his grandparents at Woodreef had he known much about his mother's involvement with the more disreputable characters and their ungodly doings. Certainly he had never been any part of it, and mother and son had gone their separate ways and lived their own lives.

By the time that Matt was a growing lad, Hannah's days were numbered. Although he knew little of her abandoned ways and wild reputation, he sensed that his parents had a certain feeling of misgiving towards her. But she was kind to him when he called on her, as he did more and more frequently, even doing little jobs for her to help her where he could.

He was seventeen when Hannah died, the year following the Fishguard invasion, and it was something which would stay with him to the end of his days. On a wild winter's night it had happened. He had been with Fred Billy Shifty and was trudging down the lane by Hannah's and was surprised to see a light in her old stable. The half-door was open and her hurricane lantern, smoking slightly and with a burnt glass, was hanging drunkenly from a nail in the beam. She was not there, nor was she in her cottage, and the door of that was open as well and banging in the wind. No answer did he have when he called her name, so he went back to the stable and took the lantern down from the beam.

A few yards down the lane, when his face hit against her clogs in the dark, by the flickering light of the lantern he found her lifeless body swinging to and fro from the branch of a tree. He managed to climb far enough up the trunk of the tree to cut her down, but although he had seen little of death previously, he saw it now in all its stark violence and horror.

He had run all the way to Woodreef to fetch his father, and then the parish constable had come. All this Matt had done as one in a dream. It was later that he began to dwell on it.

Those there were who said it was because she knew too much, and those who said it was revenge for what Hannah's children, Delilah and Josh, had once done to Gervaise Gideon. But there was no argument about the fact that it could not have been suicide, because her hands had been tied behind her back, and even the resourceful and redoubtable Hannah could not have done that, even had she wanted to.

It was then that Josh told Matt more of how Gideon had double-crossed Hannah and betrayed Seth. Delilah and Josh had never forgiven the treacherous Gideon for having their father sold into slavery, and Matt was delighted when Josh told him how Delilah had cozened Gideon, and how they had fixed him. It was a well-known fact that Hannah, not surprisingly, had been a willing conspirator in that legendary episode, and now it looked as if Gideon could well have been responsible for Hannah's murder as well as for the betrayal of her young husband all those years ago. But, however wild her way of life may have been, Hannah was Matt's Gran, and desperate enough character though she had undoubtedly been for most of her life, Matt had always had a sneaking admiration for her. Overnight almost, he had become a man and, certain in the knowledge that the Law would do nothing to bring the guilty to account, he vowed that one day he would do it himself. Josh said, 'Well, never let 'em say your mother bred a jibber', but Phoebe did not approve.

'Vengeance is mine, saith the Lord. I shall repay.' That was the text which Grandma Mona had always quoted, and Phoebe was quick to remind him of it.

10

There were those who had some daft ideas who tried to say that a man must not take the law into his own hands, but that was to take no account of all the unrest, because there was so much poverty, and so much injustice. The Frenchmen had believed that there were plenty of ordinary folk who could have been expected to offer them a bit of support if things had turned out differently when they had landed near Fishguard. As it transpired, the French had been mostly a gang of convicts, who had proved to be no more than an undisciplined rabble, and the whole venture had turned out to be a flat shot.

Now things had taken a very different course, and the great national hero, Lord Horatio Nelson himself, was coming with Lady Hamilton to dine with Captain Ackland at Earwear. And Captain Ackland set the men to picking white pobbles off the beach to make a beautiful path for his distinguished visitors, all the way down to the beach from the new doorway he had built when he had made the new driveway.

Matt saw Lady Hamilton, the renowned Emma, and Phoebe was all ears and anxious to know what she had looked like. Matt had talked to one of the serving maids, and she had described for him what her Ladyship had worn, because Matt knew that his mother would want to know the why and the how and the what and the wherefore of it all. And the serving maid said that her Ladyship had worn a white cotton Indian dress, red morocco waistband, fastened with a diamond buckle, red morocco slippers and diamond buckles.

'By gaw,' Phoebe said, 'that sound lovely.'

'Oh, hisht Mother, with thy old dullery. She's only Nelson's doxy, the same as poor li'l Leah Rhys was Gideon's doxy. An' a doxy's a doxy, an' that's that an' all about it f'rall.'

'What do'st thee know about Leah Rhys or Gideon?'

'Well, she was up at the Caban with'n wasn't she? An' I'll tell thee somethin' else, Mother.'

'What's that, hun?'

'Thicky Gideon have come back here by all account.'

Phoebe gave him a keen look. 'Who was tellin' thee that?'

'Fred Billy Shifty.'

'How would he know'n? An' what would Gideon be doin' round here now?'

'Ah, well, that's it. There's plenty of folks as remembers'n, an' Fred been watchin' 'em all down there at Earwear. All of 'em as is up in the rals was tryin' to get noticed, an' thicky Gideon was one of 'em.'

'Don't thee go near'n now. Stay thee away from'n.'

Matt said nothing to that, but he did indeed seek Gideon out. In late middle age now, and looking dissipated, he was still a dandy. Matt was able to have word with him by and by, without Gideon knowing who he was, and hinted that he knew where the notorious Hannah had hidden some of the more valuable of her booty. Eventually, Matt had revealed that he was Hannah's grandson, and said that he was the only one who now knew the secret of the cave, and that Hannah had confided it to him a year or two ago. But he said that he did not have the connections, or know how to dispose of the jewellery himself, and that was the only reason he had approached the gentleman.

The greed of the man was such that Gideon could not hide his interest. Hannah's cache, Matt told him, was in a well-concealed small cave, way up near the top of the bluff of Dolman Head. He also said that, if they were to do business, he would need a purse of forty golden guineas as an earnest of the gentleman's goodwill. Matt did not mention that the cliff rose sheer from the rocks below.

It had not been part of the deal for Gideon's shattered body to be found the following morning, spreadeagled on the rocks at the foot of the great cliff which rose to the bluff known as Dolman Head, where his horse was found wandering. By the time Gideon's body was discovered the gulls had picked out his sightless eyes and he was not pretty to look upon.

Matt had been out with a light the night it happened and, by great good fortune, had two splendid sewin to show for it. If Phoebe had her suspicions she said nothing.

For Josh the recollections came back all too vividly of Gypsy Peg and her talk of a body and a high cliff, and he recalled her words only too clearly. 'And I see the plastamengros,' she had said. 'But they will not come in your time. They will come in the time of the one who comes after you. And the one who comes after you will not be troubled by the plastamengros. I see a body and a high cliff.'

So at least she had forecast that the plastamengros would do no harm, and that was something for which to be thankful. He said to Matt when he had him on his own, 'Don't tell me nothin', son. Like th'owld sayin' of the Gentlemen in the Trade, "Them as asks no questions isn't towld no lies." I knows what thy mother would say about the Bible, but I goes by the bit where it says a eye for a eye an' a tooth for a tooth. Thicky Gideon was a bad bugger. When a done what a done to Father an' we caught'n like I always towld thee, I'd ha' done for'n myself that night only I couldn't be sure of them as was with me.'

Josh's words were a comfort to Matt, but he was beginning to wonder whether he might have brought trouble on himself and maybe others of the family. He realised that his father had been wise to put no trust in any accomplices and he was thankful he had been his own man in dealing with Gideon. He had thought about asking Fred Billy Shifty at first, but in the end had decided against it.

Some days after the tragic accident to Gervaise Gideon, gentleman, one of the famous Bow Street runners travelled from London to make enquiries. Very smart he looked in his red waistcoat with its brass buttons, his top boots and his blue spencer, but he might as well have saved his time and the trouble of such a long journey, and not wasted his breath asking questions of ignorant people who knew nothing about anything, or so it seemed. It was not even as if Gideon's horse had been disposed of, as on one previous and notable occasion, and Matt did not see any point in confusing the man from Bow Street by telling him about the purse of forty guineas, especially as Gideon had a gold watch and money in bank-notes about his person, and did not appear to have been robbed. And, in the end, the man from Bow Street said it was altogether a most unfortunate accident to have befallen a gentleman, and whatever his business could have been, it was not perhaps wise for him to have gone to such a dangerous place by night.

When the Bow Street man had gone, Josh began to feel more sure that everything was going to be all right, and he said, 'Well, Old Peg was right about the plastamengros not being much trouble f'rall.'

11

Lord Nelson was killed at Trafalgar, shortly after his visit to Earwear, and this was a cause for great national sadness. Having seen the famous admiral, Matt found his death registering more deeply than if he had merely heard about it.

The war meant, however, that there was now a demand for corn. Whilst this resulted in a measure of prosperity for those who lived by the land, rents were increased steeply to offset the better prices. Nor did all go well for those who lived in Woodreef Valley. With his great ideas for improvements, Captain Ackland drained the whole of the turbary at Earwear, where cottagers since before living memory had been accustomed to dig peat for their firing, and about which old Squire Elliot had been so generous. Low-lying, the land was subject to flooding, so the rich deposits left over the years by the stagnant floods had made the land good for tillage, and Captain Ackland could be proud of the crops this former moor was now producing.

Although the flooding meant that the peat was not of the highest quality for burning, it had, even so, been a great help to those who had lost their rights to dig turf on other land which had been enclosed. Now it was all gone, and they had to turn even more to the woodland for their firing. And the trouble was that the woodland had been ravaged by the timber fellers.

Gone were the great trees of New Inn Forest, which for so long had been such a regal sight on both sides of the valley running all the way up towards Woodreef and Clyngwyn. There was little left to occupy the charcoal burners, the tanners had more difficulty in finding the bark needed for their trade, and it looked as if the clog-makers would lose their supply of leather. True, there was some re-growth where trees had been cut down during the earlier wars with the French, but the whole chain of production was now threatened, and the life of the valley, as it had been known for countless generations, seemed doomed.

With insufficient timber for firing, coal had to be brought from the Patches at Crickdam, and it was a long haul. Sometimes, for cheapness, they brought slatch or culm from the field pits, when it was still to be had, and Josh would take 'Young' Matt with him, as Old Gramfer Matt had taken Josh himself, and show him where to find the best deposits of slime from the ancient sunken forest for mixing with the coal dust to make balls for the cottage fires which kept in all night and helped to drive out the damp. And at such times Josh would regale his son with tales which had been told to him by Old Gramfer Matt of so much which had happened in the valley over the years.

It was a hard life altogether, and when all the news was that the terrible slave trade had been abandoned at last, at least throughout the British Empire, Matt said that was hardly such a big deal as all that when you reckoned that on their own doorstep small children were having to work down the pits. They were even working, bare-footed and hungry, at Crickdam, dragging out some of the drams, harnessed like animals, or picking over the mine with their little bleeding hands until, with time, they became so calloused that they had no feeling left in them. Their poor little bare feet had become hardened almost from birth. And the children working at Crickdam reckoned they were lucky, because at least they saw something of the sunshine.

It was also only too well-known that, though the slave trade had been abolished, there was still the threat of transportation to such hell-holes as Van Diemen's Land and Botany Bay for anybody who committed the most trivial offence, even though they no longer branded such poor souls by burning them on the hand. And the magistrates still had them whipped in public.

Matt, with his little bit of schooling and some reading, thought more about things than many and he reckoned that, with the King being a lunatic, and his son, who was Prince Regent in his place, being no more than a drunken whore-master, it was no wonder the country was in the state it was. It was a common saying that the people running the country ought to be locked up in the lunatic asylums and the lunatics let out to run the country. They reckoned that even if the lunatics couldn't do the job any better, they couldn't do it any worse. Matt said that maybe it would be all right to lock up the King's son, but that would hardly be much good if it meant letting out his lunatic father.

Fred Billy Shifty had other thoughts on the subject altogether and said, 'I been talkin' to a bloke as have come back from up along as was in th'army an' knowed a man who been where th'owld King was. An' them as knowed reckoned as a was clegged half the time an' there was nothin' much wrong with'n that a dose o'salts and a good loose-down wouldn't ha' cured.'

Matt laughed and said, 'That's as maybe, fellah, but it don't alter the fact that a's mad, an' people is starvin' half the time.'

So it was no more than could have been expected that Matt's two younger brothers and their two sisters, as soon as they were old enough, set sail in the hope of finding a better land and better living overseas, for there were encouraging reports from others who had already gone to Canada. There had been much talk, too, of the New World discovered by the great Captain Cook, and the people of Templeton were full of the stories brought back to the village by John Martin.

Young Mona was the first to go, and was one of the lucky ones, having had an offer to go with a well-to-do family whose relations had already gone out to Australia and wanted help with their growing family. Two years later she sent the money home for her sister, Mary, to join her. It was to be some years later that news came that Mona had married and gone to live in New Zealand.

The two boys had other ideas. George, a bit of a tearaway, set off for America, with some sort of vague idea of trying to find out what had become of Gramfer Seth Rodda, of whom he had heard so many stories handed down in the family over the years. The last of the children, Tom, set sail for Canada with a youth of his own age from Stepaside.

A quiet and thoughtful boy, Tom had always been attached to the home and the family, and the evening before he left home, no doubt for ever, he asked that he might take with him something to remind him of so many of the stories handed down in the family. To Phoebe's surprise, and not a little to her ill-concealed disapproval, he asked whether he could perhaps have the crucifix, which had been given by Father Pascal so many years ago. For years since then it had lain in a drawer neglected.

'Aye, take th'owld thing,' she said. ''Tis nothin' but a heap of owld Popish foolery.'

'Maybe so, Mother,' Tom said. 'But 'twill be a good reminder of a wonderful owld story of Gramfer Matt.'

Sad as they were to see them all go in turn, Josh and Phoebe gave them their blessing, Phoebe shed many a tear, and prayed that they would see them again one day.

But, for all the hardships, Matt could not bear to leave the valley which had been a part of him since the day he was born, and part of generations beyond number of his ancestors who had lived there before him.

12

The year the cattle drovers brought back news of the battle of Waterloo, Matt married Jinnet Banner from Earwear, and they set up home at Hannah's, whose old cottage had long since been known by no other name. There were those who reckoned that 'Young' Matt was wise in his choice at that, rather than do as his Gramfer Seth had done and marry one of those wild ones, such as old Hannah herself, from up Pendine way. They even had a rhyme about them,

'Pendine is a funny place, a church without a steeple,
Houses built from timber wreck, and damned deceitful people.'

But, of course, the Earwear and Marros folk always spoke like that of their neighbours. There wasn't even any love lost between the Earwear folk and those in the other direction down at Stepaside. And Pendine folk, in their turn, thought nothing of any of them, including their neighbours further along the coast at Laugharne.

What the wreckers did was common knowledge, but the year the *Ellen,* a brig from Swansea, was wrecked, there was no foul play to bring her ashore on the wild beach at Marros, because there was no need of it. It was a terrible storm in the summertime, two years after Matt and Jinnet had married, and Jinnet was expecting their first baby.

The *Ellen* and her cargo had been stripped bare long before the militia and revenue men arrived, but that was one occasion on which Matt had to miss out on any wreck that was going, because Ma Probert, a grand-daughter of old Granny Hudson of revered memory, had insisted that he had to be there to keep the fire going and the kettle boiling whilst Jason was seen safely into the world.

If country folk believed that the end of the war would mean continued prosperity, they were soon to be disappointed. Prices dropped, but the rents of the farms and smallholdings remained high. Whatever poverty had been known in other years, Matt reckoned it could not have been any worse than what they experienced now. To make matters worse, the potato crop in Ireland had been struck by the blight and had failed, and some of the poor, desperate and starving Irish people were now adding to the numbers of those wandering the roads. Every day on Hannah's Plain, poor starving vagrants could be seen trudging along, with no hope, and nowhere to rest their heads. Land up in an unsympathetic parish and they might be whipped. It was small wonder that there was a steady trade for the hulks and the prison ships loaded with petty criminals for transportation.

True, those who were left in the valley and its area still had a reasonable business going for them with the smuggling, but then a dozen or so of a tough crowd from Cornwall settled in the county's coastal areas. Two of them, by the names of Truscott and Dickdelly, settled at Napp's Farm above Gilman Point, overlooking the secluded beach of Morfabychan, just beyond Marros. Cornish or not, Matt felt no affinity with them. Neither did Josh. The Roddas had been too long in their adopted land to think of themselves as belonging to anywhere else. The place was rough enough already without this lot to cause more trouble and attract the attention of the revenue men. And then a terrible thing happened.

During those years some time back when there had also been many Irish people passing through the area, some had settled. Somehow or other, Matt said, there had always seemed to be

93

trouble for the poor Irish. He knew about the building of the *tŷ-unnos* near Marros by one of the families who had settled there, because his father had told him so much about it, and how the name Teague's Dingle had come about. And, of course, Josh had talked much of Teague O'Fagan and the killing of the great bull seal, and of Old Peg's prophecies of vengeance and death in that place, and how he had often wondered whether that was why the superstitious Irishman had moved on.

At the time of the troubles after the wars with the French, long after O'Fagan had gone, there were two elderly people belonging to the Dickdelly crowd living at Teague's whose son was one of the miserable unfortunates taken away by the notorious Press Gangs. In later years there came a chance one wild night to show false lights for a vessel in distress, and the old couple were able to lure her to run ashore at Marros, but one of the crew was able to swim ashore. At first light the old couple went down to the beach and found the sailor lying face downwards. The old man said to his wife that dead men told no tales and, to be on the safe side, picked up a large stone and stove in the poor man's head. When they turned him over they found it was their own son.

13

A few years after the wreck of the *Ellen* Josh Rodda was in his seventieth year. For a few days he had not been as cheerful as usual, and then one evening he did not come in when darkness fell. Phoebe became worried, threw a shawl over her shoulders, and trudged up the lane to Hannah's. She had no need of a lantern, because a harvest moon bathed the still countryside in a golden glow, and not a ripple was there to disturb the falling leaves. But there was no sign of Josh at Hannah's. Perhaps more disturbing was the news that he had been there earlier in the day and had told Matt that he was going to take a walk as far as Teague's Dingle.

Matt, as it happened, had intended to call at the New Inn to find out from Ben Rawles whether there had been any word of a cargo of French wine which was overdue, so he set out now to look for his father and decided to walk down the valley as far as the New Inn first, in case anyone had called in there who might have seen him. It turned out to have been a most fortunate decision, because he found Josh sitting by the ball fire looking considerably bemused.

Ben Rawles shook his head slowly and sympathetically, and then told Matt that his father had arrived there an hour or two ago on his own, but had insisted that he had been brought in by a seaman who said his name was Hezekiah Trevanion. So Matt sat down by his father, who collected his wits and, perfectly rationally, told his son the same story all over again which he had already told Ben Rawles.

Josh said he had walked up to Clyngwyn earlier in the day, and then gone across the fields and walked down to Teague's Dingle to see if there was any sign of the boat they had been half-expecting. Somehow or other he had forgotten the time, darkness had fallen, then it had set in foggy as he came back up the valley and he had become lost.

It was then, Josh said, that this seaman met him and told him that he was the skipper of the *Cornish Princess*, Hezekiah Trevanion, who had sailed with his grandfather, 'Old' Matt Rodda, at one time, and had in fact put him ashore near the Blackhorn caves when he came to these parts just over a hundred years ago. Of course, Josh said, he had found such a story impossible to believe, but the man seemed to be telling the truth and had been kindly disposed towards him. Even more important, he tallied in every detail with the description which 'Old' Gramfer Matt had ever given of him. This man, who said he was Hezekiah Trevanion, was a bearded, broad-shouldered man, with an anchor tattooed on the back of his right hand and, on the little finger of his left hand, he wore a twisted gold ring with a snake's head which had a ruby for its eye. And that was exactly, almost word for word, the description of Hezekiah Trevanion according to old Gramfer

Matt. And Gramfer Matt had always said how well Hezekiah Trevanion had treated him, and how happy he had been to sail with him, and how he would have gone back to sea with him if things had not fallen out as they had, and had he not met his beloved Mona.

So Josh told Trevanion, if the man was indeed Trevanion, that he was not feeling too well and had lost his way. Trevanion said he did not know the way to Woodreef, but he could certainly take Josh as far as the Blackhorn caves, because the tide was out and they could walk along the beach. So they went down the valley, by which time the fog had cleared. After a slow walk in the moonlight they reached Telpyn Point just in time to clamber over the rocks before the incoming tide cut them off. The effort, however, had tired Josh, and Trevanion bade him to sit on one of the many flat rocks thereabouts and rest awhile. They even smoked a friendly pipe together. Then, Josh said, they realised they had tarried too long and that they would not get round the Black Hall Rock by the Blackhorn caves. He was feeling stronger by now, however, and they decided to strike up towards Tan Pits valley and, without going up as far as Hannah's Plain, walk over the top by the high cliff of Dolman Head to the New Inn and share a drink together.

By the time they came down from Dolman above the Blackhorn caves the sky had cleared and the moon was lighting up the bay like day. The tide was by now nearly at the full and he saw, riding at anchor, close in under the cliff, a great schooner. The name *Cornish Princess* was clearly to be seen painted on her bows, so he had to believe at last that it was Trevanion, however unlikely it had all seemed. And then, Josh said, which was something he had not told Ben Rawles, Hezekiah Trevanion had told him that old Gramfer Matt Rodda, whom he had loved so dearly, was aboard the *Cornish Princess* along with his beloved Mona. They had come to fetch him, and they were both waiting for Josh to join them and to sail away for ever.

There was no sign of Trevanion now, and Ben Rawles swore by everything he had ever held sacred in life, which he was prepared to admit had never been anything much, that not a living soul had been anywhere near the place when Josh had come in on his own. So, to satisfy his father, Matt walked up with him to the cliff above Dolman and, by the clear light of the moon, they could see, riding at anchor, close in under the cliff, a great schooner. The name *Cornish Princess* was clearly to be seen painted on her bows.

They went on then to Hannah's Plain, and down to Hannah's. Matt told Jinnet that all was well, and then walked up slowly with his father to Woodreef, where Phoebe was wonderfully relieved to see them. But Josh, clearly fatigued, said little and sat in his old oak arm-chair by the fire. Since time out of mind it had been his chair, and it had been Gramfer Matt's before that. Nobody could remember how long it had been in the family. All anybody knew was that it had been made in the valley, from timber grown in the valley. For a while Josh seemed to go off in a bit of a sog but, by and by, he asked for Grandma Mona's crucifix. When Matt reminded him that Tom had taken it with him when he sailed for Canada Josh smiled at the recollection and asked for her rosary. When he was a small boy Grandma Mona had taught him and encouraged him to say the rosary, but he had never bothered since those far off days.

For a little while, with a half-smile of great contentment, he sat there fingering the beads and whispering to himself. Then the whispering ceased, Phoebe held his lifeless hand and a tear rolled down her cheek.

At first light, Matt went up to Dolman Head. No sign was there of the *Cornish Princess* anywhere close inshore, but, far out to sea, against the roseate background of a sun rising in glory in the east, her distinctive rigging could be seen beginning to sink beyond the far horizon.

It was all more than Matt could comprehend, but he recognised the *Cornish Princess* as the great ship which he had seen in his vision that day at Earwear when the sea had come in far above and over him, and he had still gone on breathing and had such a marvellous feeling of joy and well-being with no thought of death in spite of all the sea, way, way above him. And he remembered again the words old Gypsy Peg had spoken to his father when he had been young. Matt had heard them from his father so often that he knew them by heart.

'I see a drowning, too, which is not drowning,' she had said, 'and it is not sad, and there will be much you will never understand until the great ship comes, because some of it is not clear to me. But the great ship will come for you, and then you will know such happiness as no mortal could ever know. And it is because you have the second sight that you will know this to be true. It is not given to many folk to know such happiness.'

Matt walked back to Woodreef, deep in thought. He told his mother he would never again be afraid of death, and said that, as the ship was sinking beyond the far horizon, he had had the joyous feeling that others on some far-off shore must surely be sending up a cheer of welcome and happy greeting.

CHAPTER 3

1820 - 1870

1

For a while after Josh died Phoebe felt she would be able to carry on at Woodreef, and Matt gave her all the help he could. Whilst the bigger and wealthier farmers were doing all right, because the new Corn Laws kept corn from other countries out and prices remained high, those who struggled for a living in the Woodreef Valley were not amongst the bigger and wealthier farmers. They were but cottagers and smallholders, who felt the poverty pinching, and pinching hard. To make matters worse, there seemed to be no end to the wet weather from one year to the next.

When Ben Knox had died up at Furlongs, Phoebe had had the land put with Woodreef, so the bit of land at Smuggler's Den went with it. The cottage at that little holding had fallen into decay so long ago that nobody could remember now when anybody had last lived there.

The place had acquired its name when an unsavoury character, by the name of Ben Scraggs, had gone there to live about ten years after 'Old' Matt Rodda had come to Woodreef. As the years went by Eli Canavan had brought odd items of news which he had picked up from seafaring people, and Scraggs' story had been pieced together.

Scraggs had knocked about the world in some rough company. A Pembrokeshire man from somewhere down Milford way, he had gone to sea as a boy with the notorious Milford buccaneer, Captain Howel Davis, whose mob of ruffians had been taken over eventually by one of his followers, another Pembrokeshire man by the name of John Roberts, who was destined to become even more notorious than Davis, and to go down in history as Black Bart. He was known as Black because of his complexion and not because of any especially dastardly behaviour. In such company his general behaviour was in fact better than that of many.

A native of Little Newcastle, a village in the north of the county between Haverfordwest and Fishguard, John Roberts was to assume the name, Bartholomew, later in his career. Matt had met and talked with him in earlier days when Roberts had been sailing quite respectably as third mate in a slave trader, oddly enough known simply as the *Princess*. Then, however, the *Princess* had been captured by Davis, the buccaneer, and Roberts had thrown in his lot with him. Shortly afterwards, Davis had been killed, and it was following this that his crew had elected Roberts as their leader. Subsequently, one of Roberts' ships, laden with captured loot, had been stolen by a traitorous former officer, Lieutenant Walter Kennedy. Scraggs had deserted Roberts, along with Kennedy, and he was lucky enough never to have fallen foul of Black Bart before Roberts himself had been killed in battle with a vessel of the Royal Navy.

In later years Scraggs spent some time in ships working off the Cornish coast before finding his way back to his native Pembrokeshire. Eventually, like most of such characters, he came ashore with nothing much left of his ill–gotten gains, but played a full part in the activities of the Trade. He had various contacts of his own, notably in the Laugharne area, from the time when he had sailed as a boy from his native Milford, and his cottage eventually became known as Smuggler's Den.

There had been no proof, but strong suspicion, that he had been involved in Hannah's murder before he, too, had come to a violent end.

No matter how high the price of food now remained, however, wages remained low, so Matt sought work and took on a contract where there was at least some money to be earned digging out the iron ore at the Crickdam Patch beyond Earwear. Being on piece work he was able to let out part of his contract to some of the cottagers from the valley who went with him. It was looking a long way ahead, but Matt reckoned that maybe one day Jason, already toddling about the place and into everything, would be able to join him and add something to the purse.

It was only natural at such a time that Matt should use as much as he could of what clothing his father had left behind, but, whilst it was one thing to wear the ancient seal-skin coat which had been made from the hide of the great bull seal killed all those years ago at Teague's Dingle, the women would not have expected him to wear the old, threadbare coat with the silver buttons. By the time Phoebe noticed, two of the buttons had been lost at Crickdam, so Jinnet cut off the remaining two to keep them safe. Not that there was anything unusual about anybody losing buttons when they were working anywhere at the Patches, for there were men there who had just come home from the wars with Napoleon. Their old army coats were all they had to wear, and the work was so rough and demanding that they were for ever losing buttons. But there was no shortage of string or a bit of wire to act as a substitute.

Originally, according to the few entries Matt made on the subject in his notebook, he had no intention whatsoever of going to live with his mother at Woodreef. More than once Phoebe had shed a tear when talking to him about the four children who had emigrated to the four corners of the earth, and his heart went out to her when he thought of all that the parting must have meant to her. But, although doing his best to help her to carry on there, any thought of moving back was a different matter altogether. Almost before the baby Ruth had started to toddle, Jinnet, a good wife and mother, was again with child, but Matt had always believed in the country wisdom of 'one dog, one bone.' He was not too sure that it would work out to have two bosses in one kitchen. Nor was he too sure about Phoebe and the Bible.

Phoebe was strong for the Church, and had done her best to instil what she could of her religious ideas into the children, and twice every Sunday she would go trudging off faithfully to Church, with her black bonnet tied under her chin, and her woollen shawl thrown over her shoulders.

There was much more to it than that, though, as far as Matt was concerned. Once, when he had been a small boy, his father had been talking to him about his great grandparents and telling him of the escape of the little French priest, and of great grandma Mona's marvellous devotion to the Old Faith. There was much about it which Josh had never pretended to understand, but 'Young' Matt had been deeply impressed and moved by everything that had happened at the time his father died, and not least by the marvellous peace which had so evidently come upon him as he so lovingly handled Mona's rosary and crucifix, and whispered the little prayers she had taught him at her knee.

Whenever he thought about the manner of his father's death he would remember once again that vision he had when he was small, which had somehow been much more than a dream. It was at one of those times when his father had been trying to explain to him about the prayer of the rosary and the bit about 'pray for us now and at the hour of our death.' It had all been very vague to him at the time, as the lady in blue had stood by the foot of his bed, with that beautiful glowing light all round her, but without speaking a word. And yet he had always had that abiding and strangely comforting memory that all was well, that everything was peaceful, and the strange feeling that she would always be there and would always take care of him. It was as he grew older that he began to think that it must have been the Mother of Jesus to whom the Catholics referred as Our Lady. And now, the more he thought about the marvellously peaceful way in which his father had died, the more convinced he was that he was right.

He was careful to speak no word of this to his mother, however, because Phoebe was very strong against the Pope and all his terrible practices, whatever they might be, and would have all the Catholics in the country burned at the stake, or worse, if anybody could think of a better way to get rid of them.

Even so, Matt tried to understand her and would make excuses for her.

'Mother's all right,' he said on one occasion to Jinnet, 'but she got it into her head that whatever the parson says is right. An' she got some funny ideas about things like that. But I knows what old great-gramfer Matt thought about things as well. An' I can mind the time Father died. I knows 'twas all a bit odd how a reckoned as thicky Hezekiah Trevanion had come to fetch'n. But I seen the ship myself. Or some ship whatever. An' I'll never forget that in all my born days an' how I had that feelin' myself of drownin' without drownin' an' bein' ever so happy about it. An' I'll never forget how peaceful a went at th'end after a'd asked for old great-granny Mona's rosary, an' that crucifix the'l French priest had gave 'em. I tell thee now, maid, 'twas wonderful to see that.'

George Banner, Jinnet's father, however, was far more interested in the rights of the workers. He was strong on that issue, and railed against the recent law which forbade Trade Unions. He also railed against the parsons and Church tithes, greatly to Phoebe's disgust, and had much to say about the fact that Dissenters and Catholics were not allowed to hold any public office. He was not in the least concerned about the Catholics but, when the Methodists finally left the Church, he became a Methodist, and to hell with all the parsons as far as he was concerned. It was no doubt only to be expected that something of his attitude would have rubbed off on his daughter, so Jinnet didn't have much love for the parsons and the church lot either, and Phoebe made it very clear that she did not hold with George Banner's way of thinking.

It was with all these thoughts in mind that Matt felt troubled whenever there was any hint that a move to Woodreef might be a good idea. It said in the Bible about blessed are the peacemakers, but he reckoned it might be easier to keep the peace if he could keep his wife and his mother apart. Come to that, if it was the Bible they had to think about, there was a passage where it said that if there was a cloud rising out of the west you knew it was going to rain, and that mother-in-law would be set against daughter-in-law, and daughter-in-law against mother-in-law.

In the end they had little choice. It was not a case of a cloud in the west, but a wind from the north-east. In later years Matt wrote a bit of Latin about it in his notebook. When he was in school, the teacher was one who had learned much of Latin from the time when it had been the language of scholarship, and it was still being used by Catholics in the Mass. The teacher had given them as an example, amongst others, a passage which he said was from the works of a great Mediaeval writer, Thomas À Kempis. The passage was, 'Nam homo proponit, sed Deus disponit,' which meant, 'Man proposes but God disposes.' And that, Matt always maintained, was exactly what had happened.

It was of an evening in November that the sky had been ominous but, so mild was their climate, snow was not something they normally expected, or for which they were ever habitually prepared. When Matt opened the cottage door by the light of the lantern at five o'clock the next morning, he was faced with a bank of snow that had fallen silently in the night.

It took an hour or two to clear a way to their small well, and by the second morning the well was frozen. It was another struggle to dig a way into their ball pit and to their dwindling pile of turf and firewood. Their diet of bread and cheese, with a few potatoes and budram was, in all conscience, meagre enough but, to compound their troubles, Jinnet was suckling a newborn babe. Whilst Jason, Ruth and the baby had to be their first concern, the cow and the pony and their few young stock had to be fed and watered as well. Before evening, the thatched roof was sagging under the weight of snow, and it was not long before the snow was dripping down on them as it began to melt in such warmth as they were able to raise.

It was on the third morning that Billy Squint and the farm servant boy from Woodreef managed to dig their way through to them at Hannah's.

Billy said, 'The missus said as we got to bring thee back with us now, all-a-both, an' the childern. So pack up thy few traps now afore it come to snow again.'

'Well,' said Matt, 'I suppose we may so well.'

The message was more of a command than an offer or invitation, but at least Jinnet understood that Matt's mother was concerned for them.

Billy Squint was a bigger man than his grandfather and namesake, and had his own cottage and few acres the other side of the lake at Donkey Hill. But his work was at Woodreef, and he was as faithful as his almost legendary forebear had been to that first Matt Rodda who had come ashore, never to go to sea again, more than a hundred years ago. Matt was thankful now to have Billy and the servant boy with him to hump up to Woodreef what few possessions they were able to gather together.

It was to be many weeks later before they could think of trying to fetch their few animals and, by the time they were able to drive them up to Woodreef, the thatch of rushes on the roof of Hannah's had caved in, and the cottage added one more to the growing number of wayside dwellings to fall into ruins. So many of the cottagers had gone away over recent years with hope in their hearts to seek a living in the more promising centres of industry, without perhaps knowing that they would be exchanging one life of squalor for another. The more enterprising amongst them opted right from the start to try their luck overseas, without waiting to be disillusioned in the search nearer home.

Fred Billy Shifty did not stay at home, however, and was not sure whether he had gone overseas, because he went to Caldey, the island across the bay.

In spite of the hard times there were limited developments nearer home, and a man with a young family had to clutch at any passing straw. There was talk of a harbour being built along the coast at Saundersfoot, and there was a plan for a fine lighthouse to be built at Caldey. Not only was there a lighthouse to be built there, but there was work to be had in the island's quarries.

Fred Billy Shifty had the chance of a job and a cottage, took it, packed up his few traps, as Matt had packed up his few traps to move back to Woodreef, and Fred's young family went with him.

Fred's eldest girl was Mary Anne, who had been Ruth's great playmate, and Ruth was sad to see her go. She was also sad to see

Mary Anne's brother Harry go, but he was just about old enough to start work, and there would be work for Harry, too, when he left school. Folks said there was reckoned to be a good little dame school on the island, so the children would be lucky there as well.

2

As it transpired, Phoebe did not live all that long after Matt and Jinnet moved in with her at Woodreef. If she found it hard sometimes not to interfere with the bringing up of the children, and if occasionally sharp words were exchanged between the two women, Matt usually managed to keep the peace. Phoebe had enough sense to realise that she was by now very much dependent on Matt, and gradually he came to be regarded as the boss.

Jason was still only in his early teens when tragedy struck. Where the fever came from nobody knew, but the general idea was that it had probably been brought by one of the foreign sailors who had been on board a French vessel which had put in with a small cargo of brandy. Billy Squint had been there with his eldest boy, and the boy had been the first to show symptoms. Ma Probert came down from Greyrock, but all her ministrations and medicines were to no avail. The boy died, so did his mother and the other six children, and they were all buried in the same grave.

Many were the stories handed down over the years, and many the tears that were shed, but the magnitude of such a blow was beyond Matt's ability to describe in his notebook, whilst Billy Squint, a desolate and broken soul, found some small comfort in the companionship of coming to Woodreef for his meals. Matt and his family did what they could to comfort and support him, but gradually, almost imperceptibly, Donkey Hill began to fall into decay, and when the thatch was damaged in the first of the autumn storms, no effort was made to patch or replace it. Eventually, Billy moved into the tallet above the stable at Woodreef, and Matt took over his few acres of land.

The tragedy did not stop there, however, for there were several deaths from the dreaded fever amongst other cottagers, who all needed help as well. Then, the following year, it struck nearer home. First of all Jason's two young brothers, complaining of headaches and aching limbs, refused their food. Then they began to shiver and sweat at the same time. Phoebe and Jinnet were the next to catch the fever, and within the week all four had died.

If there was any small grain of comfort it was that Ruth, who was now thirteen, was not at Woodreef. Word had come from Caldey that Fred's wife was ill following another confinement and Ruth, nothing loath, had been sent over to the island to help young Mary Anne.

For whatever reason, Matt and Jason survived, but the rest of the family, as had happened with Billy Squint's tragic family, were all buried in the same grave.

'Young' Matt, like old Gramfer Matt all those years ago, tried, however inadequately, to write something in his own notebook of his desolation at this time, and his heart went out, as he thought back over the years, to his namesake, who had lost his beloved Mona and written something of his own loneliness. But this was something different altogether. Mona had lived her life. Here were young tender plants mowed down before they could ever have a chance to grow. In her time Phoebe, too, had been wont to quote about Job, and the Lord giving and the Lord taking back, but the thought did little to ease the heartache for Matt at the loss of his own Jinnet. And then he would try to take heart, just like he knew Jinnet would want him to do, and he would remind himself that, unlike poor old Billy, at least, he still had some family left. He still had Jason and Ruth.

Just as it seemed to have been inevitable that Billy should have drifted back to Woodreef, so did force of circumstance cause Ruth to become a young woman almost overnight, when she returned to a grief-stricken father and brother, to take on responsibilities far beyond her years, never to know anything of the joyous years of youth.

Within months of the death of so many of his family, and of so many in the neighbourhood, Matt had another chance to think about Job and his troubles, because work at the Patches came to a sudden stop.

For some years after the wars there had been much talk about people in business going bankrupt. Then, in 1833, the iron works of Thomas Gaunt, far across the bay at Burry Port, failed, and it was to those works that the mine from the Patches had been going. So, for a time at any rate, that was the end of the work to be found at Crickdam.

Young Jason, ever the cheerful one, said, 'That's the way of the world. As one door closes another bugger slams in your face.' And Ruth would scold him about his language, and then they would laugh it off and try to look on the bright side as their troubles brought them closer together.

And indeed, just as the blow had fallen so suddenly about work stopping at the Patches, so there came now a sudden bright ray of sunshine, with news that there was work to be had on the building of a grand new turnpike road, which would replace several miles of the old Welsh Way, and which was being built by the famous road-builder, Macadam, to improve the approaches to Pembroke Dock on the great harbour of Milford Haven. There was even a magnificent bridge with high stone arches to be built, by none other than Telford himself, at Stepaside beyond Earwear. Lord Nelson had said what a marvellous natural harbour the Haven was, but it had taken a long time for anybody to do anything about it. Now there was talk of a railway coming and all sorts of things, and this would make it easier and much quicker for travellers to get to Ireland. Well, it would all be welcome, because the country people were having a miserable time of it altogether.

It had never been too good for those who had to look for parish relief in order to live, but now it became a hundred times worse, because of something they called a new Poor Law, so that if poor people wanted support they had to go into one of the workhouses which were being built. And those who ran these hellish places made life so unspeakable for the miserable wretches who went to them that, as often as not, they preferred to stay out of them and starve. There was much talk about slavery having been abolished throughout the great British Empire, but Jason reckoned it might have been better if they'd started their reforming nearer home. Small wonder that there was so much crime everywhere. They even abolished the Day for the King, *Diwrnod i'r brenin* as the old timers had called it, so that there was no longer that excuse for an occasional day off. Jason was one of those who shed no tears when the King died and the young Queen Victoria came to the throne.

Light-hearted though he was in many ways, Jason had all the sympathy in the world for those who were less fortunate than himself. And he did indeed consider himself fortunate in many ways, because he and his father had got in right at the start with the work on the new road. There had been a time when there was work to be had in hauling timber from the woods. Now, when the new road was built, Matt and Jason, having a useful team of horses, had done quite well out of the venture, and Jason even managed to put by a bit of money.

It was when the new road was nearing completion that Jason was able to find work there for young Amos Kersey from the Factory, over on the other side of the valley from Woodreef. They were the same family as the Kerseys at Tucking Mill, just across the lake from Woodreef Valley.

The Kerseys had been at Tucking Mill for generations beyond number. Their forebears had come over with one of the earliest settlements of Flemish weavers, just after the Normans, and it was their family who had established the spinning and weaving mill up the valley from the Earwear corn-mill. When the water wheel came into being they installed one and, following the current fashion, the place became known as the Factory. A thriving business it had been, too, but when times were not so good, Jason's help for young Amos endeared him to Amos's sister, Lydia. The Lydia in the Bible had also been in the cloth trade.

From all the stories and descriptions handed down over the years, Jason thought that Lydia must have looked very much like the young Mona who had stolen 'Old' Matt's heart all those years ago. She had the fair Flemish complexion, maybe bluer eyes than Mona's grey, and hair perhaps fairer than Mona's light brown. But there was the same lovely rounded forehead, the firm chin and dimpled cheeks as on the little miniature which so many years ago had been done by the artist who had painted the picture of Woodreef the year before 'Old' Matt had arrived.

Jason had known Lydia since the days when they were children and he had so often teased her by stealing up behind her and pulling gently at her long plaits of fair hair. But there was no such teasing to be now, for her hair had been swept up, and the plaits worked into a bun at the back. Overnight, it seemed, Lydia had become a young lady, and not unconscious of her charms. But it was to Jason that she gave her heart and her promise of marriage.

For some time it had been Jason's custom on a Sunday afternoon to walk down the track from Woodreef, to the place below Rose Cottage where there were stepping-stones across the ford, and walk up through the wood where Lydia would come to meet him. By the time she found herself to be with child, the work on the new road was coming to an end, and the sensible thing seemed to be for Jason to move in at the Factory, where Lydia's father had died the previous year, and where young Amos was doing his best to help their widowed mother Gwen to keep going. He thought it was wonderful to have Jason as a brother-in-law, and was more than willing to initiate him into some of the mysteries of spinning and weaving.

4

Gwen Kersey was only forty years of age when her daughter married Jason Rodda. Then there was a turn-up for the book, as the saying was, for Gwen married Jason's father, the widower,

Matt Rodda. Matt was sixty, and when Gwen now gave birth to another daughter, there was much good-natured speculation about the relationship between this new baby and the baby girl born to Lydia and Jason. As far as anybody could work it out, the grandchild was a half-sister to her own Aunt Lydia and, at the same time, Gwen Kersey had become Gwen Rodda and therefore stepmother to her own daughter-in-law. Or something like that.

'Now then, Father,' Jason said, 'thou'st better write it all down in that book o' thine in case some buggers want to know about it one day, and they'll never sort it all out.' But the chaff meant nothing to Matt, for whom his little Gwenno was more precious and beautiful than all the stars in Heaven. After the grief of his losses of so many loved ones during the terrible fever, this was for him to know happiness beyond belief.

Ruth, too, who had grieved long over the loss of her mother and the younger children from the fever, was delighted to share in the joy of caring for this late arrival, but she still found time to cross the valley quite regularly by way of the ford and walk up through the wood to the Factory, where her niece, Esther, was just as much of a delight to Jason and Lydia. Ruth was even more puzzled as to her own standing in relationship to her new stepmother, who was also grandmother to Ruth's niece. But whatever questions might arise on the involved relationships in the future, there were family matters of more immediate concern when a man turned up looking for his family, so he said. But it soon became evident that he was more probably looking for shelter.

Jack Rodda was in his thirties when he came to Woodreef. A Rodda by name, he had none of the family features, but even so, swarthy complexioned and broad of shoulder, had every appearance of being able to take care of himself should he ever find himself in a tight corner. When he had told his story and it had transpired that he was a grandson of Delilah, it did not take long for it to become evident that that harum-scarum had never married, otherwise her grandson was most unlikely to have had the name Rodda.

As a boy, Matt had always had great affection for Grandma Hannah, in spite of her reputation and her wild ways, and he had never had any real regrets for having dealt with Gervaise Gideon as he had. And he knew how Hannah's daughter, Delilah, and his father, Josh, Delilah's brother, had settled their score with Gideon. Delilah, however, had gone away with her highwayman five years before Matt had been born, and there had never been any word of the child she had been expecting at the time, or whether indeed they had married. But many were the tales which Matt had heard about her.

Delilah's man, Jack said, had been an associate of a character who had ridden with the infamous Dick Turpin, and so they had named their son Dick. Jack had no idea what had become of Delilah or her man, but he said that Dick had married, and gone to the army later on. Apparently he had taken the King's Shilling at a time when he and his family had been even hungrier than usual, and then he had been killed at Waterloo. His widow, destitute, had died young, leaving two small children, Jack himself, and a baby sister, Hannah. Some people had taken Hannah in, but Jack had gone to the workhouse before being put to work in a mill. He had no idea what had become of his sister, Hannah, but he knew from some of the stories which his father had been told by Delilah that her family had come from Woodreef Valley. Now that he was in some sort of trouble he appeared to think that it might be no bad plan to head west in his present search.

Not surprisingly, Jack had grown up a tough character and been much involved in the recent Chartist Riots in the industrial valleys of South Wales. That led in turn to involvement in the Rebecca Riots. Originally, these disturbances in the mainly rural areas had been in protest against the charges farmers were having to pay at the toll gates on the turnpike roads. It was not long before the movement provided a marvellous vehicle for those, thieves and roughnecks, who simply wanted to kick up hell's delight all round, and there were many such characters on the run. There was no knowing in which category exactly Jack had been, but he certainly seemed to be a wanted man. And he was, after all, said Matt, family.

The fact that Jack was family was one thing, but sheltering him could be risky if it meant bringing the authorities in search of him. There were people in the valley who had been involved in the skirmish at Narberth when an attempt had been made to burn down the new workhouse before it had even been completed. The militia had been called out and policemen drafted into the area from London. Rewards had been offered for any information leading to the arrest of any of those involved. Nobody had been betrayed but, as Matt said, a man could never be too careful.

It was at the time when the Penny Post had been introduced, the first steamships were now crossing the Atlantic, and word had come only a month or two previously from Matt's younger brother, Tom, who had gone to try his luck in Canada. And the word was that he was doing well and had already, by dint of sheer sweat and toil, managed to start farming on his own.

That was all right as far as it went, but there was much more news than that. They knew from a previous letter that Tom had met an Irish girl on the boat going out, but the news now was that he had married her. Whilst Tom, as was only to be expected, had been enthusiastic in his description of her beauty and her goodness, it also transpired that she was, like all her family, a staunch Catholic.

Matt, with so many of his troubles and so much of his grief put behind him, gave a wry smile when the letter came and said, "'Twas one thing for'n to ask for thicky crucifix afore a went, but maybe 'twas just as well that poor owld mother went when she did, for this would surely ha' killed her even if th'owld fever hadn't.'

'Ah, well,' Ruth said, 'let it be how it may. I don't suppose God'll worry too much about what we all was, once we gets to Heaven.'

The important thing for Jack was that Tom said there were openings to be had and he would be glad to help any of the family who wished to follow him. And, Matt repeated, Jack was family. He left for Canada before the repeal of the Corn Laws, which would lead eventually to a flood of cheap grain from the Colonies.

5

The organising of a safe departure for Jack Rodda had not been without incident, but it was accomplished in due course with the co-operation of the Squint clan at Chantry Lane, down at Earwear, and the usual contribution from descendants of Eli Canavan at the Caban. And then came a great grief for Jason.

It was the year 1853, when Lydia gave birth to Enoch. There had been two other children since Esther, who had been Jason and Lydia's firstborn, but both had died within the first week. Now it was a different story, because the baby Enoch lived, but Lydia died, and Jason was heartbroken.

At Woodreef young Gwenno was already showing signs of growing into a capable young woman, and Ruth, at the age of thirty-three, had been living in hopes of finding happiness at last in married life.

Over the years she had paid occasional visits to see Mary Anne over on Caldey, and her love for Harry had grown at the same time. More than once he had asked her to marry him, but always she had spoken of her commitments to her family. Now he had been offered the job of bailiff there, and the prospects were good.

It was a secret held close in her own stout heart when, on the face of it as cheerful as ever, she declared that there was nothing else for it but for her to move over to the Factory to look after her brother.

Ruth said, 'Anybody but a rottle dullin' would know as thou casn't look after thyself. Thee's 'ould be bugged up over there. An' 'twould be too much for a slip of a maid like our'l Esther on her own.'

Anybody with any common sense would know that, so there was no more to be said about it.

114

6

Unfitted, as yet at any rate, though Esther may have been for the management of a household as busy as her father's, she was highly skilled with the needle, as so many of her Flemish-blooded ancestors had been, and she was soon to become a seamstress whose services were sought by an increasing number of satisfied customers. She developed, too, a great skill at the fashioning of samplers of intricate design, and was for ever urging Jason to find her suitable pieces of cloth for her work.

The water wheel which gave the Factory its grandiose title was powered by two small streams which joined at the foot of the bank below the house. From the outflow the water was taken by leet all the way beneath the bank of the lane which led down to the corn mill at Earwear. It was a lovely valley, with glimpses through the tracery of spreading branches to where Captain Ackland's drainage had created the rich meadowland, opening out onto the great, wide beach with the blue sea laying down wavelets of white ribbon along golden sand. The bluebells and campion, the foxgloves and willow-herb, all in their due season, right through to the golden and copper tints of autumn, were subjects to inspire Esther's delicate patterns.

Mark Sawyer, who ran the mill, had come from the family who had worked as sawmen for generation after generation when the great forest of New Inn had been in its heyday. With the felling of acres of woodland which had never been replanted, their craft had withered and died, and Mark's surname was all that remained as a reminder of days that were gone. His father it was who had deserted his family's trade to marry the daughter of the miller and become a miller himself and eventually take over the Mill. Now Mark was following in his footsteps.

Mark had married rather late in life, and his young wife, Nelly Banner, was of the same family as Ruth and Jason's mother, Jinnet. So it was not surprising that Esther and Nelly should form a close bond. But then Nelly and her first baby both died when the child was born, and a year later, when she was still not much more than a girl, Esther became Mark's second wife.

Her baby daughter arrived a year later and Esther named her Dorcas, because, like Esther herself, Dorcas in the Bible had been skilled with her needlework. But Esther's Dorcas was still only a babe at the breast when Esther heard shouting and evident panic before the awful news was blurted out to her by a terrified apprentice who came running in to tell her that Mark had slipped and fallen under the great turning mill wheel and been crushed. Whether he had been drowned or crushed to death made little difference to a heartbroken young widow. So Esther gave up the Mill and came back to her old home at the Factory, where she would be better able to earn a living at the trade which she knew, and Ruth, now nearing her fortieth birthday, had the full care of Jason's Enoch, and for much of the time, Esther's Dorcas.

As her skills became increasingly well-known, Esther found that her services were in steady demand, and that she was being invited to the houses of the gentry to do sewing work for some weeks at a time. Ruth and her little Dorcas became inseparable, and Esther became little more than somebody who visited occasionally.

Whilst Ruth was devoting herself to the children, Jason was concerned for Esther.

'Poor sowl,' he said to Ruth more than once, 'she's grievin' terrible after Mark.'

'Maybe so,' Ruth would say. 'Maybe so.' It was only natural for Jason to try to understand his own daughter.

Then the blow fell.

Two years after the death of Mark, without any warning, Esther broke the news that she was to remarry, which meant that Ruth was to lose her little Dorcas, and she was devastated. Enoch, too, kept asking for Dorrie, as he called her. No harsh words were spoken, but Ruth felt it keenly that she had not been prepared for the blow. Though Jason was her brother, he was also Esther's father, so there was no point in trying to share her sadness with him. It was just something she would have to keep to herself, and keep on doing her best in life according to how she saw it, and as she had always done.

With a very quiet ceremony Esther had married Arthur Giles,

a man who held a responsible position in the office of the recently developed and important Bonville's Court colliery near Saundersfoot, and she tried to make light of Ruth's feelings by saying that she would not be living all that far away, so she could still see plenty of Dorrie if she wanted to.

Jason, a farmer at heart, more so than he had ever been a weaver, found solace in the fields, the crops and the livestock. Enoch, whenever he could, would be at his side and wanting to know the why and the what and the wherefore.

Ruth, too, as Enoch grew, opened his young eyes to so much of the life all round him, for the loss of her little Dorrie brought her even closer to this cherished nephew. She showed him where the blackbird and the thrush nested, where the wild strawberries grew, and warned him against the rich, shining allure of the deadly nightshade. The first time he suffered a nettle sting and began to cry, Ruth took a dock leaf and rubbed the sting, saying, 'Dock leaf, dock leaf, cure nettle thief', and the sting was suddenly better and there was no need to cry any more. So then Ruth told him that wherever there was something harmful growing, God had seen to it that the cure could always be found nearby. Ma Probert up at Greyrock had long since learned all about that as those who had gone before her had passed on their wisdom and great knowledge of such country matters.

One day, when he was old enough to go that far with her, Ruth walked with him all the way to Woodreef and tried to tell him how the once beautiful valley must have looked before so many of the great trees had been felled, and how the people must have lived. It was all so very different now, with acres of rough land where the young shoots were growing out from the stumps of trees which had never been replanted, and where masses of foxgloves were growing tall and strong, but Ruth called them dog's lugs and said that some folks called them rappers, and she called the horse violets cuckoo's shoes. She said that the cowslips which grew in the meadows were known as paugles, and the fuchsias which grew by the garden gates she called droppers. The dandelion was the piss-a-bed, and the wallflowers were bloody warriors. Enoch was quick to remind her of this when the time came, as come it had to, since he spent so much time with Jason, that he started to use words which Ruth said he shouldn't.

Here and there were the remains of cottages long since abandoned by those who had been forced to seek elsewhere for a meagre living. One such had been lived in by the Sawyers, ancestors of Mark Sawyer at the Mill, and when Ruth explained to Enoch that it was where Dorrie's people had come from, he seemed to understand what she was trying to tell him.

When they were in the shade of the high rock which towered above them, Ruth told the boy something of the escapade when his great-grandfather Seth's two children, Josh and Josh's sister, Delilah, had done what they had to a nasty, bad man by the name of Gervaise Gideon. But she made light of the story. It would be time enough for him to learn more of the truth when he was older. It was an open secret as to how Gideon had eventually met his end, but nobody spoke about these things. When Ruth showed him later in the day the remains of Hannah's old cottage, forlorn and roofless now, she told Enoch that it was where she and his father had been born, and she found it hard to fight back a tear.

It was not all sadness, though, because in the only remaining cottage in Clog Valley, there was still one old man clinging to his trade and trying to make the best of it, and he showed Enoch, as country boys had been taught since time out of mind, how to fashion a whistle by cutting a circle round a slim, short length of sycamore, sliding off one half, and then trimming a mouthpiece and holes before sliding the bark back into place. He gave him, too, a lovely wooden spinning top, which he had shaped and carved one winter evening, no doubt for some small boy who had long since followed in the tracks of so many others in the steady exodus over the years. And Ruth promised to make a whip for the top as soon as they reached home.

There was joy, too, in the welcome at Woodreef, where Gramfer Matt was delighted to take this small grandson of his to show him the newborn litter of piglets, and to lift him up onto the wall of the pig's cot and let him scratch the head of the old sow with a stick, what time she grunted her dreamy approval. Calves and a colt they had at the Factory, but they did not have any homing pigeons such as they had at Woodreef, and these had been there since way back in the time of the Normans and from the time when the dung from the dovecots had been sought after by the tanners over the way at the tan pits.

'But they be all gone now,' said Gramfer Matt sadly. 'All gone.'

His Gwenno would be going before long, too, for she would soon be marrying a young chap from beyond Marros. Preparations were in hand for the bidding, and Eli Morgans from Earwear, the last of the old talers in the area, had already been to prepare details for when he would be going round the neighbours to tell the tale and bid them to the wedding. It was mostly by the recently introduced and more fashionable post that invitations were sent nowadays, but some folk still stuck to the old customs.

Gwenno would not be moving all that far away to start with, but her mother had her own forebodings on that score, for the young man Gwenno was marrying had been talking lately, like so many others, about the opportunities over the ocean. Gwen had already buried her only other child, Lydia, so it was only natural to make some extra fuss of her grandson, Lydia's Enoch. Grandson of Matt by his son, Jason, and grandson of Matt's second wife, Gwen, through her daughter, Lydia.

No wonder Jason had once said to Matt, 'They'll never sort it all out.'

Nor was it easy for Ruth to sort out her thoughts. Always willing to give up her own home, she had rejoiced for Gwen and Gramfer Matt in the happiness they had found together after more than their share of sorrow. She had been a mother to Esther, when Lydia had died, and then loved little Dorrie with all her heart. Now she had lost them both, and Esther's going had not been without its bitterness.

Yes, Enoch, the apple of her eye, was still with her, but instinct told her that he, too, would be leaving the nest one day.

One thing Eli had been able to announce in his bidding to
Gwenno's wedding was that there would be no shortage of
victuals. With the prosperity which farmers were at last enjoying
after the long years of depression and bitter poverty, there was
now more barley being grown, and this meant that there was
plenty of malt available for the brewing of beer. At the Factory
and at Woodreef they made their fair share, the same as at most
other farms, both large and small. It was, of course, supposed to
be for their own use but, at every little ale-house where they did
not brew their own, there was a ready market for those who were
willing to sell.

'It stands to reason don't it,' Jason said. 'The buggers have put a
stop to the Trade at last, so what else do they expect us to do?'

Matt, as might well have been expected, agreed with him.
Nowadays the Trade had become no more than a memory for
the older generation, but with the ready cooperation of the
Squints and the descendants of the legendary Eli Pearce, there
was never any shortage of throat lubricant at all times as well as at
haymaking and harvest, weddings and funerals, and many other
such occasions as filled the rural calendar. The big company
brewers were far from pleased at such developments, and they
urged the newly formed police force to take steps to put a stop to
the trade. In spite of this it continued to flourish, and the home
brewing went on without let or hindrance.

Things came to a head eventually one summer when the fair
was held at Marros on land near the church. Time was when it
had been a great occasion, but times were changing. No longer
were the cattle and sheep brought in such numbers, and the stalls
were nothing compared with the old days. But there was still a
sufficient crowd for some of the farmers to find it worthwhile to
come with their home-brewed beer to sell. That was against the
law, of course, but the law had never been the greatest
consideration or deterrent for those who carried the blood of
men who, in their day, had run fearful risks in the Trade and a

variety of other nefarious practices. Never had anything been too hot or heavy for them. Many of their number had been shipped overseas in the prison hulks for their trouble, but there had never been a shortage of those who were prepared to take their chance and follow in their footsteps.

That year, the police could no longer ignore the complaints from the big brewers, and they came to see that the law was complied with. But they had not reckoned with Matt.

Old now, and leaning on a stick, he surveyed the proceedings with a wicked eye. It was to prove to be his last foray into the realms of lawlessness, but it was one which was destined to go down in the annals of history. Jason was there with a few sheep which needed his attention, but Enoch was with his gramfer, and Enoch was now a young teenager who needed little encouragement.

Living alongside the church at that time was a character who did not approve of strong drink at all, and who had recently joined one of the newly-formed temperance societies. And this character kept bees. Four hives he had, near the church, and they were known to be of the old Welsh black variety, than which there was no bee on earth reckoned to be more vicious. Withdrawing to a safe distance, Matt winked to Enoch to come with him.

When they were well out of earshot, the old man said, 'Now then, hun, get thee a couple o' them Squint cruts to come with thee an' push thicky hives over. An' once thou'st done it don't thee turn round nor look back whatever thou do'st. Just run like merry hell an keep gwain.'

Enoch needed no second bidding, and neither did the pair of Squint tyros. Matt, chuckling to himself, started walking off in the direction of home whilst he waited for the uproar and pandemonium to commence. Nor did he have long to wait. It was only later that evening that he had a full account of what he had been too wise to attempt to witness at close quarters. The retribution exacted by the infuriated bees was fearful, and Jason conceded that the pain of his own few stings was not too high a price to have had to pay for witnessing the discomfiture of the

121

police, who had been in the direct line of flight. Certain sure it was that the constabulary, as they flailed their arms like windmill sails in a hopeless attempt to keep the marauding bees at bay, had neither the time nor the inclination to concern themselves with the miscreants.

Matt, in fact, went so far as to claim that the miscreants were nothing of the kind, but were in fact public benefactors.

'I'll tell thee one thing, hun, an' that's not two,' he said to Enoch. 'Thou ca'st venture to reckon as the buggers won't ever suffer much from the owld rheumatics.'

The more worldly wise amongst the victims had used a finger nail or the blade of a knife straightaway to scrape the stings out gently, but great was the use made of the blue-bags in many a farmhouse and cottage that evening, and a steady stream of sufferers made their way to Greyrock, where old Ma Probert was a staunch believer in the efficacy of woad as a balm in such emergencies. And there was still plenty of that to be had down at Tucking Mill, although nowadays there was little enough dyeing or any other work being done where the last of the Kerseys had long since recognised that the weaving trade was in its death throes.

As it transpired, the epic of the last of Matt's inspired ideas also marked the end of the Marros summer fair as well. In any case, folk said, it was just about dead anyway. And only a year or two later old Matt died. He was eighty-eight, and still known in family lore, as he would ever be, as 'Young' Matt, to distinguish him from his great grandfather, the old patriarch of the *Cornish Princess*.

8

Enoch was fifteen when his Gramfer Matt died. They had always been close and, as Enoch had developed into a fine youth, he had spent more time at Woodreef, where his help and growing strength meant much to those who had grown old. Even Grandma

Gwen, twenty years younger than Matt, was approaching seventy and not these days in the best of health.

Enoch had had a fair schooling at the old school at Earwear and, like so many of his forebears, was reckoned to have a good head on him. In his last two years he had been the monitor first of all and then the pupil teacher, teaching some of the younger children. The teacher had taken a special interest in him, making sure that he read as much as he could, and he could speak well, though he tended to lapse into the broadest dialect when he was in the company of the older folk. Jason and Ruth had urged him to keep up his studies, and his father had been prepared to pay. There was no shortage of money these days, but Enoch was one for the fields, and the animals, and growing things.

He knew a bit about the Bible, though, because he had been to Sunday School regularly when he was younger, and he went to chapel sometimes, if only to please his Aunty Ruth. So he knew who Enoch in the Bible was, and his lot were just like the Roddas, with ancestors going back for hundreds and hundreds of years, and since Enoch in the Bible was the father of Methuselah who lived to be nine hundred and sixty-nine it was no wonder so many of the Roddas lived to such a great age.

During the last winter of Gramfer Matt's life Enoch had spent many evenings at Woodreef, sitting on the old oak skew in the warmth and comfort of the chimney breast of the great open fire-place, and listening to the old man reminisce as he sat opposite to him in the arm-chair in which Gramfer Josh had breathed his last. Towards the end of his life Matt talked a great deal about all that had happened over the years, both in his own life, and in the lives of those who had handed down their own stories, sitting there in the smoke-blackened corner, just as they were sitting now. And he told Enoch how it had come about that he had done away with Gervaise Gideon and the manner of it.

'Maybe I never ought to ha' done it,' he said, 'but if I haves to answer for it when I stands afore my Maker, then I'm willin' to do it f'rall. The world's better off without the likes of thicky. A was a bad bugger. An' I can never believe that a just God would ha' wanted a tack like that to go on livin' and blastin' the lives of innocent young maids.'

Matt puffed his pipe for a while until the silence was broken by the sound of ash trickling from the ball fire. The only other sound was the slow, heavy tick of the grandfather's clock in the corner. Matt reckoned that it had been there before ever 'Old' Matt had come to Woodreef and that it had belonged in the first place to Great Grandma Mona's father, Seth Barlow. All they knew for sure was that it had been made by a well-known watchmaker by the name of John Maurice of Haverfordwest, because his name was on the face of the clock in gilt lettering.

'Owld Seth Barlow was the one as my Gramfer Seth was named after. My Gramfer Seth was thy great great gramfer. An' thou'st heard tell often enough about my Gramfer Seth an' what it was as that tack Gideon done by'n, an' Gramfer was never heard tell of again. Aye, a bad bugger thicky Gideon was f'rall. Mind thee, I knows what it says in the Bible, and by all account 'twas what Great Grandma Mona alus used to say, "Vengeance is mine, saith the Lord. I shall repay." I knows that. But Father alus towld me as a would ha' done it hisself that night when they stripped'n an' stole his horse an' his clothes, only there was others with Father, an' a was afeart as they might ha' blowed the gaff. An' I vowed as if ever I had the chance I'd do for the bugger. Any road, a went away for a spell after that, an' then when a come back into the area you knows what a done by poor old Hannah. She was my Gran. Oh, she was wild, I knows. But there was good in her, too, an' she was wonderful kind to me. I tell thee now, hun, I loved her. We never knowed for sure as Gideon was there when she was hanged, but we knowed the ones as a paid to do it. An' paid 'em well by all account.'

'Who was it done it then, Gramfer?'

'Ben Scraggs. Another bad bugger by all accounts as I've towld thee about afore. The one as had sailed with Black Bart as they called'n.'

'So what happened to Scraggs after?'

'Aye, well, that's it. They says there's honour amongst thieves, but owld Gramfer Matt alus reckoned 'twas the punishment met out to pirates if they ever stole from their own kind was one hell of a death, so 'twasn't so much honour as that they was afeart to steal from their own. Well, I wouldn't reckon to know about that, but I knows one thing f'rall. When thieves falls out there's one hell of a owld cabal an' fandango betwixt 'em. Any road, thicky Ben Scraggs was found drownded only a few weeks after Hannah was done in. They found'n in the lake just below the pompren. They reckons as a had a fit an' fell in as a was crossin', but whether a had a fit an' fell in or not his neck was broke.'

'Who done it, did anybody know?'

'Another of his own sort, but a cleared off out o' the district an' was never heard tell of again.'

'Did they steal Hannah's money, Gramfer?' Enoch asked.

''Tis funny thou should'st ask that, hun,' Matt said. ''Twas alus reckoned as she had a tidy bit hid away f'rall, but there was never no talk about money in the wrong hands after. Her bit of a cottage had been ransacked, but them as knowed more about it reckoned as the ones as done it was afeart to hang about too long. I'll tell thee about 'em sometime. By all account Scraggs was tied up with the same family as thicky tack from down Cornwall way as betrayed owld Hezekiah Trevanion all them years ago.'

Matt knocked out his pipe and said, 'She told me once when I was not much more than a bitty crut as what she had would be for me when she was gone, an' she said there was enough to make sure as I'd never want. An' she said as when I was older she'd tell me where 'twas all hid.'

'An' didn't she never tell thee, Gramfer?'

'No, hun, never a mewk. That bugger Gideon done for her, poor owld sowl, afore she could tell me many things as I knows she would ha' towld me. But she had money put by f'rall, an' if ever thou should'st come across it, it's thine, an' don't never let nobody try to say otherwise.'

'But she never told you where the money was?'

'No, never. But I knows there was money because she told me

there was a key to the box. An' I found the key when we searched her cottage after. But there was never no sign of the box. So whether thicky Scraggs found'n or not I don't suppose we'll ever know now.'

'Do you still have the key?' Enoch asked.

'A's in thicky lustre jug up there on the top shelf of the dresser. Thou may so well take'n now. Anythin' that's in the box is all thine hun, if ever anybody should find'n. Not as anybody's likely to after all this time f'rall.'

'Was you never afeart though, Gramfer, as you might be found out?'

'Aye, indeed, hun. But that was only when I was younger. Until I could see as nobody'd found out. Mother knowed all right, but never said nothin'. An' like I towld thee. Father admitted a would ha' done it hisself if a'd had the chance. But after thicky Bow Street man had gone back I was alus main sure I'd be all right.'

'But wasn't you afeart as thy image would ha' been seen in his eyes when they picked'n up? Don't they alus reckon as when somebody's killed there's a picture in their eye of the last one as they looked on?'

Matt chuckled. 'Aye, they says that f'rall, but that's only owld superstition. Like they says that when a babbie dies an' the next is named after'n a won't live long. Well, look at me, hun. I was named after the bitty mite as was drownded when a was only a frit, an' I'm gwain on for ninety. An' there was no need to worry about any image in thicky Gideon's eyes, for the gulls had done a noble job on 'em f'rall.'

Matt refilled his pipe thoughtfully, and after a while as Enoch pondered on what he had been saying, the old man said, 'Aye, I was afeart at the time. I was only young, mind, an' I just pushed'n an' ran an' hardly looked back. But I heard'n hollin' an' screamin' as a went over the cliff. Many the time at first I'd wake up in the night in a wopple an' think I could hear'n hollin', like when a went over the edge after I'd pushed'n. Mind thee, hun, I've thought many a time as well about what I done in takin' a

126

man's life, but there 'tis. I'm still ready to meet my Maker, an' I got a strong feelin' as I'll manage f'rall.'

He took a piece of stick and lit his pipe slowly from the fire. When it was going to his satisfaction he told Enoch again of the wonderful experience he remembered from when he had been a small boy and had the vision of the lady in blue.

'I didn't understand it then,' he said. 'I was too young. But I had the feelin' somehow that everythin' would be all right, an' I reckons I understands it now f'rall.'

He closed his eyes then, lay back his head and, in a voice not much above a whisper, said, as if to himself, 'Pray for us now and at the hour of our death.'

Enoch could see that his gramfer had dozed off, as he often did of an evening, and Grandma Gwen had already gone to bed. So Enoch lit the lantern, let himself out, and set off for home.

Sam Canavan told him afterwards that there was a wonderfully peaceful look on the old man's face when he was found in the morning, apparently still asleep, but with the coldness of death on him.

9

Enoch had been to funerals before, but this was the first time for him to be involved. Now, as the custom was, it was his duty to be alongside his father to be one of those 'with his shoulder under the coffin' as it was carried from the house. A new black suit had to be hastily acquired, and that meant a journey of ten miles to Narberth. For the first time in his life he would be wearing long trousers, and he had to have a black tie and black crêpe for his new bowler hat as well. Everybody was in black and, in the case of the family, black would have to be worn for another twelve months.

He was surprised, too, to realise how many relations there were in one way and another when they were all gathered together in the one place, what with a sprinkling of Roddas from here and there, plus the Kerseys and the Banners, and even some of the Skeels from old Grandma Hannah's family, to say nothing of all the Canavans and the Squints, and so many others from all the families over a wide area. But Gwenno, who had been the joy of her father's heart, was not there. She and her young husband had long since left, as had so many others, to seek their fortune overseas.

As Ruth had feared, they had seen little of Dorrie since Esther had remarried, but she was there now with Esther and Arthur Giles. Enoch was so conscious of his own responsibilities and duties on such an occasion that he saw little of Esther or of Dorrie, but he realised when he thought back later over the day's events how his niece had suddenly grown into a young lady. Very grown-up and dignified she looked in her long, black gown, and with her hair piled high under her black bonnet. There had been some comment, he recalled, from one or two of the older women, that she had been dressed unseemingly for a girl of her age, and there had been the whispered hint to go with it that Esther had always been a bit of a fancy dresser herself. But there would always be those who were willing to do some back-biting wherever you went in life and whatever the occasion. Dorrie had a young half-brother and half-sister as well now, but they were not brought to the funeral.

There had been plenty for everybody to eat, and then the coffin was carried out and placed on trestles whilst the crowd sang a hymn. It was a hymn which had recently been written by John Henry Newman and set to the tune known as Belmont. Enoch heard no more than the first verse, before his mind, dwelling on the words, began to wander.

> '*Help, Lord, the souls that thou hast made.*
> *The souls to thee so dear,*
> *In prison for the debt unpaid,*
> *Of sins committed here.*'

Eventually, after words of prayer, they set off for the church, taking turn and turnabout with others to share the task of carrying the coffin. There was a service then, with readings and long prayers, and more hymns and words of great praise and thankfulness for the wonderful life and qualities of Matt Rodda, but never a word was there of any sins he might ever have committed.

Enoch heard none of it until there was another hymn with a line about sin which went, '*Though sin has touched them, yet their weakness spare*', and his mind went back again to his last long talk with his gramfer, when the old man had said, 'If I haves to answer for it when I stands afore my Maker, then I'm willin' to do it f'rall.'

Yes, what he had done had weighed on his conscience, but he had come to terms with it.

Just before he had fallen asleep, he had told Enoch once again of that wonderful experience he remembered from when he had been a small boy and had the vision of the lovely lady in blue, and the beautiful, almost heavenly, light which had surrounded her.

Then, as Enoch looked at the coffin below the altar, his eyes misted over, and of a sudden, he saw as it were a marvellously bright, shining light surround it and he knew, he knew for sure, that, whatever sins his gramfer had committed, those sins had been forgiven. And he was more glad of that than any words of his could tell, because he had loved his Gramfer Matt so much.

10

'Young' Matt Rodda died in 1868, and by that time the railway, so long talked about, had at last come to Pembrokeshire and had been operating for the last four years. Not surprisingly, there were the Jeremiahs, who were always against any sort of change, who said that no good would come of it, but for most people it was reckoned to be a great era, and they all said what prosperity it would bring. They had not reckoned on the cheaper coal which could now be brought from the more efficient collieries of the South Wales coalfields, nor the cheap goods being mass-produced in the factories of the great industrial centres, and what a calamity that would be for the rural areas. What the felling of the timber over the years had already started for those who lived and moved and had their being in Woodreef Valley, the coming of the railway finished off.

Cobwebs had long since festooned Tucking Mill across the lake from Woodreef, and now Jason had the unhappy task of breaking the news to the last of the Canavan boys who still worked at the Factory that there was no longer any work for them. But at least the railway provided an easier and quicker means of escape for them than had been available to those who had gone before.

There was another consideration, too. After so many years of depression, farming fortunes had for some time been on the mend, so maybe it was not too much of a sacrifice for the Roddas, Jason, Ruth and Enoch, to uproot and move back to Woodreef where Grandma Gwen was daily becoming more and more frail and needed someone to care for her.

Ruth, now nearing fifty, had long since given up any ideas of ever being able to marry Harry over on Caldey. Harry, for his part, had also abandoned any such hopes and, having decided to wait no longer, had married a young governess who had taken employment there caring for the master's children. Whatever sorrow there may have been in Ruth's heart, she did not speak of it.

Jason, even whilst he had combined his weaving with his farming, was still a farmer at heart, and there was more land at Woodreef than he had at the Factory. Enoch was positively eager. Woodreef and farming were in his blood, and never had he needed any second bidding to go there on any mission whatsoever.

Fond though he was of his Grandma Gwen, it was his gramfer who had been his boon companion, and his passing had been Enoch's first real experience of death. Even so, it was a matter of sadness to him to find that he needed his black suit, and the black tie and the crêpe, so soon after the death of his Gramfer Matt, because Grandma Gwen followed him to the graveyard within the year.

So they were left on their own with the farm servants. Just Jason, who had never looked at another woman after Lydia's death, Ruth, devoted to her brother and the family and ever sacrificing herself for the sake of others, the only ones left of Matt and Jinnet's five children, and Enoch. They heard from the families in Australia and America and Canada from time to time, especially with long, sad letters full of news when the old people had died, but little hope was there that they would ever be seen at Woodreef again.

There was still one bright spot, though, Jason reckoned. About twenty years ago some Mormon missionaries had come to Earwear and all along the parish down towards Stepaside, and a good many people from the parish had gone off with them to the Salt Lake city in Utah.

'By all account,' he said, 'there be some funny owld capers with 'em out there altogether, with men havin' four or five wives and a heap of children swarmin' all over the place. I reckons as 'tis a blessin' they never found their way up as far as this.'

Whatever was happening to those of the family who had gone 'out foreign' there was no word of anything like that ever happening to them.

Occasionally, as the years went by, his Aunty Ruth, in an unguarded moment, would let slip to Enoch a hint here and there of her unrequited love, and as he began to know her story he sometimes wondered was there the hint of a tear in her eye when she came back from the top fields from which Caldey could be seen across the bay. On clear nights, too, the beam flashing from the lighthouse was plainly to be seen, and Enoch wondered whether it held any sort of message for Ruth.

CHAPTER 4

1870 - 1875

1

Before the coming of the railway was to make its impact on the rural areas the future looked good. Woodreef was by no means a big farm, even with the extra land, amounting to no more than a few small fields and a burgage or two, which had come with Furlongs, Smuggler's Den and Donkey Hill, but there was once again a fair living to be made from the land.

There was a bonus, too, especially for Jason with his love of the horses, when it became known that an oil-works was to be built in the wood by the stream above Greyrock, up towards Clyngwyn. It was known by the people who built it as a portable plant but, as far as Enoch could make out, when he saw the kiln and the metal cooling tanks and pipes, that was only to distinguish it from some big factory. Whatever they called the whole set-up, it would mean work and activity in the forest and the valley once again.

It was more than a hundred and fifty years since the first onslaught had been made on the great oaks of New Inn Forest, and the stools were growing well to provide another useful crop. There were places, too, where mature trees had, for one reason or another, been allowed to stand. There would be no shortage of timber for the new breed of charcoal burners, and Jason was there on the spot to contract for their timber hauling, as well as to cart the drums of naphtha and pitch out to the road for the waggons to collect.

For Ruth it was a home-coming, and Jason, grateful as ever to this self-sacrificing sister of his for all she had done for him and the family, was more than happy to have any jobs done to improve the place and to do much of the work which had been so sadly neglected during the years of financial struggle.

To Enoch's delight, one of the innovations was a tread-wheel for turning the spit over the fire in that great open fire-place where he had sat to listen to the reminiscences of his Gramfer Matt in the old man's last years. And, thinking of the tread-wheel going round and round and round, he found himself thinking of the vagaries of life itself and how it had this habit of turning full circle. He remembered well all the stories going way back to the time when 'Old' Matt Rodda had come to Woodreef, and how Eli Canavan had loomed large in his life-story, in the Trade, in the droving, in the escape of the little French priest, and so much besides. Eventually a Canavan had come to the Caban, and now the family had seemingly become fixtures there and almost a part of their way of life at Woodreef, indispensable and always on call.

Sam, who had taken over when his father, Will Canavan, had died, said he knew the very man to sell Miss Ruth a dog for the wheel.

'Another Laugharnie, I expecs,' said Jason. 'Rob Jesus Christ of his boot-laces, and then come back for the lace-holes.'

'Why, no, fellah! Don't go thinkin' things like that. That's only some owld yarn them lot from Pendine puts about. Some o' them buggers ought to be had for definition o' character. The Laugharnies got more sense than to try somethin' like that on one o' their own. An' I knows a cockle-picker up there as got the very sort o' dog as Miss Ruth'll be lookin' for.'

And so, indeed, it turned out. Enoch went off with Sam, and they came home with the brightest looking mongrel anybody would make sure never to leave on his own near an open food cupboard. Part lurcher, part corgi, and probably part anything else which happened to have been passing at the time, his smooth coat could perhaps have been called brown, with a touch of black, and a shade of grey, so maybe he was not much of any sort of colour at all. But his brown eyes were alert, his stump of a tail looked as if it would have wagged if only there had been enough of it to wag, and he had, Sam assured Ruth, already been trained for his work on the wheel. And, for good measure, he was not a year old.

He had come from a cottage on the banks of the Taf, which Sam pronounced 'taav', so Tav was the only name he was ever given. When he arrived, Ruth immediately gave him a bone, and he was imbued with sufficient native cunning to recognise a sure touch when he saw one.

2

As Sam had predicted, Tav took to his work on the tread-wheel as if he had been born to it and, as the turning joint dripped its juices, his eyes would brighten, and sometimes he even gave a bark of sheer delight. Jason reckoned it was because Ruth rewarded him with a tasty morsel after every stint.

In the garden, too, Tav was never far from her side, and Enoch was as delighted about everything as Tav seemed to be. Not that he had ever been all that excited about the gardening himself, but it was always good to be with his Aunty Ruth, and it was better still to see her so happy. Even as a small boy he had been aware that there was something special in the air at springtime, but now, in their new home and with the prospects being so good, everything seemed better than ever. And, to his own self-wonderment, he found that he was really looking forward to the gardening, enjoying it, and taking a pride in it.

Not that every aspect of life consisted of all joyful and exciting thoughts. There were times when Enoch would see the cottages, long since derelict, along the banks of the lake, where the families who had lived in them were no more than names and a memory these days for the older generation. And some of the older ones not even that, but forgotten altogether.

Amidst the brambles and nettles it was marvellous how the apple trees, and even the currants and the gooseberry bushes, survived somehow and still bore fruit, to the delight of the handsome, red-breasted apple birds, as well as the children of what few families remained. And every springtime the daffodils and snowdrops, and the summer blossoms, pink and blue, and natural primrose colour, were there as a happy reminder that life would go on like the waters of the lake, flowing towards the sea, or maybe eternity, who knew what or where, which was also like life itself.

The potatoes were planted early in spring, and Enoch, using the traditional Flemish shovel, took great pride in opening the drills as straight as a line. The shovel, with its pointed blade, had a long, slightly curved handle, and was of the type which had been brought over by the original Flemish weavers. Enoch's first efforts, as he levered the shovel on his thigh, were not as good as Sam reckoned they should have been, even if they were not, as Sam also said, as crooked as Tav's hind leg.

The children from the Caban and Greyrock did their share, too, with the older ones sometimes staying home from school to earn a copper or two. After the garden had been planted, Enoch would take charge when the time came to 'lock up' the fields for hay, and the children bent their young backs to pick the stones ready for haymaking time in June when the men would be coming with their scythes to mow.

One springtime Sam happened to mention that he had been sowing some parsley seed in his garden at the Caban, and Jason said, 'Thou'rt a dull bugger, askin' for trouble like that. Thou know'st th'owld sayin', sow parsley sow a babby.'

'Why, no, fellah,' Sam had laughed. 'There's nothin' in that. Only a lot of owld foolery like Ma Probert used to talk.'

Ruth said, when Jason told her, that maybe Sam was right at that, but nine months later, just before the Christmas of 1871, Eli Canavan was born at the Caban to increase Sam and Maggie's growing family.

3

It was the following August, not long before his nineteenth birthday, that Enoch met Drusilla Warren. Not surprisingly, some would have said, it happened down at Earwear at the Big Day for

Amroth parish, where so many such meetings had taken place over the years in a holiday atmosphere of hail-fellow-well-met, and where everybody seemed intent on enjoying themselves.

On the first Friday following the Thursday of the great Narberth horse fair in August they held Big Day when, with any luck, the hay had been safely gathered in, and corn harvest was yet to come.

Not only from all over the parish and from local farms and hamlets did folk converge on Earwear for Big Day, but from way up in the Welsh parts they came, too, from Maenclochog, and Llandissilio, and Clynderwen, and all over the place, and it was a point of honour amongst the croggans to see who could be there first every year. And the traps and gigs, the milk-floats and gambos, were all spanking clean and fresh-painted, the harnesses fresh done with saddle-soap, and the brasses polished and shining to see your face in them.

Straight from the day in Narberth the showmen came with their stalls, the coconut shies, a stall where you could throw a celluloid ball into a glass jar to win a goldfish, or a stall where you could throw quoits to win a china ornament. Lovely looking ornaments they were under the bright naphtha lights, but maybe not so good, if you happened to win one, once you had it in your hand. But there were other stalls, where you could buy good quality material to occupy the needles in the long, dark evenings of winter. The spinning wheels of the cottage wives, who for generations had spun their own wool, were already beginning to pass into history.

There was a brass band, too, and a man with his face blacked with burned cork, who played the bones and the spoons, before switching to a musical saw.

All this, however, was by the way, because the real business of the day, apart from the food, was the racing and the tug-of-war, and the big wash-in-the-tide, the old Pembrokeshire term for bathing.

In the evening there would be a concert on the village green by Squire Elliot's old school house, outside the wall of the mansion opposite Billy Shifty's. Whatever name the old cottage might have had in the past, for many a year it had been known by no other name, just as Hannah's and so many other cottages, long since abandoned, had come to be known by the names of those who had lived in them. There was talk now that the school started for the children of Earwear by Squire Elliot would be closing as well, because a Mr Forster had passed an Act of Parliament about education, and a new school was to be built up Chantry Lane at the top of the hill by Amroth parish church, and this new school would serve the whole parish.

At Woodreef on the morning of Big Day they were early astir, for there was crockery to be wiped, and cutlery and food to be packed in baskets, boiled ham, beef and mutton, cold potatoes, pickles and cheese, and lashings of bread, butter, jam and a rich fruit cake. The linen was snow-white and spotless. Ruth could have tolerated nothing less than what she saw as perfection. Fires burned on the beach, where kettles were boiled, tea was taken round in large cans, and there was home-brewed as well.

Although it was the year when Enoch met Drusilla, when he could have been forgiven for being oblivious to all else, he was so attached to his Aunty Ruth, and knew her story so well, that he was sufficiently observant to notice that the romantic side of the day was not so good for her. She had passed her fiftieth birthday the previous year, but Enoch had no doubt it would have aroused strong feelings in her when she saw Harry Billy Shifty with his wife and two small children. The word was that they had managed to come over from Caldey for the week-end, and Harry certainly looked prosperous in his suit of broadcloth and his belltopper hat, with his wife in a fashionable blue gown and bonnet. Nor did it escape Enoch's notice that Ruth somehow contrived to avoid a face-to-face meeting. There were so many people swarming all over the place that it was not too difficult to avoid anybody you would rather not meet.

For that matter, the crowd was big enough for him to have avoided Drusilla had he so wished, but he did not so wish. The day was far advanced when he caught sight of her across the green, where her attention was fully concentrated on the wares of a stall-holder selling wool and lengths of cloth. Dark, with a complexion like milk and roses, she was not tall, and yet had a commanding presence. Her straight nose was that of one of breeding, and she wore a fitted bodice and full skirt of wool check, pleated into a waist-band, and trimmed with gold braid, which would have become a princess. Or so thought Enoch. She wore laced-up boots and a wide-brimmed, white sun bonnet with ribbons in it.

It was no difficult matter to move over to where she was standing and to examine a length of cloth himself. Then, whilst she was still intent upon her possible purchase, Enoch engaged the man in conversation and they were soon talking about selvedge and weft, and shuttle and warp and woof, and the man took the piece of cloth in which Drusilla had been showing an interest to illustrate his point, and the next thing anybody knew all three were talking together.

'Thou looks like a farming man to me,' the man said, 'so how come thou know'st so much about this business?'

'I was born and brought up at the Factory,' Enoch said.

'Not here at Earwear?'

'Why, aye, of course.

'Well never muv from here alive again.' The man eyed him keenly, then said, 'Thou'rt not Lydia's boy?'

'Aye, indeed I am, but I never knew her, of course. She died when I was born.'

'Aye, indeed, fellah. I remembers it well. A terrible sad job 'twas. My missus an' her was wonderful big friends an' she grieved about it terrible. She'll be main sorry she wasn't here today when I tells her.'

Then there was talk of the Kerseys and the Roddas, and somehow the man seemed to think that Enoch and Drusilla were together, and Enoch did nothing to discourage the idea, and the upshot of it all was that Drusilla bought the length of cloth in which she had been so interested for not much more than half the price that had been mentioned in the first place. The deal done, it seemed the most natural thing in the world for Enoch and her to walk off together, and Enoch carried her purchase for her.

4

Enoch was to see little of Drusilla again until they married four years later. That first evening they did not stay for the concert, but Enoch walked with her to the station at Kilgetty where the wonderful new railway ran. He had been, as had many others, to stare in wide-eyed wonder at the great steam trains which now belched their smoke across the countryside, but this was the first time he had been with such a crowd who were going back 'down-line' following an outing to Big Day. He walked with Drusilla by way of Pleasant Valley and the ironworks at Stepaside, and he found it hard to believe that the way could have been so short or time have sped on such wings. And then she had gone.

Her story was a sad one, but not entirely without hope. Nothing had she known of family life such as had been Enoch's, even though he had never known his mother. Jason had been a good father, and there had always been his Aunty Ruth, to say nothing of his Gramfer Matt for the first formative and impressionable fifteen years of his life. Sella, as she had soon asked him to call her, had been a foundling knowing nothing but the rigours of the workhouse and the harshness of existence there until she was eleven years of age. Then her luck had changed and good fortune come her way.

A bright and pretty child apparently, which Enoch found it easy to believe, she had attracted the attention of a charitable lady who was in the habit of visiting the workhouse, and who had taken Sella into her employment. She it was who had then gone to some trouble to find out the child's background. Little enough was there to know except that the mother was considered by her well-to-do family to have married beneath herself. Disowned by them, she had died young in childbirth at a time when her husband had just been lost at sea. All that Sella possessed of value which had belonged to her mother was her beautiful gold wedding ring, and this she cherished.

So well had Sella responded to her benefactor's interest and kindness that the good lady had seen to it that she was educated and taught music and needlework, for which she had shown a particular aptitude. Her intention had been to do even more for Sella, but she had died the year previously just after Sella's seventeenth birthday. There had been a small endowment, provided that Sella did not marry before the age of twenty-one, but a dishonest lawyer, entrusted with the handling of the lady's modest estate, had feathered his own nest whilst keeping in with the lady's family, and robbed Sella of anything else she might reasonably have expected to inherit.

Her accomplishments, however, and the grounding which she had been given, stood her in good stead. She still had a touch of her rich Pembrokeshire accent, but she was well-spoken, and had found employment as a nursemaid and seamstress with a family who had a small estate near Pembroke. They had treated her fairly enough and in many little ways with kindness. In a week's time, Sella said, they would be moving to London for a few months and she would be going with them. As if that were not bad enough for Enoch to hear, she also said that one of the sons of the family was soon to be married and would be taking over the estate, so the parents, by whom Sella was employed, would be spending their time between their London house and another estate in Cornwall, because they were wealthy and had a great financial interest in the copper and tin mines.

Certainly she would write to Enoch. She would be having a day off next week, too, so she agreed to his suggestion that they could meet in Tenby and spend the day together. She could come by train from Pembroke, and he could ride the ten miles or so to Tenby on horseback.

Then, with a great gush of steam from the engine, there was a last minute slamming of doors, a clatter of carriage couplings as the train jerked and shuddered, and finally drew out of the station. Enoch stood and watched it go, until the red tail-light of the guard's van, winking in the gathering dusk, had disappeared round the bend towards Saundersfoot and left him standing there on the platform which was destined to be the scene of so many sad partings and joyful reunions in the coming years.

Darkness had fallen long before he had walked further than Pleasant Valley, but a red glow from the ironworks lit the sky and, by the time he had topped the rise at Pleasant Green, the moon was riding high over the bay. As he came down the hill to the Burrows and walked on to Earwear with his heart as light as his step, there was a great golden swathe spreading across the sparkling ripples to Gower Peninsula in the far distance. On the green at Earwear the debris of the day remained, but only a few young late night revellers were still there from the crowds of earlier in the day.

A barn owl screeched somewhere in the distance as he came up the track by the high rock, and small nocturnal creatures scuttled through the undergrowth. By the time he reached home Woodreef was as silent as the grave.

5

However intent Ruth had been on avoiding Harry Billy Shifty and his wife, she had evidently not been too preoccupied to have kept an eye on Enoch and the young lady who had so absorbed his attention. There was nothing much in anything she said, but more perhaps in the things she had left unsaid. Enoch had been left with the distinct impression that she did not entirely approve.

His father, if anything, appeared to be amused. Later in the day, when they were on their own, Jason said, 'Don't thee worrit thy head too much about thy Aunty Ruth. Whoever thou should'st bring home here'll never be good enough for thee in her eyes.'

'Aye, but she seemed to be hinting that Sella looked a bit filty fine.'

'Why, no. She certainly wasn't that.'

'Did you see her then, Father?'

'Why, aye. O' course I seen her.'

'An' what did you think of her?'

'She looked a main tidy sort o' maid to me.'

'Well, that's all right then', said Enoch. 'But what d'you reckon's got into Aunty Ruth?'

'Why, fellah, think for thyself. Thou'rt still her only'l molly lamb, an' she can't abide the thought o' losin' thee. But once she've met the'l maid she'll change her mind no doubt.'

It was to be many a long day, however, before that would come about.

Over the coming days Enoch had little thought in his head other than his meeting with Sella, keeping a watchful eye on the weather and worrying in case she would not be there if he went to Tenby. Shanco, the big Welsh cob, namesake of that Shanco of long ago, who had played his noble part with those legendary characters in the oft-told story of the escape of the little French priest, had extra special grooming, and the saddle and bridle yet another good polishing.

Enoch rode down the track to New Inn and, when he came in sight of the shore, he could see that he need not have worried about the weather because the tide, which was on the ebb, was running down from Telpyn, and that was always a sure sign of good weather. Enoch got down to lead Shanco down the bank of pebbles, then remounted and cantered him along the beach all the way from the Blackhorn caves below New Inn to beyond Earwear and the Burrows. Once or twice he walked him in the sea, with the health-giving salt water coming up to above Shanco's knees. Every horseman knew that there was no better exercise in all the world for strengthening a horse's muscles.

At Crickdam, although the roof of the thatched cottage had fallen in and the cottage had been abandoned, there was again work going on at the iron ore patches. But no boats came to the open beach these days to load the mine as they had in earlier years, because it all went to the ironworks along Pleasant Valley at

Stepaside, and the whole of the cliff-face and the beach were alive with great bustle and stir. The tide was far enough out for Enoch not to have to stop to talk to anybody, so no one could ask his business as to where he was going all dressed up like a real young gentleman.

Out in the bay, hove-to off Monkstone, a full-rigged schooner rode at anchor, waiting for the tide to answer so that she could come into Saundersfoot harbour. Above the walls of the harbour, dry at the moment, a small forest of masts could be seen sprouting skywards from vessels being loaded, and some, already with their gear stowed and hatches in place, ready to sail on the evening tide.

At the foot of the cliff from Wisemansbridge to Saundersfoot a railway now ran, and this had necessitated the building of three tunnels. The drams taking the iron and coal to Saundersfoot harbour from Stepaside, and the firebricks and iron goods from the brickworks and foundry at Wisemansbridge, were drawn by horses, but there was talk now that new rails were to be laid and that the horses were to be replaced by a steam engine. Jason, talking about it a few evenings previously, had seen a dark cloud on the horizon for those who reckoned to make some part of their living out of horses. So maybe the Jeremiahs had been right after all when they had said that no good would come out of it when the steam trains had come into being. But had it not been for the coming of the railway Enoch doubted whether he would ever have met Sella, and certainly he would not have been on his way to meet her now.

At Saundersfoot, Enoch gave a passing thought to Dorrie, and to his sister Esther and Arthur Giles, and wondered how they were doing. Little had been heard of them at Woodreef for some time and it was long since they had been there. For no more than a fleeting moment he wondered whether to take Shanco up off the beach and see whether Arthur was somewhere in the office on the village green, but very quickly dismissed such a foolish thought when he was on a far, far more momentous errand. So he took Shanco across the stream which flowed onto the beach at the mouth of the harbour, out beyond the great wall of the pier head, and cantered gently along the last short stretch of sand to come up into the Glen below Swallow Tree Wood. Some of the toffs had recently built some very nice houses in the Glen but, today of all days, Enoch felt as big a toff as any of them. In less than another half-an-hour he was in Tenby.

Shanco, stabled for the day at the hostelry in Upper Frog Street, once his saddle and bridle had been removed and he had been rubbed down and fed and watered, with a net of sweet-smelling hay left in front of him, settled to his strange surroundings without any undue fuss or apparent misgivings. Enoch took out his new half-hunter watch from the pocket of his embroidered waistcoat and saw that he had more than an hour to kill, so he wandered round the town and looked down at the harbour where some fine boats were lying high and dry. Others, including a few of the distinctive Tenby luggers, were about their business or at anchor out in the bay.

The sun shone, the sky and sea were blue, the whole town seemed to be thronged with folk of quality come to take their ease at the popular seaside resort, and the bathing machines on the North Beach were doing a busy trade. As the clock on St Mary's Church struck the hour, Enoch looked at his watch again, feared that he might have dallied too long, and then more or less ran most of the way to the station, only to find that quarter-of-an-hour was apparently another word for eternity when it came to having to wait.

6

Whether his Aunty Ruth would have described Sella as filty fine today or not, Enoch was not sure, but she looked even more beautiful than he had remembered her from only a matter of days previously. A less besotted observer could have told him that she was wearing exactly the same clothes as when they had met.

Now that the moment had arrived Enoch had clean forgotten

all the things he had been planning to say to her and could do no better than to take the basket she was carrying and, when she exhorted him to be careful not to drop it, ask her what was in it.

'Our food for the day, of course', she laughed, 'what else?'

That broke the ice, and for the rest of the day there was never a doubt as to their burgeoning love for each other. Enoch had already had some vague thoughts as to where they might eat, or what they could do, but if Sella had been sufficiently practical as to bring food, then that was bound to be a good idea.

Having walked up to the town and looked down at the crowded beach, there seemed to be an unspoken agreement between them that it would be no place for young lovers who would be interested only in each other's company. So they walked down to the harbour, where there was no great activity at the moment, since the tide was out, and then round the Castle Hill, which was evidently a popular place for the ladies to parade in their finery, with their gaily coloured dresses, fashionable bustles and many-hued parasols. On St. Catherine's rock opposite, where until recently, Enoch said, there had been a mediaeval chapel, a great new stone fortress had been built, apparently in case there should ever again be wars with the French.

Thinking they might be able to view the fort they walked down by the old lifeboat house to the Castle beach. The fort not being open to the public, however, they decided instead to explore along the golden sands all the way to the South beach.

Close across the water the lighthouse on Caldey stood out white and prominent against the blue sky. The island had been bought recently by a gentleman by the name of Mr. Hawksley, who was spending large sums of money there on the farm, with new buildings and machinery, and the quarries on the Island were busy as well. Of greater interest was the fact that the bailiff was Harry Billy Shifty, so Enoch told Sella something of his Aunty Ruth and his own family, and his Gramfer Matt's story of his boyhood experience of a drowning which was not a drowning when the tide had seemed to come in over the cottage of Matt's friend, Fred Billy Shifty, and then the incredible story of the coming of Hezekiah Trevanion and the *Cornish Princess* when Gramfer Matt's father, Josh Rodda, had died.

For a long time whilst Enoch was telling Sella all this, as they walked along the beach where there were far fewer people, they had been holding hands, until eventually they reached the seclusion of the sand-dunes. There was a profusion of marram grass, scrub willow and burnet rose now in the hip stage, and there was, too, a wealth of flowers which, in spite of all that Ruth had told him when he was a boy, were new to Enoch. But he had other things on his mind than trying to identify unfamiliar plants, and it was there, in a sheltered corner, that he kissed Sella for the first time. For the rest of his life, which was not by any means destined to be all happiness, Enoch was never to forget one moment of this perfect day.

7

They had eaten their picnic in some shyness after that first kiss but, by the time Enoch had kissed her several times again, and Sella's dark hair was tumbling down below her shoulders, their feelings for each other were clear to both of them. When he asked her to marry him, though, she laughed, not unkindly, and said, 'Don't be silly. We're too young.'

'How d'you talk like that?' Enoch said.

'And where would we live?'

'What's wrong with coming to live with us at Woodreef?'

'What? With your Aunty Ruth?'

Enoch seemed to ponder on that, and then Sella said, 'What was that you were telling me about your Gramfer Matt talking about one dog, one bone?'

'That was different,' Enoch said.

'What's the difference then?'

'Well, Aunty Ruth is special.'

'Of course she is. She brought you up, didn't she? Worships

you, I shouldn't wonder. And what d'you reckon she'll think of any woman taking you away from her?'

'But you wouldn't be taking me away. We'd be together.'

'That's right, two dogs fighting over one bone. Only in this case it would be two bitches, I suppose. Same thing, though. Only worse maybe.'

They both went quiet for a while then, until Sella took Enoch's hand and said, 'All right, I'll marry you. But wherever we live it can't be yet. We haven't got any money.'

'I thought you said not to be silly. I've saved a bit already. Everything on the farm's between Father and me, and 'tis paying pretty good money these days.'

'So they tell me. But the Agent for the estate knows what he's talking about, and he reckons that now the steamships have started bringing in things from abroad, wheat and butter and all that, times could soon turn bad again for the farmers.'

Enoch did not try to argue. His father had recently been talking about the effect the small engine for the colliery at Bonville's Court would have on the horse trade, and everybody could see already what was happening in the area, with the railways bringing in cheaper coal and factory produced goods.

'That's fair enough, I suppose,' Enoch said. 'Gramfer Matt always used to say 'twas money made the donkey gallop, but I'm not all that sure.'

'You would be if you didn't have any money. Hungry, like they used to be in the old days. Like I was when I was only a child in the workhouse. Starving half the time.'

Enoch's heart went out to her and he held her hand and kissed it.

'That won't happen to you again as long as we're together.'

'Not if I can help it. If we were daft enough to rush off and get married now I'd lose the bit of money I'll have coming to me when I'm twenty-one. There's an old saying down Pembroke way, "If they haves thee once, shame on them. If they haves thee twice shame on thee." That lawyer had me once, but he won't have me a second time.'

There was an old saying, too, as Enoch remembered it, 'If you canna feed a child afore a's fourteen, it's not a bit of good for you to start after.' The thought hardly disturbed him now as he looked at Sella, her face radiant and the picture of good health, but it was understandable if the hardships of her childhood had left a scar on her mind. Please God, he would help her to make up for it all one day.

'That's sensible enough, I suppose,' Enoch said, 'but are you bound to go away with your people?'

'No, I'm not bound to. But I'm going. I've told you before, they've been fair enough with me, and they've always treated me well. Three years'll soon pass. If anything's worth having, it's worth waiting for.'

Enoch had to acknowledge to himself that there was sense enough in what she was saying. They agreed that she could probably come to Woodreef for a holiday or two during those years, but three years seemed a life time away. Still, she promised faithfully to write to him every week. So maybe the wonderful new railways had something to be said for them after all, carrying letters all over the place in no time at all.

There was one last, long passionate kiss then before Sella got up, smoothed down her crumpled skirt, and began to put up her hair, what time she complained laughingly of the mess Enoch had made of her.

The afternoon was far advanced by the time they strolled back to Tenby. The carriages of the gentry were much in evidence, and Enoch could not help but stand and admire a few of the horses. But even that could not distract him from the real business of the day and he suggested to Sella that he should now buy her an engagement ring. Sella, as ever, essentially thrifty and practical, said there was plenty of time for that, but to buy her a piece of ribbon. She knew it was an old fashioned custom, but it meant that they were sweethearts. There was time afterwards for a snack in a pleasant little tea-room which they found near the town's historic Five Arches, and then it was a lingering stroll back to the station to wait for the train, which came far, far too soon,

149

and left Enoch standing forlorn and lonely on the platform. Then he bestirred himself and walked slowly back to the town to where Shanco was waiting for him.

The tide was at the full now, so there was no thought of crossing the sands anywhere. At Saundersfoot, Enoch dismounted to lead Shanco through the three tunnels along the dramroad, and from Wisemansbridge he took the cliff road above Crickdam and the patches. Shanco was no doubt puzzled at the leisurely trot which was the most that was required of him when he was not walking, and the shades of night were falling by the time the smoke from Woodreef's round chimney came in sight.

8

For the next two years Sella's weekly letter was a constant source of comfort to Enoch, and he always replied to them just as faithfully, telling her of all that was happening at Woodreef and in the area. He kept every one of her letters, written in a small, neat hand. Often, there was not much to be told other than of her work and of the members of the family and what they had been doing, but she never failed to proclaim her love for him and stress how she was looking forward to their life together.

In the meantime, however, there was work to be done, and life had to go on. If Ruth had her misgivings, she said little when Enoch had announced their plans for marrying. It was always more by what she did not say that Enoch thought he could fathom what she was thinking. On the other hand, with Sella being so far away, for much of the time it was a case of out-of-sight out-of-mind, and life went along smoothly enough.

Jason was understanding and that meant a great deal to Enoch. He was understanding of his sister, too.

'Thou'st got to mind as she've gave up a lot an' put herself out for us', he said on one occasion. 'Wanted to marry an' have childern of her own, but 'twas never to be for her. So don't think too bad of her.'

'Good God, no, Father. I don't think bad of her. It's just that you can see she thinks Sella isn't up to much. Says things about her not looking healthy and all that sort of thing. And she doesn't know her or anything about her.'

Not for the first time, he wondered whether he should tell his father and Ruth about Sella's childhood, but decided not to. Let Sella tell them for herself if she wanted to when the time came. No doubt it would all come right in time.

The profitable years on the land continued, with good crops safely harvested, and good prices being paid for the stock and produce. Even the workers in the hayfields looked more prosperous in their white or yellow corduroy trousers or breeches, grey or brown homespun coats, and well cleaned and greased tack-boots. Enoch told Sella of all these things in his letters, and he told her, too, of the pleasure amongst the workers at Stepaside ironworks and in the pits that the trade unions had been legally recognized at last. That would have pleased George Banner, the old campaigner, no end if only he could have lived to see it. And the new Education Act meant the building of new schools as well. The school where Enoch had done so well at Earwear had already closed, and now the old school at Marros was to close and a new one was being built nearer to Pendine. At Crunwear there was to be a new school nearer to Woodreef, so the children could walk there now to go to school every day.

Until then the school at Crunwear had been run by old 'Billy the Gate'. For years Billy Oriel had kept the toll gate on the new turnpike road, whilst earning his living as a cobbler, and he combined these duties with the use of his little house for the keeping of a school for about twenty pupils. His cobbler's leather knee-strap had been adapted when needed as a powerful instrument of correction, and he had turned out some useful scholars, but now there was to be a proper school with a proper teacher.

Enoch told her, too, of some of the preachers who came to the chapel, including the one who came on horseback. There was

151

such a powerful offering of hell fire and brimstone with him, as well as a full measure of fear and punishment mixed up with it, that Enoch said it might have been more sensible if he had come on a donkey and then, if the donkey had been as sharp as Balaam's ass, he could have preached his sermon for him. But Ruth did not care much for that sort of fun to be made of the preacher. Apart from all that, the same preacher was hot and strong against the Pope with his pink stockings, but whenever Ruth looked like following down that road, Enoch would remind her of what she herself had said when the news came from Canada that Gramfer Matt's brother, Tom Rodda, had married a Catholic.

'Ah, well,' Ruth had said, 'let it be how it may. I don't suppose God'll worry too much about what we all was, once we gets to Heaven.'

'Now come on, Aunty Ruth,' Enoch would say. 'Tell the fact. That's what you said, wasn't it?'

But Ruth was strong for the chapel these days and, every Sunday, would be there faithfully in her lilac gown, well-flounced and expanded with crinoline, a wide ribbon fastening her bonnet, and tied in a large bow under the chin.

9

About this time Ruth said they should put headstones on the graves of any of the family who had died recently, and Jason agreed with her. Usually this was something to be done a year after the funeral, but times had been hard and money tight. Then, it was so easy to forget, and nothing was done. There was no reason now for them not to do what they could not afford to do at the time.

There was, of course, only one man to go to, and that was the renowned stone mason, old Thomas Morris, over at Morfabychan, who had become almost a legend in his own life-time. Life was very different at Morfabychan these days from what it had been before the Trade had been brought to an end, when the Dickdelly crowd and Ben Scraggs and his kind had made free of the secluded bay, and where there had been many a rough encounter. Tom Morris was a different sort of character altogether.

This renowned old mason was fond of working with a particular type of stone from the quarry at Pwll, near where the cockpit had been in the days of Seth Rodda and Gervaise Gideon. He used to polish the stone until it came up in a black lustrous surface flecked with white shells, which he called snowdrop marble, and his lettering and scrollwork were beautiful to behold.

His wife, Jenny, was also a character from another age. One of Nature's ladies, with a gentle manner and a sweet smile, she wore a Welsh high-crowned hat, with full-frilled cap and the native woollen shawl. Not only were they self-supporting with their geese and pigs and chickens, but Jenny also spun the wool from their own sheep and wove it to make their own clothes and blankets.

Of all these things Enoch wrote to Sella, but it was because of Tom Morris as a musician that he knew she would be interested, for he was more than just a country artisan. He was also a musician of repute, known as the Bard of Morfabychan, who played the bass viol and sang many ballads of his own composition.

At the time when Jason and Enoch went to see him about ordering the headstones he was under threat of having to quit the cottage which had been his home for so long, and he had composed a ballad because of it. Before they left he sang it for them in a surprisingly strong voice for one of his age, and Enoch was able to remember a couple of the verses and write them down for Sella when he next wrote to her.

Oh, the old house at home, where my forefathers dwelt.
Where a child at the feet of my mother I knelt;
Where she taught me the prayer, she read me the page
Which if infancy lisps, is the solace of age.
My heart, 'mid all changes wherever I roam
I think of the past in my old house at home.

Oh, I mourn for the cot where I spent all my time,
From the first day of childhood to the height of my prime,
But now to my sorrow it's no home for me,
In that lone little cot that's so near to the sea;
But it is my desire ne'er from there to roam,
But to spend my last days in my old house at home.

Enoch was pleased to be able to tell her in a later letter that the notice to quit had been withdrawn, and Sella wrote back to say that she would love to go with Enoch to see the old couple when she came to stay, and to hear the old man play his bass viol and sing. And that was when great preparations were afoot at Woodreef for her visit, almost two years after she had gone away.

10

Fair play to Aunty Ruth, Enoch said, whatever misgivings she might have had over his choice of a wife, she made quite sure that Sella would be shown a good welcome and have no cause to complain about her reception at Woodreef.

It had been part of their promise to each other that day in Tenby that she would come to stay for a holiday, and now, two years later, the time had come at last, and Ruth immediately began to busy herself having everything put in order. Then Ruth rather spoiled it all, as far as Enoch was concerned, by saying, 'If we're gwain have a grand lady to stop with us then we may so well aim to make the place look filty fine and clicksy.'

Enoch said nothing, but smiled to himself as he thought that one day she would know the truth about Sella's childhood, and he wondered what her reaction might be to that.

It was known that when 'Old' Matt had come to Woodreef best part of two hundred years ago, he had been given the little bedroom at the back, overlooking the wild acres of heather and gorse running up, beyond the hovel known as the Caban, towards

Crunwear and the quarries below Llanteague. But things had changed since then. At the time of the enclosures land had been reclaimed, fields had been created, and the Caban, following the improvements effected by Gervaise Gideon, was no longer a hovel. The same room as 'Old' Matt had been given was now being made ready for Sella, and it was indeed a room with a pleasant outlook. With new wallpaper, and a new quilt on the bed, to say nothing of a beautiful new wash basin and water jug of finest quality Staffordshire pottery, with an extravagant pattern of roses, Sella should at least receive the outward impression of being welcome.

With the date of her visit fast approaching there had not been the usual letter from Sella throughout the week, and then, on the day before Big Day itself of all days, that memorable occasion of their first meeting, the blow fell. Instead of the looked-for letter from Sella, a letter came in a rather unlettered hand compared with Sella's, from one of the housemaids who worked for the same family to say that Sella had a fever and the doctor had said that probably she would be unable to travel for some weeks, but she would write as soon as she was well again.

Enoch had no heart for the fun of Big Day after that, but stayed home and went for a walk through the woods and the fields with Tav. At least he could talk to Tav and confide in him, and pour out all his troubles to him, whilst Tav would not be asking a heap of questions when Enoch wanted only to be quiet.

Even the itinerant workers at the oil-works had taken the day off to go to the Big Day, so there was no point in walking up that way. He went up instead towards the Caban, and round by Furlongs to come back down the lane towards the lake and over the pompren. And that was where Enoch noticed, not for the first time when he came to think about it, that Tav's behaviour was strange beyond rational understanding. He stood still, he was tense and alert in his every look, and the hairs along his back stood up. Nor would he cross the pompren. Sam Canavan always reckoned that dogs and horses were aware of evil things that had happened, and Enoch recalled yet again one of the last talks he had ever had with his Gramfer Matt just before he died.

'Thicky Ben Scraggs was found drownded only a few weeks after Hannah was done in', Gramfer Matt had said. 'They found'n in the lake just below the pompren. They reckons as a had a fit an' fell in as a was crossin', but whether a had a fit an' fell in or not his neck was broke.'

Whatever evil spirits were there, Tav would seem to have been aware of them, for he would not cross the pompren, but stood and growled, so Enoch walked on and left him. Tav caught up with him shortly afterwards, all dripping wet and shaking himself vigorously, so he had evidently preferred to cross the lake by coming through the water at some other point.

A fortnight later a postcard came from Sella to say that she was feeling better, there was no need to worry, and she would write as soon as she could. The following week there was a long letter saying that she was now much better, apart from a silly little cough, that Squire Legassick and Madame had been wonderfully kind to her, paid for all the doctor's visits and medicines, and now insisted that she go with them for a long stay to their place in Cornwall, where the fresh air, the doctor had said, would do her the world of good, especially after the miserable weather of the previous winter in London.

So there it was, and Enoch prepared to face the long nights of the coming winter and tried hard to remember that it said in the Scriptures, 'In your patience possess ye your souls.'

Of a winter evening, when the cattle had been fed and watered, and bedded down for the night, the family would sometimes be joined by Sam Canavan and some of his family, and the old stories were told round the fireside again and again, and they played drafts or dominoes or quoits. But for Enoch the time hung heavy on his hands as he counted the days and the weeks and the months to next August.

11

It was the following year, in the early summer of 1875, when the woodlands and the meadows were quick with life, the trees bursting into leaf and the spring flowers ready to give way to the richer growth, that Enoch eventually married Miss Drusilla Warren. Sella had just passed her twenty-first birthday, and Enoch was a year older. His Aunty Ruth was not there, neither was his father, nor anyone else of his family or friends, and in his heart Enoch was not entirely sorry. The wedding, as quiet as it was possible for any wedding to be, which was what Sella wanted, took place in far distant Cornwall. Although he did not know at the time, it was not far along the coast from the area where 'Old' Matt Rodda had been born and bred, and where Hezekiah Trevanion had ended his colourful career

Of recent years weddings had tended to become occasions for much wild behaviour. Prior to the wedding day there would have been the taler going round with his rammas, and even when the custom of the taler and his rammas had really become outdated, it was still harmless enough and in many ways no more than good fun and a reminder of days that were gone, whereas some of the old customs had now grown out-of-hand. There was much blowing of hunting horns and chasing about the place on horseback, seizing the bride and dragging her out of the church, and all sorts of nonsense besides. On more than one occasion there had been nasty accidents, sometimes fatal, and for all his normally cheerful nature, Enoch had never wanted any part of that sort of caper. Much as he would have liked to have had his family with him, he was thankful to have been spared the antics which had now become part of such occasions. And Sella, bless her, had no family anyway, so maybe it was as well for them to be on the same footing.

Sella had kept him informed of all the arrangements, and the residential qualifications, which made it sound like good sense to be married in Cornwall, because that was where she had been resident throughout the summer. The banns had been duly called in both parishes, and Enoch had been to Narberth for a new suit of best quality broadcloth. The same day he bought for Sella a delicately carved gold locket on a fine gold chain.

Now that the railways had arrived, he had thought at first of trying to go by train, and that was what his father and even his Aunty Ruth had urged him to do, but old habits died hard and, according to Enoch's reckoning, it was a case of the devil you knew being better than the devil you didn't. To have set off on such an unknown venture was not something which he was anxious to undertake, when all he was certain of was his longing to be safely with Sella once again. And 'Old' Matt Rodda had come from Cornwall by sea had he not?

So Enoch went down to Saundersfoot and saw his brother-in-law, Arthur Giles. Arthur had done well in his job and was now in charge of the busy office on the harbour. Esther and Dorrie had both gone by train to Carmarthen for the day, so there was no talk of calling to see them as well. Arthur said he was sure they would be pleased to hear Enoch's news and was more than pleased to help. The iron-works at Stepaside was in serious financial trouble and closing down, but there were other possibilities. Leave it to him, Arthur said, and he would fix something.

Sure enough, a few days later a letter arrived to say that Arthur had been able to arrange a passage on John Twicey's coastal trader, the *Mary Darling*, a fifty ton dandy sailing from Saundersfoot the following week with a cargo of best fire-bricks from Stokes' brickworks at Wisemansbridge, and bound for Wadebridge, up river from Padstow in north Cornwall. That part of the journey would cost him nothing, and from Wadebridge, Arthur said, Enoch could go most of the way by train all the way down to Truro in the south. Enoch was delighted, for he knew Twicey well, a cheerful character with a reputation as a sound and trustworthy sailor. His name was really John John, so he was known as Twicey.

The joy of being on his way to Sella at last had made the whole world seem a different place altogether. That alone would have been enough for Enoch, so the ten hour voyage on such a day was one great bonus. The sun shone, and a steady off-shore breeze from the north carried them along on no more than a gentle swell.

As they rounded Monkstone and hove in sight of Caldey, Enoch gave a passing thought to Harry Billy Shifty and wondered how he was doing. It was a long time since Ruth had as much as mentioned his name.

For a short distance a bewhiskered seal swam alongside the boat and inspected them carefully with great eyes like saucers. Enoch recalled briefly the stories of his great-gramfer, Josh Rodda, and the episodes at Teague's Dingle of the bull seal that was killed, and of the beautiful girl and the silver seal skin coat. Then, apparently satisfied, the seal dived and shortly afterwards they disturbed a raft of shearwaters which took to the air and swept round on their long, scything wings. Enoch had never seen one before, but had heard the story times beyond number of the cocklynave calling at the time of the stories of the seals at Teague's Dingle. Every word of what Josh had said had been imprinted on Enoch's mind when he had listened as a boy.

When they were off Lundy there were other sea-birds to be seen and John Twicey knew them all and told Enoch what they were and of their feeding and breeding habits. The little hook-beaked, clown-like puffins, which the sailors called sea-parrots, fascinated him with their busy wing action as they whirled about all over the place. Twicey said that they were very much synonymous with Lundy, and then the great white gannets, with a six foot span of their black-tipped wings, began to circle the boat. Their breeding season had already started, but John Twicey said that their numbers had been dwindling of recent years and that they had begun to desert Lundy and nest in some numbers on the little island of Grassholm off the west coast of Pembrokeshire.

As far as the history of Lundy was concerned, Twicey had heard of the notorious Tom Salkeld, the pirate who had held the island as a fortress at one time, but Enoch told him stories he did not know of Hezekiah Trevanion and the Roddas, of Black Bart and Ben Scraggs, and much else which interested him, until the time had passed so quickly that, with the tide on the flood, they were running up past the sandy beaches of the Camel Estuary to Padstow, and on up the river all the way to Wadebridge.

There, having bade farewell to John Twicey and his crew of three, Enoch set out on his journey by train to Bodmin, where there was a change and a short journey by coach to join the train for Truro.

Inland there was much evidence of mining and quarrying, the country was dreary, and the journey tiring. Darkness had long since fallen before Enoch arrived at Truro, weary in spite of the excitement, to be met by Jem Pascoe, the family's young coachman.

In her letters Sella had often referred to Jem and his wife, Marianne, who had been so kind to her and made her feel welcome and at home, from the time she had first come to what was to her a strange land. Not knowing exactly what to expect, Enoch was thrown into some confusion to find a coach and four-in-hand waiting for him, but he had no time to admire the handsome greys before there was a flutter of petticoats as Sella hurled herself out of the great coach into his arms.

For all the light shed by the fine brass carriage lamps, Enoch, his weariness forgotten, saw nothing of the countryside as the coach rumbled through it in the dark. It would have been all the same if it had been broad daylight. They were still close held in each other's arms when the coach finally came to a halt outside the Pascoe's cosy lodge near the stables.

In due course all was made clear. Squire Legassick and Madame had both insisted on Enoch being met in style, even to the extent of having a dog of the fashionable Dalmatian breed trotting along proudly at the rear step. But equally, to Enoch's relief, they had also insisted that the young couple's wishes should be respected and that they should be allowed to marry as quietly as ever they wished. And so they did, the following morning, in the beautiful little church of Mylor in its lovely setting looking out across the great sweep of the Carrick Roads to St Just and the Roseland Peninsula.

Enoch had spent the night with the Pascoes, whilst Sella was still at the mansion. For most of the night he felt the steady roll of the *Mary Darling* and the swaying of the train, but towards morning he fell into a dreamless sleep, to wake to the song of a myriad birds, and with the sun already shining in through the latticed window as it set out on its day's journey in yet another blue sky above green fields where sleek cattle grazed.

12

With the memory still fresh in his mind of so much dreary and depressing countryside on the train journey the previous evening before darkness had fallen, Enoch was completely unprepared for the beauty of everything around him. There were all the great trees which had once been the heritage of his native valley, but there were also rhododendrons of many colours, eucalyptus and mimosa, camellias and magnolias, dense thickets of rustling bamboos, and so many truly exotic plants and shrubs which were new to him. Ruth would have been in her seventh heaven of delight, and a tear came to his eye as he remembered all she had meant to him, and all she had taught him about the plants and the wild creatures of the wayside and woodland when he was a small boy. And he said to himself, 'Please God, there will be no friction between her and Sella.'

Jem drove Enoch to the Church in a smart little phaeton with a well-groomed, high-stepping chestnut pony in the shafts. To Enoch's complete bewilderment he was told that the Squire would be bringing Sella to the church himself and would even be giving her away. On that he had insisted.

A smart young stable-boy was waiting at the church to hold the pony until the end of the service, and there was plenty of time for Jem to point out the various landmarks and tell something more of the various creeks which ran so far inland in places. The previous evening, tired though he had been, Enoch had talked to Jem and, amongst other things, had asked him of the old smuggling days. Jem did indeed know of 'The Ship Aground', and he said that tales of the smuggling Parson Tregellis were still told, but 'The Ship Aground' was much further down the coast near Marazion. Years later Enoch was to learn that it was from a secluded creek in that area that the first Matt Rodda had come.

Enoch looked anxiously at his watch, and Jem said not to worry and for them to go on into Church. There they were met and welcomed by the warden, Matt Doble, who said he had succeeded Stephen Doble twenty years ago, and assumed that Enoch would want to know all about the beautiful church. Enoch, however, deemed it expedient not to ask too many questions, because he was becoming very anxious and fidgety and taking another look at his watch.

Matt Doble looked at his own watch then and shuffled off into the vestry. Yet again Jem had to reassure Enoch that he had the ring in his waistcoat pocket, because Sella had already entrusted her mother's wedding ring to his safe keeping. It could not have been more than five or ten minutes, but seemed more like an eternity, as Enoch's heart pounded whilst they sat there waiting. They heard then the rumble of carriage wheels and the stamp of horses' hooves. Then there was a whispering at the door, and the Squire, a tall and distinguished white-haired old gentleman, came proudly down the aisle with Sella on his arm. Marianne walked behind them and, as Enoch turned to take Sella's hand he had to catch his breath, so beautiful did she look in a pale blue gown of taffeta silk, delicately embroidered, and with a little bow of red ribbon at the bodice. He recognised it straightaway as being the ribbon he had bought for her in Tenby on that day when they had plighted their troth, and he knew instinctively that the gown would have been of her own skilful making. It was low–cut, and she wore the locket on the gold chain which he had given to her the previous evening. Then she gave him a smile full of love from beneath the wide brim of her bonnet.

Quiet though the wedding was, most of the servants made a point of being there to add their blessings and good wishes. The Squire and Madame shook Enoch warmly by the hand, told him what a jewel he had gained, just as if he didn't know, and he did his best to thank them for all their kindness. Then they insisted on leaving the happy couple to themselves, which was what Sella wanted and, with Enoch at the reins, they drove off together in the phaeton to a great cheer from those who had been there to witness what some of them fondly and foolishly believed was a typical Welsh wedding.

Jem and Marianne followed them back to the Lodge, where Marianne had prepared a beautiful meal, and Enoch and Sella spent their wedding night there.

13

Such had been Enoch's excitement over the preceding weeks that he had given little thought to the return journey, because Sella had said they could arrange it after the wedding. The Squire, as it transpired, had insisted on taking a hand in that as well, and the arrangements had already been made.

One of the Squire's ships was sailing from Falmouth the day after the wedding with a cargo of copper for North Wales. What more sensible, he had said, than for the young couple to take ship and be put ashore at Pembroke Dock. At least, as Enoch had to admit, there was something to be said for the railways after all, because there was now an electric telegraph at Kilgetty station. So a groom was dispatched to Truro station first thing on the morning after the wedding with a message to be sent from there to the effect that Mr and Mrs Enoch Rodda would be arriving at Kilgetty by train from Pembroke Dock the following afternoon, and please inform Mr Jason Rodda of Woodreef.

Sella's packing had all been done, and that included, she told Enoch, a beautiful dinner set of Wedgwood china which had been the wedding present from the Squire and Madame. There were some other presents from the servants, and also her clothes. All these, safely packed, could accompany them on their voyage to be delivered at Woodreef by the weekly carrier.

Their farewells having been taken, and many a tear shed by those to whom Sella had endeared herself, at midday they set sail in the three hundred ton barque, *Pride of Falmouth,* to begin their new life together.

Many were the memories of that voyage, but chiefest for Enoch was Sella's bright-eyed enthusiasm as she told him something of the people with whom she had been living and working at different times over the last three years, and what she had learned of the place, but any regret at leaving such friends had soon been forgotten as the great ship surged from the Carrick Roads and round the Black Rock and Pendennis Point for Falmouth Bay and the open sea. It was an awe-inspiring and thrilling sight to see the great sails filled and towering above them.

Three-masted, square-rigged on the fore and mainmast, and fore-and-aft rigged on the mizzen, the *Pride of Falmouth* was far bigger than any ship spoken of by the old characters who had been involved in the Trade round the Blackhorn caves, and the ships of so many stories to which Enoch had listened as a boy. It was sad to think that such beautiful vessels, built originally for sailing anywhere in the world, had become little more than coastal traders, reduced to such status by the advent of the great steamers which were now so much in evidence.

Sailing in style, Enoch and Sella had been provided with their own cabin, but in no time at all the motion of the great ship under the influence of a steady and gentle breeze caused Sella to hold her stomach and say she was starting to feel sick. Brought up on so many stories of the sea, Enoch said, 'The only chance now, my love, is to go up on deck. They always reckon you've got a better chance up on deck and standing up.' And so indeed it proved.

''Twould be a shame anyway,' Sella said later, 'not to be up here on a day like this.'

The sun shone and the slight breeze of previous days had gone round from the north to the south east. Sailing conditions could not have been better and there was the prospect of a following wind all the way.

Sella, recovering her brightness, told Enoch much about the people and the various landmarks, and then, as they sailed wide of the dreaded Manacles, she told him of the terrible disaster when a ship called the *John* had been wrecked there twenty years previously. Out of nearly three hundred people on board, only ninety-one had survived. Most of those on board had been emigrants bound for Canada. The steamships were taking them in greater numbers these days, so at least it meant they could travel in greater safety and with a better hope of reaching their destination.

The steamships, however, were also bringing in ever more cargoes of cheap corn from Canada, and dairy produce and meat in refrigerated ships from as far away as New Zealand. But Enoch was in no mood at the moment to allow such thoughts to worry him or spoil his happiness.

Such thoughts prompted him instead to tell Sella more than he had already had a chance to tell her of those of his forebears who had long ago sailed for Canada and New Zealand, of how Jack Rodda had turned up, of Delilah and Grandma Hannah and all the rest of them. By this time they had rounded the Lizard and, sailing on across Mount's Bay towards Land's End, Sella spoke of Marazion, and Enoch had so much to tell her of Hezekiah Trevanion and Matt Rodda and Grandma Mona, and of all the stories which had been told of the family down through the long years. And Sella nestled her head on his shoulder and said how blessed he was to have been told so much about his family. Of her own family she knew next to nothing. And Enoch held her close and said they would make up for all that from here on.

At last, having rounded Land's End, with the sails re-set, they were in the Bristol Channel, heading north and for home at last. As darkness began to fall, and the wicks of the great lamps had been trimmed, and the red and green lights of the *Pride of Falmouth* lit, they saw on their starboard bow the towering lighthouse on the height of Lundy begin to flash out its warning to those who travelled the high seas by night, and Enoch told Sella more of Black Bart and Ben Scraggs and the death of Hannah and Gervaise Gideon.

As the air grew chill, Sella went below to fetch her travelling cloak and a ship's blanket from their cabin, and they sat enfolded in each other's arms in the pale light of a new moon to doze fitfully as the wind sighed in the riggings, the nocturnal cocklollies and the little storm petrels, which the sailors called Mother Carey's chickens, flitted wraith-like in the darkness, and a myriad stars turned the canopy above to magic.

They were well set for the Pembrokeshire coast before the cloudless dawn of a new day and sailed on for the great harbour of Milford Haven to find, to Enoch's intense relief, that the water at the dreaded and notorious St Ann's Head was on its best behaviour. He had heard old sailors say that at certain times the seas there could be as bad as anything to be found coming round Cape Horn. But that would be when a spring tide was on the ebb and the waters of the two rivers Cleddau came rushing down to a narrow bottleneck to be met by the fury of a sou'wester. Today the *Pride of Falmouth* arrived at slack water and there was no wind to speak of.

At last, their voyage, which Sella said had seemed to her like a fairy tale, was over. Their thanks expressed to the skipper, who refused point blank to take the money which Enoch proffered, and having bade farewell to the other passengers, they were on the train at last and drawing ever closer to home.

The electric telegraph had evidently done its work well, for there was Shanco, groomed and shining, with his brasses polished, in the shafts of the high spring trap, and Jason clean-shaven and suitably dressed for the occasion. As Sella walked down the platform he took off his bowler hat and put his arm round her. No need was there for any words for her to know that she was welcome.

Shanco pricked his ears and raised his head at the sight and sound of the steam monster, and gave every indication of regarding it with disdain.

166

14

Whatever Ruth's feelings or misgivings may have been, she had a good meal waiting when the newly-weds arrived towards evening. Not over enthusiastically perhaps, she kissed Sella, whose first words were, 'Will it be all right if I call you Aunty Ruth? Because that's all I've ever heard Enoch call you, and it would sound a bit funny for me to call you Miss Rodda, wouldn't it?'

'Well, I'm his aunty aren't I?'

Enoch wondered if it could have been his imagination, but he sensed a touch of coldness about the greeting.

'Of course.' Sella said. 'So that means you're my aunty as well, doesn't it, now that we're married?'

Sella held out her hand to show Ruth her wedding ring, and Jason wondered if it hurt Ruth to know it was something which she had denied herself in life for the sake of others. Ruth said, a trifle disdainfully, 'Oh aye, 'tis a lovely ring. That must have cost a mint o' money.'

'I wouldn't know about that,' Sella said with a slight, a very slight, break in her voice. 'It was my mother's.'

'Who was thy mother then? Enoch have never towld us nothin' about that.'

'I don't know much about her. She died when I was born, and my father had been drowned just before that.'

'Oh? Who brought thee up then?'

'Nobody.'

'How could it be nobody?'

'I spent the first eleven years of my life in the workhouse.'

There was a silence broken only by the ticking of the old grandfather's clock. Ruth's eyes filled with tears as she looked at her and, of a sudden, she said, 'Good God!' and Sella, to her complete bewilderment, found herself being enfolded in a pair of loving arms.

Enoch went out quietly, certain at last in the knowledge that he had done the right thing by waiting for Sella to break the news herself. It would surely be a happy household from here on.

CHAPTER 5

1875 Onwards

1

Towards the end of the voyage from Falmouth Sella had said that everything had been like a fairy tale. And so it had. But fairy tales have happy endings, and life is far from being all like that. It would have been good to write about years of prosperity and happiness for Sella in her new home, but it was not to be.

It had been a source of great comfort to Enoch to see the bond between Sella and Ruth grow closer with every passing day, and Sella even started going to chapel with her. Church, Sella had always been, if anything, but as she said, that was because the Squire and Madame and the family and servants had all gone to Church as a matter of course. Sella had no strong feelings about any of it. Chapel and Church were all the same to her. She was content to thank God anywhere for the good things that had come to her in life because it had not always been like that.

It was a great thing, too, that Sella had learned music, so they bought a harmonium, and Sella could play, and they could all spend Sunday evenings singing hymns and that was marvellous.

Nor was it only hymns, because of a weeknight they would sometimes have a singsong, and Jason would usually weigh in with one of the favourites about the fox,

> *A fox looked out one cloudy night,*
> *wishing that the moon would shine out bright,*
> *For he had a long way to go that night,*
> *before he reached the town-o, town-o, town-o.*
> *Before he reached the town-o.*

There were several verses, and everybody joined in with the

chorus at the end of each verse. As far back as anybody could remember, the song had been in the family, since it had first been sung by 'Old' Gramfer Matt when he came up from Cornwall, and he reckoned that the song had been sung all round the coastal areas, no doubt by sailors as they went from one port to another. He said he had heard it sung as far over to the east as Suffolk, and in fact it was in a harbour tavern at Lowestoft that he had heard it for the first time. Sella had a good ear for music and had soon picked up the tune, and sometimes put in a couple of twiddly bits to add to the fun.

Had anyone said there was never a dull moment it would have been an understatement, and never could it have been more true than before their first summer of married life had run its course.

It was in September at harvest time that a very smart landau, drawn by a very smart pair of black horses, and bearing a very smart lady of indeterminate age, came up the track from the New Inn, and the lady's name was Hannah Rodda. She had come by train to Tenby, where she was now staying, and had engaged the landau and coachman for the day. Twice married, and twice widowed, without children by either marriage, she was now, in her own words, foot loose and fancy free. Her name now, she said, was not really Rodda, but for reasons best known to herself she had reverted to her maiden name because her name had been Rodda before she had been daft enough to marry. All her two fools of husbands had done was to leave her well provided for financially, and thank you very much for that. She looked the part, too, in her high-necked mulberry velvet dress with its bustle, her expensive pearl choker, her beflowered bonnet and her parasol.

Dark of eye, with jet black hair, it took little for those who had heard the stories of her legendary namesake to realise that this Hannah Rodda was very definitely her descendant and a chip off the old block. Yet she knew nothing of her, had never even heard of her, nor had she known of her grandmother, Hannah's daughter, Delilah. They had learned at Woodreef of this Hannah's existence from her brother, Jack Rodda, when he had turned up, before they had managed to help him to get away to Canada. All Jack had been able to tell them about his sister Hannah was that 'she had been taken in by some people.'

The people who had brought her up had looked after her well, and it was from them that she had learned that her father was Dick Rodda, who had taken the King's Shilling and been killed at Waterloo for his trouble. They had known no more about him than the fact that he was the son of a girl who had come from this place called Woodreef. It was not strictly accurate, but near enough for her to hit upon the truth now that she had arrived.

Her first surprise, which was one of delight, was not only to discover that she had a brother who was, the last they heard of him, alive and well, but that he had in fact already been to Woodreef ahead of her, albeit something like forty years previously. It mattered not to her that Jack had deemed it expedient to depart for Canada. When she was told of the nature of his departure, and the story of a similar spiriting away of the little French priest long ago, she thought it was all the stuff of real romance. It would be a matter of small inconvenience for her, too, she said, to sail for Canada. All she needed was Jack's address, and she left her own, along with a promise to keep in touch with them.

Hannah Rodda, as it transpired, was destined to be too late to find her brother. Truth being stranger than fiction, as folk were inclined to say, within weeks of her visit, and long before she could have had time to be thinking about arranging a voyage to Canada, there was another visitor to Woodreef who had come in search of his family or any information about them. He was a young Canadian, George Rodda, who brought the news, amongst other things, that his father, Jack Rodda, had died the previous year. He also brought news of the late Tom Rodda and his Catholic family. So he was delighted to take to the road again in search of his Aunt Hannah, and Jason reckoned that he could be doing a good thing for himself at that.

171

That first autumn, as it moved on to winter, was a source of great contentment for Sella, and there was so much which made her feel at home and gave her a sense of security. In the china display cabinet was the lovely Wedgwood dinner service. There were hams hanging from the ceiling, a couple of flitches, and a bladder of lard along with bunches of dried herbs. Some of the brasses belonging to the best harness were there on the wall, too, polished bright and shining to keep Satan and the evil spirits away from the horses.

Then there was the gun, which was also kept on the wall. The gentry did not have much sporting interest along the valley, so nobody worried unduly that Enoch enjoyed going out with the gun now and again. There was a great fashion, too, for stuffing various of the wild creatures, and the cases displaying the taxidermist's art increased steadily in number.

There was one specimen, though, which was not the prey of the gun barrel, nor even of the rod-and-line. It was a handsome trout, somewhere near three pounds in weight, and he had been delivered to their feet one crisp autumn morning when Sella had walked with Enoch in the meadow that ran down to the lake as they fetched the cows in for morning milking. And, as they walked hand-in-hand, unheard until the last moment, a heron, startled from his business, rose from the river bank within feet of them with a frantic beating of his great wings, as a few feathers floated down, and he dropped the great trout, which had been destined for his morning meal, jumping and kicking, right in front of them. Enoch's only regret was that he didn't have the gun with him so that the heron could have been stuffed as well.

Jason had moved out of the big bedroom from the day that Enoch had brought Sella home as his bride, and it was there, a year after their marriage, that Seth, their first child, was born, and Enoch was grateful that his father had the pleasure of nursing his grandson. Often he would ride him, crowing with delight, on his shoulders when he went to the fields, or to look at some of the animals. Enoch had always realised how his father had grieved for Lydia. For his own part, even though he had never known his mother's love, Enoch had always had Ruth to cherish him.

Whilst Jason had ever been one of the most cheerful people in life, now that he had little Seth to occupy his time it gave him an even greater zest for living. And yet, through one of life's ironies, when he was still but sixty years of age, he caught a heavy cold which settled on his chest. There was no Granny Hudson or Ma Probert at Greyrock nowadays as there had been long ago, so Ruth made up some mixture of hot mustard and rubbed his chest and put hot flannel on it. It availed but little, the cold turned to pneumonia and, before the seriousness of it had been fully realised, he had died. In the same month, Sella gave birth to a daughter, to be followed by another girl a year later.

It was in the spring that Jason had died, and even the weather seemed intent on casting a gloom over the place. Day after dreary day throughout the summer, rain followed more rain, and out in the fields the hay was sodden and turned black as the new grass grew through the crops which would never be harvested. It was then that the Jeremiahs shook their heads once again and said that they had been proved right at last, that they had always known that no good would come of it when the railways came, with engines belching smoke and steam to the skies all over the place, and people began to write letters to the papers explaining how this was causing all the rain.

There was another thing about the railways as well, and not everybody said it was a bad thing. There was good money to be earned in the industrial cities and the railways made it much easier to get to them. So farm wages went up as well, which was good for the farm-workers, but it was not so easy to keep a man.

Indoors, too, they had their troubles, with steam and damp everywhere as they struggled with the well-nigh impossible task of drying the washing, and another baby girl being born. Sella said that without Ruth she could never have coped. There were three such summers, and then, whatever the Jeremiahs may have said about the railways and the weather, there was no doubt about the threatened recession which came with a vengeance at last as the steamboats brought in ever more of the cheap corn and dairy produce, and the railways delivered them to the remote and far flung stations of the countryside.

It was then that Sella began to cough. When there was no sign of an improvement, she was even persuaded to go with Enoch in the phaeton as far as the New Inn, and walk down to the beach by the Blackhorn caves as the tide was going out, in the belief that the ebbing tide would take the cough with it. It did not, and to be fair to her, she did not think it would, but at least nobody could say she had been unwilling to try.

It was not the only superstition, and it was not long after she began to cough that a robin was found fluttering about in the bedroom and hurling itself against the window in a frantic effort to escape. Some said that this presaged a death, and some that there would be blood in the coffin. But nobody in the household dared speak their thoughts.

When Sella began to cough up blood the doctor, a bluff character, was sent for, and he came several times in his pony-and-trap, and each time he left medicine. Sella took the medicine dutifully but continued to cough, and was even persuaded to try a faith healer. Ruth had instilled so much of the Bible into Enoch as a boy that it was not perhaps to be wondered at that he had become, like his namesake in the Bible, a man of great faith.

As Sella became more ill Ruth had to take more care of Seth. One day when he was with her she came across an old prayer book of Grandma Mona's. In it was a little card with a picture of a beautiful lady dressed in blue, and holding a string of beads. Ruth said the lady was Mary, the mother of Jesus, known as the Madonna, and said that some people believed that she had the power to help and heal the broken-hearted. But, although Ruth was always willing to talk about the Bible and Jesus, she did not seem to want to talk about the beautiful lady in blue, and she put the picture back in the prayer book and put the book back in the drawer.

Then Enoch, more perhaps in desperation than with any great

conviction, and perhaps because of some almost superstitious belief in the man's name, spoke of Enos Hodge, the faith healer who lived near Wisemansbridge. Enos in the Bible was the son of Enoch, which Enoch Rodda hoped might be a good omen. Enos Hodge, however, was the seventh son of a seventh son, which should be even more potent. Because he was the seventh son of a seventh son he was reputed to have the gift of healing, and he had indeed wrought many notable cures and used his gift as a charmer to rid folk of some serious complaints where the men of medicine had failed. Although he did not use it he even possessed an old-fashioned cockalorum which had been handed down in his family for many generations. On every seventh day from the date of her first visit for seven weeks running Sella, well wrapped up against the weather, went with Enoch in the phaeton, and Enos Hodge placed his hands on her head and whispered his incantations. But still Sella coughed, and the cough grew worse.

Ruth had been suspicious of Sella's lovely complexion from that time at the Big Day when she had seen her but not met her. There was never a doubt in her mind now that Sella was suffering from the decline, or consumption, or whatever it was they called it. Small wonder, really, after the malnutrition, the hardships and deprivations of her childhood, and the awful damp in which they were now having to live. No amount of firing seemed to be able to dry the place properly.

Heart-breaking it was to hear the poor soul cough, cough, cough, and to see her wasting away. She had been a bride of just six years when, with a weak, pain-racked cough that was half rattle, she breathed her last as a distraught Enoch sat tearfully by her bed and held her hand.

Now that Ruth had been having to give so much time to the two smaller ones, Seth had spent more time with his mother and, at the impressionable age of five, he, too, was going to be devastated. He had been too young to understand when his Gramfer Jason had died, but day after day he had brought flowers for Sella and wondered what was happening. Then the bedroom door was shut and Enoch took him into the parlour on his own to tell him that his Mam had gone to be with Jesus, and Seth thought that was bound to be a good thing.

He pondered on this for a while before he said, 'When will she be coming back?'

'Oh, she won't ever be coming back,' his father said.

'Not coming back at all? Not never?'

'No indeed. Oh no, she won't ever want to come back. Not now that she's with Jesus. You wouldn't want her to come back to all that coughing and everything now that she's so happy with Jesus would you?'

The little lower lip trembled then and the tears came slowly.

That night he cried in the dark when he thought about never seeing his mother again. Then a strange thing happened. He woke, and was sure he was not dreaming, and there was a lovely lady in blue standing by the foot of the bed with a beautiful glowing light all round her. She did not speak, but gave him a feeling of great comfort, as if she would always be there to take care of him, just as he had once heard in the story of the same thing happening to Gramfer Matt when he had been a small boy.

It did little to comfort him immediately, or later, when Enoch lifted him up to take his last look at his lovely young mother in her coffin, with her face like delicate wax, at peace at last. It was in later years, as he grew to man's estate, that he was glad that he had that memory of her at rest, rather than to remember only what she had suffered, and how ill she had looked with all that pain and all that coughing.

He had already lost his doting Gramfer Jason. Now he had lost his lovely mother. He sensed somehow that his father had his own grief, so who else was there to turn to for comfort but Aunty Ruth?

3

That summer the weather improved slightly, but nothing else seemed to improve much, and Ruth, in her sixties now, began to stoop a little and complain of her aches and pains. Her hair had gone very grey, too, and sometimes when she was sewing she would hold the needle and cotton up to the light, sigh, and then ask Seth to thread the needle for her. She felt the loss of her brother keenly, for she and Jason had always been close, and she felt the death of Sella more than she might have expected at one time. So Seth was as great a comfort to her as she was to him.

On one occasion when she was spring-cleaning and turning out the drawers, just as Grandma Phoebe had once been doing, Seth found old Grandma Mona's rosary and was full of curiosity, for the beads were like those which the beautiful lady in blue had in the little picture. Ruth could not tell him what the prayers were which were said by the people who used them, but she was able to tell him about Grandma Mona and what the beads had meant to her, even if she didn't go much on the idea of it herself because she was strong chapel, and she was able to tell him of the little French priest's crucifix which Tom Rodda had taken to Canada, and Seth listened to it all with wide-eyed wonder. Then she had to tell him as well as she could, according to what she had been told herself, about Gramfer Josh and the beads when he fell asleep in the old wooden arm-chair for the last time, and how Gramfer Matt had seen the big ship sail away the morning after Gramfer Josh died.

Much time did they spend together that summer, and Ruth began all over again with the stories and the lore of the countryside which she had told Seth's father when Enoch had been the same age as Seth was now. Before ever he started school there was hardly a wild-flower or tree, or a creature of the fields and woodlands, which he could not name. She taught him, too, how to bore a hole in the horse-chestnuts and thread a string through them to play conkers, and she began to tell him brief snippets of the stories which had been handed down in the family since time out of mind.

Apart from the stories of the family, though, one of the stories he liked best was when there was a great rainbow right across the sky in front of them the day after rain, and Ruth told him that if they could get to the rainbow's end they would find a crock of gold. They were up in the top field at the time, and the rainbow could be seen clearly all the way from where it started on Lundy on the far horizon. But the other end was way up over the land somewhere, so that wasn't much good. Even so, there was always hope, and Seth said he was sure he would find the other end one day. Every time there was a rainbow he would try hard to find the end of it, and then, as he grew older, he forgot about such ideas.

One of the first jobs he and his Aunty Ruth did together was to put a cluck hen to sit. They knew she had started laying away, so they watched her carefully without the sly old thing knowing it, and then they followed her quietly a couple of times until they found her nest with thirteen brown eggs, and they took them and put her to sit on them in a cub near the house where the old fox couldn't get at her. One of her mates, though, was too many for the watchers, and they knew nothing about it until she came clucking proudly home out of the nettles with eight fluffy chicks in tow, which was two fewer than the one they had put to sit.

Sometimes by candle-light, when Ruth had put him to bed, they would play at making figures on the wall by holding up their hands to cast shadows in all sorts of shapes like butterflies, and horses' heads, and birds with big beaks. Then they would say their prayers together and Ruth would wait, and not many minutes would it be, for him to drop off to sleep before she would blow out the candle. Occasionally, he would think of the time when the lady in blue had appeared in a kind of dream, but she did not appear again.

If the house had seemed desolate and empty without Sella, especially so soon after Jason had died, it seemed emptier still when summer was over and Seth started school. What would happen when the time would come for the children to leave school scarcely bore thinking about. From Greyrock and the few cottages left in the valley they were going out into service or to work on the bigger farms, when they were hardly any age at all. All the news seemed to be of young people packing their meagre belongings and heading for the towns and cities or overseas, with the farmers complaining there was not enough money to pay those who stayed behind.

The two girls, Nan and Ellin, were into everything and Ruth had her hands full. Young Lily Canavan from the Caban had been spending time at Woodreef, back and fore helping, and now she came to live. The two girls adored her, so Ruth, in spite of all she had to do, was able to take Seth to school for the first few days until he settled. The day he started she walked with him all the way to Crunwear where the new school had been built. He would soon be all right, because there would be other children with him. There would be a couple from the oil-works up by Greyrock, who would be crossing the fields towards the Caban, and then they would be meeting up with a couple more from Garness. From there they could all go on together.

It was a mild day in September, when for once in a while it was not raining again, and Tav went with the pair of them as they walked the track to cross the stream by the pompren. Old now, and grey about the muzzle, Tav had lost interest in his tread-wheel. As Enoch said, it hardly mattered all that much, because the way things were going it was doubtful whether they would have any meat to roast.

When they reached the pompren, however, where the lake was in full spate, Tav whimpered and growled, the hair along his spine bristled, and, much as he was devoted to Ruth, he refused to cross with them.

'All right, then, boy,' she said, 'wait thee there till I comes back. I shan't be long f'rall.'

Then, as they walked on up the lane, she told Seth something of Tav's refusal to cross the pompren one day with Enoch, and of how dogs and horses were reckoned to be conscious of the presence of evil. But when Seth wanted to know more, she said, 'Oh, Lord sowls, hun, thou's'd have to ask thy father about that. 'Twas some character as lived up at Smuggler's Den a mortal long time ago. There be some in the family as haves the second sight as they calls it, but don't thee worrit thy l'l head about it.'

179

The following spring Enoch decided that it was time to see about a headstone for his father and Sella who had both been buried in what was to be a new family grave. Already, because times were so bad, the money she had left had started to dwindle. A cruel thought it was somehow that she had been so careful with her money as a girl, and so keen never to know again the deprivation of her miserable childhood, and it had all come to nothing. The least he could do now was to ensure that she had a worthy memorial stone above her where she had been laid at rest so young. There was a wonderful fashion these days for the iron headstones being made at the foundry at Wisemansbridge, but only the best would be good enough, and only old Tom Morris could turn out the best.

It was a sad thought for Enoch that Sella had looked forward to the time when they would be married and able to go together to Morfabychan for her to meet the old gentleman, and talk to him about music, and hear him play his famous bass viol. But it was not to be. There had always been so much else to do, and now it was too late.

Seth was going to go with him and, with a full moon due over the next few days, Enoch said the tide would be far enough out for them to go on horseback along the beach. And that in itself was a great adventure for Seth. In the winter, Tav had gone to his last, long sleep and been buried in the garden beneath the damson trees. He had been sadly missed, but the loss had been eased for Seth by Sam Canavan finding a quiet little Welsh mountain pony for him. A grey roan Jenny was, with a mouth like velvet, and not a wicked thought in her head.

Shanco was still going strong, and Ruth found it hard to hold back a tear as she watched the pair of them set off side-by-side, with her precious little one sitting very straight-backed and proud in his new saddle. Only the other day, or so it seemed to her, Enoch had been a small boy holding her hand as they went everywhere together. There he was now, lonely, with the cares of the world on his shoulders, and soon, soon, all too soon, Seth would be out in the world and making his own way in life. The years had a habit of going by so fast, and of recent years they seemed to have been going by faster than ever.

Up the lane past the long-since derelict cottage at Hannah's they went, and crossed Hannah's Plain to go down the track by the old tan pits to the beach below Telpyn. Seth had heard fragments of the various stories at different times, but often they had been no more than snatches which his young mind had not yet been able to grasp. Now that they were down on the beach Enoch was able to point out to him where so many of the legendary happenings had taken place.

Seth listened to it all and thought especially of those with the second sight who had seen visions, and he wondered again about his own vision the night when his mother had died, and the belief that the gift of second sight ran in his family.

5

Much could have been said about their time at Morfabychan. The venerable old Morris couple, childless themselves, made a great fuss of their young visitor, and dear old Mrs Jenny Morris plied him with scones of her own baking, well buttered with butter of her own churning from the milk of their own cow, and spread with honey from their own bee-hives. And pleased indeed was she to be told that the name of his lovely little pony was Jenny.

The business with the renowned old mason was quickly done. The inscription on the headstone was to be simple . . . *Until the day dawn.* That had been Ruth's choice, and Tom Morris approved. It was certain that his beautiful scrollwork would do justice to it.

So long did they spend with the old couple that there could be no thought of returning along the beach, so they set off up the long track for the Greenbridge Inn, and so on home by way of Clyngwyn and the oil-works at Greyrock.

6

Seth was eighteen when Ruth died and he could not have believed it possible to feel so devastated. When his mother had died he had been broken-hearted, but they reckoned that the hearts of the young, like their hurts, healed quickly. And there had been Aunty Ruth to take her place. Aunty Ruth had been there always, even when his mother had been ill for so long before she died, and now, at the age of seventy-four, worn out, she laid down the burden of caring for others which all through life had been her lot.

'Poverty's no disgrace', she had been wont to say of recent years, 'but 'tis a bit inconvenient.'

Over the years he had learned much from his father of the sacrifices she had made for others. He had seen a verse somewhere recently,

> *'Others, Lord, yes, others*
> *Let this my motto be:*
> *Help me to live for others*
> *That I may live for Thee.'*

There had been far more to Aunty Ruth's beliefs than just going to chapel, and she had lived them to full measure and overflowing, even as it said in the Bible, 'Good measure, pressed down, and shaken together, and running over.' And, like Ruth in the Bible, she had been wonderful for family. Three generations would never be out of their debt to her. Never a wife, and denied the joys of marriage and motherhood, she had yet been a mother, and more than a mother, to Seth and to his father before him. Yes, both of them.

For days the curtains were pulled across, and then Seth was alongside his father when the time came to carry the coffin, just as Enoch had been there as a boy to become a man when his Gramfer Matt had died. But Esther was not there. Arthur Bridges had moved on and up in the world, with a well-paid job in the

Midlands. For years they had been growing apart, and Enoch had long since forgotten about his beloved playmate, Dorrie. But he had not forgotten the criticism of the fashion display at Gramfer Matt's funeral. But they sent money to buy flowers, and they were not the only ones. Seth saw a wreath on the grave later, when everything had been made neat and tidy, with just a name on it. All it said was the one word 'Harry', and Seth knew the story, because his father had told him all about Ruth's only love when he had been telling of all the sacrifices she had made. If Harry Billy Shifty had been at the funeral nobody had seen him, but it was nice to know he had not forgotten. By-and-by they would have to see about having her name put on the headstone, but it would not be Tom Morris to do it, because he had earned a headstone of his own nearly ten years ago.

In the good years for farming they had been comfortable at Woodreef for a while, but never well-off. Nan had found a good job in service with a family in Tenby, but Ellin was still home, and Lily Canavan had been found to be indispensable. Then the wet seasons had come, and the shortages, and now they were in the grip of what people would one day come to speak of as the Hungry Nineties. Geese were selling for no more than five shillings each, beef was sixpence a pound, you could buy a dozen eggs for a shilling, and butter was under a shilling a pound. It was hardly worth churning it. So it was something of a windfall when the dealers heard about the field of Tenby daffodils at Woodreef. For years they had been going round looking for the bulbs of these fashionable little flowers, and there had been a steady sale for them on the English markets. A cash payment of twenty sovereigns was too good to refuse. All they had to do was dig up the bulbs. Enoch thought that it might have made Ruth sad, had she been there to see it, but twenty sovereigns were twenty sovereigns.

There was no connection between the two but, the year the dealers came to buy the field of Tenby daffodils, the oil-works packed up. That meant that there would be no more work for the horses hauling timber, although even that had been little enough for the last few years. Then the thatched roof at Greyrock fell in, and one more cottage was abandoned.

The disappearance of such a landmark, though, was as nothing compared to what happened two years later in the autumn of 1896.

7

Never in living memory, so the old people said, nor indeed in any story of the past which had ever been handed down, had such storms been known.

Sheltered though they were at Woodreef from the south and south west winds, such was the fury of the gales that they experienced some damage even so. A few slates here and there, and thatch from one small shed, however, amounted to nothing compared to what had happened further down the valley. Where a few of the great trees had for one reason or another been left standing, they were uprooted and hurled like match-sticks. Eventually there was prolonged lightning and huge claps of thunder. When at last the storms had abated a boy from Earwear, going round his rabbit traps, came with such a story as they found it hard to believe. So Seth went with his father and walked down to the Blackhorn caves. Whatever stories had been told of all that had happened there in the past, there would never again be any smuggling there, because the caves were no more. Great chunks of rock were strewn all over the beach and it was an awesome sight. Just one pinnacle had been left standing, and that was to be demolished by the sea in later years.

Out across the bay the spume was still flying, and great waves were crashing and rolling as though intent on wreaking even more havoc. The garden wall of the mansion at Earwear had a great gap in it, and a mountain of pebbles had been thrown up where the road had once been. Never in a hundred years would anybody ever be able to shift that lot, so they would simply have to make a new road on top of them. Further along, the sea had in reality come in over Billy Shifty's as it had in 'Young' Matt's oft-told of vision. This time there would have been no feeling of well-being, especially had anyone still been living there, because the tide had claimed a new stretch of beach where previously the sand dunes had been. Apart from a few scattered stones and what had previously been roofing timbers, there was little evidence that there had ever been a dwelling there.

Later on word was to come of the damage to boats at Tenby and Saundersfoot. It was the age when photography had come into being, and pictures were being sold of great fifty-ton boats thrown up on breached harbour walls like so many little cockle shells, and some smashed asunder beyond any hope of repair.

Nor would it have been only at these two local harbours that shipping would have suffered. For days on end the locals were busy all along the beach from Crickdam and Earwear, to beyond Telpyn and Marros, collecting timber. There were folk with horses and carts, too, from further inland, intent on picking up their share, and their presence was not welcome. The Earwear people tended to regard such wreck as theirs by divine right, so there were one or two heated confrontations, but only one fist fight developed from one of them, and that was between characters with an old score to settle from a long-running family feud.

It was later in the winter, after another brief storm, on a day which began as a real fox, that Seth walked with his father up to Dolman Head. The lighthouse on Caldey was rising white and bright against the background of a blue sky, and the great hump of Lundy was clear on the far horizon.

Seth had heard the family stories as he had grown up, and could remember them word for word. He knew how Hannah had died, but Enoch said that maybe he was old enough now and that the time had come to tell him more than he had ever heard previously, and he told him of his last talk with his Gramfer Matt before the old man died, and how he had admitted to having done away with Gervaise Gideon.

Then, Enoch said, Matt had told him about Ben Scraggs. Seth

had heard about Scraggs and Black Bart, and knew of the stories about Lundy, but Enoch said he did not know who else might have been involved apart from Scraggs.

'I can remember every word of what Gramfer told me like yesterday,' Enoch said. 'Gramfer said, "They says there's honour amongst thieves, but owld Gramfer Matt alus reckoned 'twas the punishment met out to pirates if they ever stole from their own kind was one hell of a death, so 'twasn't so much honour as that they was afeart to steal from their own. Well, I wouldn't reckon to know about that, but I knows one thing f'rall. When thieves falls out there's one hell of a owld cabal an' fandango betwixt 'em. Any road, thicky Ben Scraggs was found drownded only a few weeks after Hannah was done in. They found'n in the lake just below the pompren. They reckons as a had a fit an' fell in as a was crossin', but whether a had a fit an' fell in or not his neck was broke." That's exactly what Gramfer said. So I said to Gramfer, "Who done it, did anybody know?" And Gramfer said to me, "Another of his own sort, but a cleared off out o' the district an' was never heard tell of again." And those were his very words.'

Seth asked his father then about the money, just as Enoch himself had asked his Gramfer Matt, and Enoch told Seth how Gramfer Matt had said that Hannah had told him that she had money put by and one day it would all be for him.

'No money was ever found,' Enoch said, 'but Gramfer said to me, "She had money put by f'rall, an' if ever thou should'st come across it, it's thine, an' don't never let nobody try to say otherwise." But he told me about finding the key, and that was kept in the lustre jug. Come to think of it the key's still there. Not that it'll do you or me or anybody else any good. Unless you should ever find the box, and you can forget about that f'rall!'

It was as they stood talking and looking out to sea that there came a cloud across the sky and, suddenly, there was the rainbow rising vividly from Lundy and sweeping over them in a great arc to finish quite clearly and definitely way up at Smuggler's Den.

'If only we could have been there now,' Seth laughed, 'we might have had that crock of gold.'

'I don't know anything about the crock of gold,' Enoch said, 'but if you should ever come across what Hannah left, then it's yours. And as Gramfer Matt said to me, don't let anybody try to say otherwise.'

8

A year after all these momentous happenings there was news from beyond the seas to occupy their minds when the word spread like wildfire that gold had been found in the Klondike, and people sold up their few possessions in a mad rush and took the first available boat for Canada. Enoch had been proved right on that count sooner than he had expected.

It was of more than passing interest that a young man from Stepaside wrote home to say that he had met up with one of the Roddas whose family had gone out to Canada from Woodreef years ago, and he was one of the prospectors to have had a lucky strike. They were not lucky enough at Woodreef to have had any word of the great gold find themselves.

Seth had thought many times about his talk with his father that day a year ago up at Dolman Head, and all the talk of Klondike gold had somehow brought back thoughts of Hannah's gold which had never been found. It was an evening in August when he had walked to Crunwear with a pair of boots for repairing. As he came back down the lane towards Garness it was just going dusk, and the stars and a faint moon were beginning to light his path. He was close to Smuggler's Den when a man came hurrying up the lane, furtive, but urgent of movement, sly of look, and dark of visage. He wore the striped jersey and flat round hat of the old-fashioned sailor, and answered in every detail to all the descriptions Seth had ever heard handed down from the old people of Ben Scraggs. Even his hair was done in a sailor's pigtail.

There was a gold ring in his ear, and he was carrying a small brass-bound box.

Not knowing what to say, Seth stood rooted to the spot. He was certain beyond any shadow of doubt that the man must have seen him, yet he passed within feet of him and ignored him completely, showing no sort of interest whatsoever. His mind was intent only on whatever it was he was doing. At a discreet distance Seth followed. Crossing the burgage by the cottage at Smuggler's Den the man put the box down by the winch from which the water was drawn. What puzzled Seth was that the cottage, which had for years been in ruins, seemed to be in fair condition with a neatly thatched roof, and the winch, which nowadays had a pump on it, tonight had only a wooden cover. In a few minutes the man came back with a slight roof ladder, tied it to a post with a plough line and, removing the wooden cover, lowered the ladder into the winch. He went back to the cottage, then returned with a lantern, picked up the box and went carefully down the ladder into the winch.

Scarce able to believe the evidence of his own eyes, Seth stood and waited. It was not long before the light appeared again coming up out of the earth, as it were, and the man's head and shoulders emerged, but without the box. He put down the lantern, drew up the ladder, untied it and replaced the wooden cover. Seth still stood, momentarily bewildered, and then the man had gone and Seth had not seen the going of him.

He walked home deep in thought, but long before he reached Woodreef he had decided to say nothing to anybody. Lily Canavan was a good sort, but so full of fun there was no knowing what she would have made of it, or to how much leg-pulling he might be subjected. Maybe later on he would tell his father.

The following day Seth went up to the fields at Smuggler's Den to look at a few young cattle that were grazing there. He was not yet twenty-one, believed he was in possession of his mental faculties, and had never been drunk in his life. Yet there was the abandoned cottage, as delapidated as ever, and there was the familiar pump over the winch where the previous evening there had been an old wooden cover. What was it his father had once said to him? . . . 'And sometimes poor old Ruth used to reckon that you might have the second sight as well. The same as Gramfer Matt, and old Josh before that.'

It was a disturbing thought. And a few weeks later it was even more disturbing. A harvest moon was high in the sky, the lake was full to the banks, and Seth had gone down in search of a couple of trout. He was under a bush, just down-stream from the pompren, his eyes well adjusted to the light, when he had a strange presentiment of the figure of a man crouched in the shadows behind the trunk of a tree. An owl hooted twice, and there was a single hoot in return. It was almost like the stories which had been told of 'Old' Gramfer Matt when he had gone to the aid of the little French priest who had been helped to escape. Within minutes, Seth had a strange feeling of being in the presence of the sailor man who had been carrying the brass-bound box.

The man who had been crouching behind the tree stepped out and, in the clear light of the moon, Seth could see that he, too, had all the looks and bearing of a sailor.

'So, Benjamin, my old shipmate,' he said, 'you thought as maybe you'd diddled us.'

The vision faded again then, but there was a feeling of evil, and Seth heard a sudden cry of pain. There was a splash of water, and then all was calm, and there was a great peace where the moon cast its shadows amidst the trees of the forest.

9

For a long time Seth thought frequently and deeply about everything that had happened. The morning after the second incident he had walked down to the pompren. No sign had there been of any footmarks or disturbance in the grass or undergrowth, and no sign of any dead body or anything unusual anywhere down-stream. Still he had kept his own counsel.

On Sundays he went to chapel, as Ruth had always encouraged him to do, so did his father and the two girls, and life went on as usual through all the seasons of the year, with little improvement in farming fortunes. Ellin had started keeping company with young Eli Canavan from the Caban, but Lily Canavan said she was waiting for a handsome prince to come riding up the valley in shining armour and with a sack of gold on his back.

It was the year 1905, when Seth was nearing thirty years of age, and Bostock and Wombwells great travelling circus came to Kingsmoor Common near Kilgetty. People from all over the place, it seemed, were flocking to see the wild beasts from foreign lands. But there was even more to it than that. The great Queen Victoria had died at last and the country had been at war with the Boers in South Africa. All the news nowadays was of the money being spent to restock the farms there after the ravages of war and to reopen the gold mines. And, believe it or not, for a penny you could see miraculous moving pictures at the circus of the soldiers when they had gone marching off to the war.

On a Sunday round about that time there had been a great revival meeting in chapel, and the preacher had given it to them good and strong on the subject of Calvary and the Cross and its power to save. There were things in life far more precious than silver and gold, for it was only the Cross that could save them, and they all had to meet at the Cross. A great number of sinners, many of them well-known to be very great sinners indeed, had gone forward to be saved that night.

Had anybody asked Seth which of all these things had been in his thoughts when he went to sleep he could not have said. It could have been the talk of foreign lands, or the gold mines, or even the preacher's sermon on gold and silver and the power of the Cross to save. Whichever of them it was, the vision he had that night was as vivid as anything he had ever had previously.

From deep in a dreamless sleep he was suddenly aware of the lady in blue, surrounded by a beautiful light, just as had happened to him when he was a small boy, when he had had that wonderfully comforting feeling that she had been trying to tell him that she would always watch over him, even though his mother had died. And then, as suddenly, it was old Grandma Mona who was standing there. There was never a doubt in his mind as to who she was. He had so often seen the delicate little miniature painting of her by the same artist as had painted the picture of Woodreef the year before Matt Rodda had arrived. Grey eyes and light brown hair, with that lovely rounded forehead, the firm chin and the dimpled cheeks.

And there she stood now with the rosary beads and the crucifix. The beads he had first remembered seeing when he had found them in the drawer that time when dear old Aunty Ruth had been spring-cleaning. Of the crucifix he had only ever heard how Tom Rodda had taken it with him to Canada. But, for that matter, there was a little crucifix on the end of the beads as well.

Ruth had not been able to tell him what the prayers were which were said by the people who used the rosary beads, but she had told him about Grandma Mona and how it was well-known that the beads had meant a great deal to her, even though Ruth had said she didn't go much on the idea of it all herself because she was strong chapel. Seth had heard the story many times, too, of Gramfer Josh and the beads when he fell asleep in the old wooden arm-chair for the last time, and how Gramfer Matt had seen the big ship sail away the morning after Gramfer Josh died.

For a while Grandma Mona gazed at Seth lovingly and tenderly, and yet sadly.

'I'm glad they named you Seth,' she said. 'Seth was my little boy, named after my father. He was Seth, too. My little Seth went astray, I'm afraid, but his wife left a whole box full of money for you. That Hannah, she was a wild one.'

Then the vision faded to become more of a dream, and Seth woke. After that he slept fitfully, half-dreaming, and not sure of anything amidst the jumbled images. There was a young woman who looked exactly as Grandma Mona looked in the little painting as a young girl at Woodreef when that first Matt Rodda had come ashore.

But this girl did not have the rosary beads, only the crucifix, and then everything became all mixed up again with a passing vision of a man sailing away for Canada and some other people sailing away to New Zealand. And the crucifix and the beads seemed to be all drifting apart and coming together again, and Grandma Mona's voice in the background saying that her prayers would be answered.

For days Seth puzzled his head over what it could all mean. It had all been at once so vivid and yet so vague. Then he gradually began to push it all to the back of his mind and forget about it.

In that same year Ellin Rodda, of Woodreef, married her long-time sweetheart from the Caban, Eli Canavan.

10

There was an old country saying that one wedding usually led to another and, sure enough, at Eli and Ellin's wedding, Seth met Theodosia Escott from Earwear. To say that he met her would not have been strictly true in the sense that he had not known her previously. But she was working at a big house in Tenby, and this was the first time he had seen her for a couple of years, and certainly the first time that he had spoken to her properly. Seth was thirty-three at the time, so nobody could say he was too young to know his own mind, and they married a year later. The year after that Eli and Ellin's first child, Lena, was born at the Caban.

Seth and Theo's son, Jason, was born at Woodreef a few months later.

Enoch delighted in the new young lives, with two grandchildren to occupy him, but there was hardly ever a time when there was not some concern about the future and the lack of prospects, with many vague references to the possibility of emigrating. But it took much courage to set off for a foreign land with little or no money, and small mouths to be fed. It was all right for young people who were single, but for those with family responsibilities it was different.

All sorts of stories were told about life in the far-off lands, but nobody knew for sure. They knew only too well at Woodreef that one of the daftest stories to be told was not true. It came from the same source at Stepaside as the old story when somebody had received a letter from Canada. But this time it seemed that the man who had gone out from Woodreef had not only made a fortune in the gold rush but had sent much of it home. The tale lost nothing in the telling as it was passed from Stepaside to the Burrows, and from the Burrows to Earwear. From Earwear it went to Marros, and on from there to Pendine and Laugharne. By the time it reached Woodreef everybody knew that the family at Woodreef were rich. Everybody that was, except the people at Woodreef. Yet the rumour was to prove before long to be rather beneficial.

The bit of land at Smuggler's Den had gone with Woodreef ever since the time way back when Ben Knox had died up at Furlongs. Long before that Ben had taken over Smuggler's Den, so when he died, his daughter, Phoebe, married to Josh Rodda, had both lots of land put with Woodreef. The cottage at Smuggler's Den had fallen into decay so long ago that nobody could remember now when anybody had last lived there.

There were a few bullocks grazing there of a mild autumn day when Seth had gone to check on them, and he was satisfied that there would be enough grass to last them for some weeks yet. The following day Bertie Butter Jaws, the rabbit trapper from Crunwear, began setting his traps. Always happy to be the harbinger of ill-tidings, he came to Woodreef the following morning at first light to say that a bullock had fallen down the winch.

Calling to his father, Seth went straight to the Caban to collect Eli, and the three of them hurried up to Smuggler's Den. It was bad but, fortunately, not nearly as bad as Bertie Butter Jaws had suggested. A hole of a foot or so wide had opened near the pump on top of the well, and the animal's two front legs had gone right

193

down until he was resting on his breast-bone. It had been a lucky escape as long as there was no further collapse. Bertie Butter Jaws went off across the fields about his business for the day, to start picking up the rabbits caught overnight and resetting his traps, and left the three of them to start work. He would have a good story to tell as he went his rounds of the farms where he was catching.

It took best part of the day to fix up a roughly contrived gantling to take the block and tackle with the endless chain, and to work a strong sack under the animal's chest as a sling. It was well into the afternoon by the time their task was completed and, to their relief, they saw the bullock limp away apparently not much the worse for his narrow escape. It was useful to have the winch and the old pump for water for those couple of fields, but the few cattle had to be moved to another field until such time as the covering of the winch could be repaired.

Maybe it was because the October moon was shedding a wonderful light over the woodland and the fields, and bathing the valley in mysterious shadows, and maybe it was because of the winch itself, but Seth found it all so reminiscent that the memories came flooding back vividly of his two visions of Ben Scraggs, as he had always thought of the evil sailor-man, of the night he had gone down the old winch with the brass-bound box, and that other night when he would seem to have been killed. Whatever the reason, Seth felt he had to tell somebody, and the obvious person to tell was his father.

The baby Jason had been fractious, Theo had taken him into her bed to peace him, and Lily was over at the Caban. Enoch and Seth were on their own by the fire, and Enoch was in the old oak arm-chair, where his Gramfer Matt had always sat, and where he had been sitting when he told Enoch so much just before he died. And Enoch himself, a young teenager at that time, had been sitting on the old skew opposite to him where Seth was sitting now, as generations of their ancestors beyond number had sat before them. That old arm-chair, like the chair in the old song, could have told some wonderful tales if only it had been able to speak.

Lily had come in and stummed down the ball fire for the night, and it was late when Enoch and Seth went to bed. Their plan had already roughly taken shape.

Enoch had listened intently as Seth's story had unfolded. Not for one minute did he think there was anything far-fetched about it, and he thought it was good that Seth had spoken no word of it over the years.

'Aunty Ruth always reckoned you had the second sight the same as Gramfer Matt and old Josh had. By all account some of the Roddas have always had it. And Ruth knew thee better than anybody because she'd watched over thee growing up f'rall.'

'I don't know, Father. 'Tis a funny owld feelin' to have, an' yet 'twas all so clear, an' Grandma Mona was as real as if I'd knowed her all my life.'

'Ah, well. I've told thee many a time what Gramfer Matt said to me as Old Hannah said to'n. A dear owld man Gramfer Matt was. I can hear'n now saying, "She told me once when I was not much more than a bitty crut as what she had would be for me when she was gone, an' she said there was enough to make sure as I'd never want." I've towld thee as well as if what she left was ever found 'twould be thine.'

'Good God, Father! If you think there's anythin' in it there's only one way to find out.'

11

The biggest decision they had to make was whether to tell Eli. The great Benjamin Franklin, who was sometimes known as 'the wisest American', had said nearly a hundred years ago that three could keep a secret if two of them were dead, and that was no doubt still true. But Eli was family. He was married to Ellin. And another Eli Canavan, his forebear, had been a wonderful ally of the Matt Rodda who had come to Woodreef two hundred years ago. There were ties here that had lasted right down through the years and were so close that no outsider would ever understand. If Eli couldn't be trusted with such ties as bound them, then no man in this world could ever be trusted.

When they told Eli he was so matter of fact that they could scarcely believe it.

It was an ancestor of his who had helped to dig the winch. The water diviner had come and told them where they would find water. They had not gone down more than about fifteen feet when they came across a very big stone which it took them all of one day to shift. It had been a major operation, much talked about at the time, to hoist it out. That done, they went on digging, and there was a great hole left in the side of the winch where the stone had been.

Then they had gone down another twenty feet or more without striking the faintest sign of a spring. When they came up that night, one of the two men brought his pick and shovel with him and stored it in the hole where the stone had once been. The other man said there was no point in bothering, and he left his tools where they were at the bottom of the well.

'An' that,' said Eli, who had heard the story told so many times, 'is where the buggers are to this day, for when the men went to work the next mornin' the winch was full right up to thicky hole in the side, an' a've never been dry since.'

It was not an unusual story, because the same thing had been known to happen in other places where a winch had filled up overnight. The difference at Smuggler's Den was that, once the water reached the level of the bottom of the hole, it overflowed into the hole itself and soaked back down into the ground. The winch had been sunk, perhaps not all that long, before Ben Scraggs had hove-to at the cottage which, because of his activities, had soon become known as Smuggler's Den. That was in the days when there was only a wooden covering, long before the pump had been fitted. And Eli knew when that was as well. Yes,

196

Eli said, Scraggs would have known all about the convenient little hidey-hole, long since forgotten by subsequent generations.

Bertie Butter Jaws had done his job well in spreading the story of the bullock, and it did not occur to anybody within viewing distance, from near or far, that there was anything at all odd to see Enoch and Seth and Eli busy at the winch with pickaxe and shovel, ropes and a ladder.

It was Seth who went down, as dusk was falling, and came back up with Hannah's brass-bound box, mildewed and dust-encrusted, but still securely locked. And they had the key, if it would work, in which case there would be no need to smash the box open.

No word was said in the house, and after supper Enoch and Seth went out to the stable where Eli met them. The key to the box did not work, but they were patient with the application of paraffin and oil. Then, at long last, there was a click and, as the lid was lifted, they looked at each other in awed disbelief.

They had no need to start counting the money to realise that, whatever false tales Hannah might or might not have told in her lifetime, she had never said a truer word than when she had said that there was enough to make sure they would never want. Use it wisely and there would be enough to keep a few families.

'We'd best go in from here,' Enoch said. 'This is family business now, so we'll have to tell Theo.'

Later they would have to tell Ellin as well, but Enoch said to both of them in turn, 'For God in Heaven's sake don't say a mewk to a livin' sowl.'

Lily had already gone across to the Caban for the evening, but all four of the family went into the front room out of the way even so, lit the big brass lamp, and turned the key in the door.

There was no paper money in the box. Nobody was sure whether bank-notes had been introduced during Hannah's lifetime but, to judge from every story which had ever been handed down about her, it was doubtful whether she would have valued them as she did gold. Nobody, even in her own lifetime, had ever known the extent of her dealings and earnings, whether in the respectable profits from the smuggling, however illegal, or in the reprehensible harvest from highway robbery. But there would be enough in gold coinage of the realm to buy a couple of good farms and stock them. And no matter how much it was all worth it was bound to be infinitely more than when Hannah had acquired it.

The coins were mostly in sovereigns, and there were more than eight hundred of them. These had all been loose in the box, but there were also three velvet bags. In one of them there were over a hundred spade-guineas from the reign of George III. The second bag had an assortment of gold coins of much older dates and a number of Spanish doubloons. The third velvet bag was smaller, and contained more than a dozen diamonds of varying sizes. If there was not one as big as a hen's egg or anything spectacular like that, there were three which looked as if they would assuredly appeal to any discerning lady.

Late into the night they talked, until Enoch said, 'At least what we've got have been come by honestly as far as we're concerned, whichever way old Hannah came by it, and nobody'd ever be able to say about that now f'rall. But we don't take any chances. If we don't give folks cause to ask questions we won't have to tell no lies nor give no answers.'

How to dispose of the treasure safely would be a question for another day.

12

Enoch had once heard a wise old country saying, and for the life of him he could not remember who it was had said it, that if anybody told you a secret, or if anything exciting or unusual or unexpected happened, to say nothing for twenty-four hours. Keep your mouth shut for twenty-four hours. In the light of this staggering find that was much easier said than done, but all four of them were very conscious of it. They even tried not to speak of it to one another. But they all knew what the others were thinking.

Eventually Enoch wrote to the bank manager in Narberth to say that he wished to come in to discuss some business, and would he please let him know when it would be convenient. The manager wrote back to say that there were severe restrictions on lending at the moment, but he would be pleased to have a chat with Mr. Rodda next Narberth Fair Day.

Enoch said that, as far as humanly possible, they would have to take no chances of any sort of mishap on the way, so Seth and Eli went with him in the trap. Eli stayed with the horse whilst Enoch and Seth went in to do the business. They were kept waiting longer than Enoch thought might have been necessary, which was irritating, but he said to Seth, 'There's worse things happening in the Atlantic every day.'

Eventually they were ushered into The Presence, morning-suited, wing-collared, and cadaverous in appearance. He was one of those from up Carmarthen way. Some of them from up there were all right, but not Waldo Tomas. Not in Enoch's reckoning anyway. Enoch had met him no more than a couple of times and had never much cared for him, but today the world seemed a more cheerful place altogether, and he felt well disposed towards mankind in general. Even the dark mahogany of the bank's furnishings and counter seemed to sparkle with good cheer, until it brought back memories of youth and that joyous feeling of the day he had sailed off to Cornwall in the *Mary Darling* to marry Sella and bring her home. It was a shame she could not have lived to share their good fortune but, according to what they were supposed to believe, she would no doubt be praying for them and rejoicing for them where she was now in Heaven. And so would Aunty Ruth.

'They tell me trade's been slow again today, Mister Rodda,' Waldo Tomas said.

'Aye, so I've heard.'

'Oh? You haven't been selling then?'

'Not today. We've come to do business today.'

199

'Ah, business. And how can we help you?'

'Well, times are main bad as you well know, so we've decided to put our savings to better use. Gold's all right as far as it goes, but it don't earn much stored away.'

'Oh, d'you have a few sovereigns stored away then?'

'Aye, we've got a few. Nearly all sovereigns. But there's a couple of spade guineas as well.'

'Very good. Very sensible of you. Make the money work for you, however little it may be.'

'That's exactly what I said to the two boys and their wives. Look to the future.'

'So how many sovereigns and guineas do you have, Mister Rodda? A few, you said.'

Enoch turned to Seth, who had been sitting quietly and trying not to smile, and took from his hands the bag which Seth had been careful to keep out of sight on the floor beneath the manager's desk.

Seth said to Eli much later in the day, 'You've got to hand it to th'owld man. Drop dead, now. He led that bugger on a proper masterpiece.'

'We haven't put 'em all in,' Enoch said. 'We've kept a few back. Just in case, like. But between the two there's just over a thousand of 'em.'

'Good God! Where did they all come from?'

'Oh, they been in the family for years.'

The eyes of Waldo Tomas, sticking out like organ stops or, as Seth said later, 'like th' eyes of a lobster on a stalk', were riveted on the bag. Casually, with an air of utter indifference, Enoch put the bag on the desk, and stroked the coins out with his hand as though they were so much dross.

Waldo Tomas cleared his throat and said, 'This is most unusual, Mister Rodda. Most unusual.'

'How do'st thou mean, unusual?'

'Well, our function is really lending money when it comes to a sum as large as this.'

'Well, drabbit man, thou hast to have it from somewhere before thou ca'st lend it.'

'Oh, yes, yes, of course. Quite, quite. Yes indeed.'

'So thou ca'st reckon that lot up, and then we can talk about what to do with it. Then there's some much older coins and some doubloons. So what d'you reckon they'll be worth?'

'Worth?'

'Aye, worth.'

'How d'you mean, Mister Rodda, how much are they worth?'

'Well, folks reckons as they'll be worth more these days.'

'Ah, I see what you mean. Well, of course I wouldn't know about that exactly. But if you'd care to leave them with me I can have them valued for you, and we'll credit you with the full amount.'

'No, no. Don't thee bother about that. We may so well hang onto 'em.'

'Ah, I see what you mean. Yes, of course. Well maybe I could buy them from you privately. Strictly between ourselves, of course.'

'An' what do'st thou reckon as they'd be worth in that case?'

Waldo Tomas seemed to ponder before he said, 'I suppose I could give you five sovereigns each for them.'

Then, as an afterthought, he added, 'Well, maybe I could stretch a point and make it six.'

'Ah, well, we'll think about it. There's no hurry like that.'

'No, no, of course.'

It was a young clerk who came in to do the counting along with Waldo Tomas. When it had been checked yet again for a second time, the clerk withdrew and Enoch said that their intention was to place the money in three separate accounts. There would be four hundred-and-fifty in the name of his son, Seth Rodda, and four hundred-and-fifty in the name of his son-in-law, Eli Canavan. The balance would be in his own name. His son-in-law, Eli Canavan was in town, Enoch said, and would come in later to sign his name.

As Enoch said to them on the way home, they could talk about the old coins and the diamonds another day.

13

It appealed immensely to Enoch and Seth's sense of humour when Eli came over from the Caban a fortnight later to say that it was right enough after all that the people at Woodreef had just had a lot of money from the relation in Canada who had made the rich gold strike in the Klondike. Eli said he had found it hard to keep a straight face as Bertie Butter Jaws had told him all about it. A farmer where Bertie Butter Jaws had been trapping rabbits had told him, and this farmer knew because he had just come back from Narberth, and his sister's daughter was going with a clerk in the bank at Narberth, and he had told her in strict confidence that the Roddas had paid in a lot of gold sovereigns the previous week.

With a news vendor like Bertie Butter Jaws about the place, the three of them agreed that it was just as well that it was Bertie Butter Jaws who had brought the news that the bullock had fallen down the winch. Oddly enough, it was a cousin of Bertie Butter Jaws who had first brought the good news of the Klondike from Stepaside. So it only remained now to dispose of the old coins and the diamonds, and Enoch told them he had an idea about that as well.

He said that when Sella had died so young old Squire Legassick and Madame had both written to him showing great sympathy and concern, as had their son, Jonathan, who had taken over the Pembrokeshire estate. It had been evident that the whole family had had great affection for her. Apparently Sella had done some beautiful needlework for Master Jonathan's wife, and she had never failed to remember them at Christmas time. So the time had come, said Enoch, to take them up on their offer to be of help at any time. Over the years, after old Squire Legassick had died, Squire Jonathan Legassick had been highly successful in his financial affairs in London and would be more to be trusted than any bank manager or solicitor. Nobody in his right mind, Enoch said, would trust Waldo Tomas, and he remembered only too well Sella's experience as a girl even to think of going near a lawyer.

Then, before they could follow up what it was agreed was Enoch's good idea, and just as if there had not been enough excitement already, a letter came from New Zealand.

It was years since they had heard from any of the family out there, but now, here was this letter from a girl who signed herself Phoebe Randall, and who said she was trying to trace her relations 'back home'. Her grandmother was the Mona Rodda who had gone out to Australia as a girl years ago and then married a man Randall and gone to New Zealand. One of their sons was this Phoebe's father, so she had been named after her grandmother's mother, Phoebe Rodda, who had lived at Woodreef. It was simple enough to understand. Phoebe Rodda had been the wife of Josh Rodda, and within days Enoch wrote to her and told her many other things she would have wanted to know.

Within a couple of months another letter came, full of news of their farming activity out there, and how well they were doing, and the great opportunities their country offered for anybody willing to work.

'So that's it,' Enoch said. 'There've been enough talk about it for long enough. There's no future here f'rall, and the money won't last for ever.'

'Would you come with us, Father?' Seth said.

'Think thee about it first for thyselves. 'Tis something for them with their lives before 'em. I'm sixty now f'rall. That's no sort of age to be uprooting. But 'twould be a wonderful chance for the rest of thee.'

For days practically nothing else was talked about, and Enoch went as far as to promise that, if the four of them went out with the two small children, maybe he would think about going out to join them later on if everything went well.

One evening when they were talking about it Enoch opened the big family Bible at random and put his finger on a text, as had ever been the custom with the old people in days gone by, and the verse on which he put his finger was Matthew 25: verse 14, which said, 'For the kingdom of heaven is as a man travelling into a far country, . . .' It seemed to be a fair omen.

There was another consideration, too. Nan's husband, up in the coalfields of the valleys, had started to cough, and the doctor had told him the best thing for him to do would be to go to live in the country. That, normally, would have been no easy or simple matter, but it would be a Heaven-sent opportunity now for him to do that, for Nan to come home, and bring two grandchildren to replace the two little ones going off to New Zealand. Enoch had been dreading that loss more than he would ever have told them.

'I suppose really,' Enoch said, 'God knows His business better than we do. But then, of course, that's not surprising, because He've been around a lot longer than we have f'rall.'

Apart from the thought of Nan and her family coming home, there was still the ever cheerful, ever faithful Lily, and there was Eli's family at the Caban. There would still be plenty of young life and plenty of help.

Squire Jonathan Legassick had been away in London when Enoch wrote to him. Eventually there was a reply from the Agent who said that the Squire would look forward to seeing him the next time he was back in Pembrokeshire, which would be in a couple of months. There was more than enough money to give them a start in New Zealand, and they knew they could rely on Enoch to realise the best possible price for the rest of Hannah's treasure.

Then everything was suddenly all bustle and excitement. Theo's sister and her husband came up from the Burrows, and prayers were said, and the house seemed to be always full of people. And they had to take with them the lovely picture of Woodreef which had been painted so long ago, just as a reminder. Enoch also insisted that they should take the family Bible, with all the names written in it, and Seth said they had to take the rosary beads because old Grandma Mona had them in her hand when she had appeared to him in the vision, and the tradition was that they had meant so much to her.

So it was, after all the tears and the laughter and the excitement that, in the year 1912, the two young families sailed off into a new life in a new land.

14

Sailed off would not perhaps be the exact term compared with the pioneers of old, who had taken their chance on board the great sailing ships, because nowadays they sailed on grand ocean liners. Suffice it to say that the new emigrants prospered in New Zealand. They all had a good farming background, they were all prepared to work, and they had enough money to ensure that they had a good start. To make matters even better, word came from Enoch of the excellent deal for the old coins and the diamonds which Squire Jonathan Legassick had arranged for him, and they all had their share.

In due course, when they grew up, having gone out as not much more than babes-in-arms, Jason Rodda married Lena Canavan, whose mother had been a Rodda anyway, and it was Lena who was reckoned by the family to have inherited the Rodda's gift of second sight if anybody had.

During the second World War news came that the apparently indestructible old Enoch had died in his ninetieth year, so neither he nor his son, Seth, managed the nine hundred and sixty nine years of Methuselah in the Bible. From there on there was little or no news of the family at Woodreef.

Jason and Lena had a large family, and I, Matthew Rodda, born in 1955, was the youngest of them.

EPILOGUE

1

It has been said more than once about something or other in life that if you put it in a book people wouldn't believe it. Well, all right then, in that case don't believe it. All I know is that I am going Home.

What is more I am far more excited than when I set off from New Zealand for what I had foolishly thought of as Home. Maybe that was because I had been brought up listening to all the old, old stories and had fondly imagined that Woodreef was Home.

I am sitting in my hotel in Tenby writing this before setting back off for what I know now to be Home, and Woodreef and Earwear and all the rest of it has turned out to be a fair cow as we say down under.

I wrote at the beginning that I needed a good holiday. I saw no need to write any more, and it would have been difficult to find the words anyway. At that time I had been a widower for just over twelve months. For five years I had been married to my beautiful Kiri. Her mother had been half Maori, and her father a third generation New Zealander from original Pembrokeshire stock. I was not yet forty, and Kiri was in her early thirties, when it seemed we were to be blessed at last with our first child. Then it happened.

A policeman came to the house to drive me to the hospital, and told me only that Kiri had been involved in an accident. I tried hard to prepare myself for the worst, which was maybe as well, because by the time we reached the hospital Kiri was dead. They told me later that she had been dead on arrival. The fact that it had been nobody's fault was neither of consequence nor consolation, and I do not intend to write any more about it. The parents of the little girl Kiri had tried in vain to save from drowning have already suffered more than enough.

People were marvellous to me. Well, some of them were, and I certainly found out who my friends were. It was not long before some of them were trying to find a wife for me. The best advice I had was from our chapel minister who said to do nothing for twelve months. The twelve months were up when I finished writing what I had promised Mother I would write, and the writing was a great therapy. Call it escapism if you like. Then I set off for the long-delayed holiday to talk to the old people over here and fill in the gaps.

Although I had been so familiar with the names, which all my life had been a part of my very being, I realised when I arrived here that they were in fact no more than names to me. So the obvious place to stay seemed to be the holiday seaside town of Tenby, and this is where I made my base. In the month of May there was no difficulty in finding accommodation. Come to that, most of those to whom I have spoken bemoan what has happened to the holiday trade and assure me that it would be just as easy in the height of the season.

I mentioned at the beginning about the chap with the metal detector who had found the silver buttons, and I had written to tell him I was coming. I telephoned him the evening I arrived and he said he would be delighted to come to dinner with me the following evening and would bring the buttons with him.

I walked round the town next morning and enquired in a couple of shops if anybody could tell me where Woodreef was. Nobody had ever heard of such a place. Perhaps I should not have been too surprised, but it came as something of a shock to find that neither had anybody heard of Earwear or the Burrows. Then I came across the bus station and found that it was no more than a ten or fifteen minute journey by bus to Saundersfoot. So rather than bother with the car I went there by bus.

I had some vague notion of trying to find the house where Esther and Arthur Giles had lived, but it did not take long for me to realise that I was wasting my time. I had this fond picture of Saundersfoot as a pleasant little seaside village. Indeed, I had seen many attractive postcard pictures of it from the days before the first World War when Gramfer Seth and Eli and their families had left for New Zealand. Now it was far worse than anything I could ever have imagined. I chatted to a few people, who were all friendly enough, but not one of them had been born in the place.

The harbour was no more than a couple of hundred yards from the bus stop and the awful gaming machines and blaring noise, which according to taste might have been classed as music. And it was when I reached the harbour that I realised the cloud cuckoo land in which I had been living. The picture I had in my mind had been painted for me by the words of those who had known it a hundred years ago, when it had been a busy little port, exporting coal, with coastal traders and a few fishing boats. Now it was all spanking white motor launches and yachts, with their radio aerials and what-not, and characters with pseudo sailors' caps strutting about the place, and it was all a million miles from any likeness to the *Mary Darling* on which Enoch had sailed away to Cornwall to marry Sella more than a hundred years ago.

Meeting Gad Skyrme could in many ways have been the highlight of my trip had it not been for what was to come later. His name was pure Pembrokeshire, everything about him was Pembrokeshire, and the thought occurs now that he was about the only real Pembrokeshire person I was to meet. It was refreshing beyond words that evening when he came breezing in to the hotel foyer. A broad shouldered man, not quite as tall as I am, he was in his early sixties, with a weather beaten face, and dark crinkly hair going grey at the temples. From the moment he shook hands with a firm handshake I knew that we were kindred spirits.

When I told him I had been to Saundersfoot he laughed his infectious laugh and said, 'Good God, how did you want to go out there?'

'Don't you like Saundersfoot?'

'Aye, Saundersfoot! The home port of the Birmingham navy.'

It set the tone for much of his conversation.

'Did you have any trouble booking in here?' he said.

'None at all.'

'No wonder. The whole area's plastered with caravans, and every other house is a second home for some bugger from off. All part of the joys of the place being designated a National Park. It's no wonder the hotels are half-empty most of the time. Half the houses empty in winter and then a heap of dull talk about a housing shortage.'

Having worked hard to build up his own business in agricultural plant hire and contracting, he had much to say on the state of the economy, with its burden of the bureaucrats which the self-employed had to carry. The way he told it he made it sound humorous, but there was a serious side to what he had to say, and he had an almost apologetic air when he talked about Europe and the way Britain had betrayed the farmers of New Zealand.

I knew what Gad, as I was soon calling him, was trying to say, because our own family's money is in a successful agricultural merchants' business as well as a few farms. Metal detecting, apparently, was his one hobby and relaxation, and over dinner he told me of some of his interesting finds. We had a bottle of good wine to go with our meal, and then, the meal over, he put his hand in his pocket and took out the two silver buttons and put them on the table.

I picked them up and handled them in disbelief. As with the pair which had been handed down in our family over the years, the letters G.G. were embossed on them, surrounded by the intricate pattern of a crown and a sword.

'How much do you want for them?' I said.

'Do your pair match 'em, d'you reckon?'

I took from my pocket the pair of buttons, which had been cut from the coat of Gervaise Gideon so long ago, and passed them to him. Gad Skyrme gazed at them in his hand and said, 'Tell me all about 'em.'

I ordered a pot of coffee and a couple of brandies, and we went into the lounge and talked for a long time. It was late by the time I had told him the full story of all those who had gone before, and I did not think that 'Young' Matt would have minded too much about my telling of his part in it.

At the end of it all there was no talk of payment. Gad belonged to some metal detecting society whose members prided themselves on their integrity. As far as he was concerned he was returning the buttons to their rightful owner, and all he asked was that when I went home I would write a piece about them for their magazine.

It was encouraging to learn that Gad also had an interest in local history. He had found the silver buttons, along with many others of different types, on the beach at Crickdam, so he was able to tell me where that was, and he knew a fair bit about Earwear and the Burrows as well. Nowadays, he said, they were simply known as Amroth.

On the question of Woodreef he was not too sure, but he had a rough idea as to where it was because he knew exactly where to find the remains of the oil-works. The way he spoke made it sound as if there would not be anybody living at Woodreef these days, and certainly not at the Caban.

The upshot of our talk was that he said he had to go to Carmarthen the following day and it would be no trouble to take the coast road and drop me off on the way. With a few succinct words about the breathalyser and the local gendarmerie he declined any idea of 'one for the road', and told me to be ready at half-past-eight the following morning. I could, he said, get a bus back to Tenby from Amroth, or even Pendine should I decide to go on as far as Morfabychan.

The hotel proprietors were happy to provide a splendid early breakfast and a packed lunch. On the stroke of half-past-eight Gad Skyrme walked in through the door and I went forth with him to that which my mother had predicted for me. No wonder I said at the beginning it was too ridiculous to write it all down. But I reckon she had the second sight all right.

His plan, Gad said, was to put me on the right track from Marros, and afterwards, on the way back, I could see all I wanted to of what had once been Earwear.

He was as good as his word and cheerful company, pointing out so many landmarks, the names of which were familiar to me, as we went. He slowed down as we passed the New Inn, where the first Matt Rodda had that splendid breakfast when he came ashore. Although he had lived in the area all his life, however, and had a great interest in such things, he had never heard of Squire Elliot's tunnel.

There was no need to tell me when we had reached Hannah's Plain because there was a sign there proclaiming a camping site in the field adjoining the road.

We had gone far beyond Telpyn when Gad turned inland down a farm track and eventually stopped by a gate into a field which sloped down towards a wood. He told me where to pick up the stream, and assured me that if I followed that it would take me to what was left of the oil-works. As far as he knew, Woodreef would be some way well beyond that. He also promised to tell the good people at the farm who I was and what I was doing there. For my part, I promised him I would let him know how I fared.

In a dense part of the wood, much overgrown and difficult of access, I found the oven, and the rusting iron pipes and tank of the long abandoned oil-works, so I was happy that I was heading in the right direction. From there, remembering the details of the stories we had been told over the years, I followed my sense of direction until I came to a field of rough growth in the corner of which was all that was left of what must have been at one time a substantial little house or cottage, with an overgrown area which had been a garden. Something in my mind from all I had ever heard told me it was the Caban.

I stood and looked about me and saw little but a valley of eternal conifers. There was the sound of chain saws and tree-felling going on somewhere in the distance, but this forest with its depressing, sterile darkness would know nothing of the wildlife which had thrived there when Matt Rodda arrived nearly three hundred years ago, nor would it provide any sort of living for cottage dwellers.

It was with mixed feelings that I headed for where I believed I would find Woodreef, sick at heart, because I had seen enough to realise that the whole area had long since been abandoned and deserted by those who had ever lived there, yet my heart was thumping for reasons I could never have explained. Crossing a small stream, which I sensed could not have been the site of Ben Scraggs' demise, I climbed a steep track until I came to another rough field. In the bottom corner the crumbling remains of the house and buildings told their own dejected story. It was clearly the Woodreef of the lovely old painting, but drawing closer I realised that I had approached from the opposite direction from that in which Matt had come when he came ashore from the *Cornish Princess*.

There were primroses in the hedges, and the old cabbage rose still struggled for survival. There were the damson trees, and there was even a gnarled old apple tree with blossoms on it, and a red-breasted apple-bird was enjoying himself amongst them. Further down there was a chestnut tree in bud and my mind was far away as I wondered whether that could have been the tree from which Ruth so long ago had picked the horse chestnuts to show Gramfer Seth and his father Enoch before him how to play conkers.

Then, close behind me, a gentle voice said, 'Excuse me . . .' and I turned, and there stood the beautiful Mona Barlow who had married Matt Rodda and become Grandma Mona of all the stories which had been handed down to countless generations since.

In one blinding moment I recognised her from the painting on the miniature. And I knew that I would love this girl and would willingly follow her to the ends of the earth.

When, a little later, she told me her story it was small wonder that she should have broken off in mid-sentence as I turned and she stood staring at me.

She was not dressed as the Mona of old, but wore well-cut pale blue jeans and a close-fitting jumper of a slightly darker shade. Over her arm she carried a lightweight jacket, and a hold-all was slung over her shoulder. There the difference ended, for the grey blue eyes, the light brown hair, the forehead, the chin, the dimples and, above all, the shining goodness and gentleness, were gazing straight out at me from the miniature.

We stared at each other for so long that, as a slight colour rose to her cheeks, it became a question of who would be the first to speak, and then, hardly knowing what I was saying, I said, 'Are you really Mona?'

She laughed, and then she said, 'In that case, you must be Matt Rodda. Are you really Matt Rodda?'

I stared at her in disbelief, and all I could say was, 'How would you know that?'

'You're not going to believe this, but my grandmother was a Rodda and she had the family's second sight.'

'Yes, I've heard a fair bit about the Roddas' second sight,' I said.

Then, as we talked, she told me how her namesake, Grandma Mona, who had been born at Woodreef, had been a devout Catholic in days when that had been dangerous, and had treasured her rosary beyond words. Many years later, she said, a Tom Rodda had gone out to Canada, and she still had the beautiful little crucifix he had brought with him. He had married an Irish Catholic girl he had met on the boat going over.

'I'm a descendant of theirs,' she said, 'and my grandmother told me not long before she died that if I wanted Grandma Mona's rosary I would have to go to Woodreef myself and maybe Matt Rodda would give it to me.'

Like some sort of fool I said, 'So this really is Woodreef then?'

'I suppose it must be. But that was what I was going to ask you when you turned round and stared at me, gaping like a landed fish.'

Then we both started to laugh at something which was beyond

214

the comprehension of either of us, and from there on our conversation was easy.

I told her then of Gramfer Seth's vision when Grandma Mona had appeared to him, and how it had brought him comfort. Mona had the crucifix which had gone to Canada, and I had the rosary which Gramfer Seth had taken to New Zealand with him. It was with Mother's possessions when she died, and she had been with Kiri and me for the last months of her life. Sella's wedding ring was there as well, along with the locket and gold chain which Enoch had given her.

It would be tedious to go over all the stories which we exchanged, for it seemed that the Roddas in Canada had handed them down just as faithfully as those who went out to New Zealand. She told me later of the harum scarum Jack Rodda, and the Rodda who struck gold in the Klondike and soon spent his way through it all. So the talk went on and the time sped by until I said, 'I'm hungry.'

'Come to think of it,' Mona said, 'so am I.'

She, too, had brought a picnic and we found a shady spot and shared our first meal together. At twenty-eight years of age, Mona was twelve years younger than I was, and she said she was a nurse. She had been staying in Haverfordwest where she had spent some time in the Records Office, only to find that many of the registers and records she wanted to consult were in Carmarthen. Then I told her of all the playful arguments Mother and Father used to have as to which was the County from which their families had come, until we decided it was time to explore. But first of all Mona said she would take a picture of what was left of the old place for what it was worth and would I stand in front of it. So she took the picture and seemed to fumble a bit in doing it.

Down by the lake we went then until we found the crossing where the pompren of Ben Scraggs' day would have been, so then I had to tell her that story, and we found the ruins of cottages, the leaves of daffodils and snowdrops which had bloomed in the spring, stray gooseberry and currant bushes, and flowers which still fought for survival somehow, and brighter parts of woodland where bluebells bloomed.

The afternoon was well advanced when we came to a damp patch where I offered Mona my hand, and then we walked on without her making any effort to take her hand away. When we came to a fallen tree which barred our way I had to help her over, and as I eased her to the ground I took her in my arms and kissed her. Nor did she try to resist exactly, and I said, 'Will you marry me?'

She gave a shy and nervous laugh and said, 'It's a bit sudden, isn't it?'

'Not if all those Roddas with the second sight have got it right.'

'Would you give me Grandma Mona's rosary?' she laughed.

'Would that mean I'd have to become a Catholic?'

She held me at arms length and said, 'Don't be stupid. That's got nothing to do with me. If God wants you for a Catholic He'll have you. And what does it matter about anybody being a Catholic or not anyway? It's the same God for all of us.'

'Ah, well,' I said, 'if you want the rosary you'll have to come to New Zealand.'

'I suppose I could do worse than that', she said.

'Yes, but you haven't answered my question yet. Will you marry me?'

'Don't rush me,' she said. 'It's all quite ridiculous anyway. Ask me again tomorrow'

I shall not write much of the rest of the afternoon, because I am still old-fashioned enough to believe that what passes between a man and a woman is private and very much their own business. But later on, when we had collected our belongings, we walked up by what we both felt must have been the remains of Hannah's cottage to where Mona had left her hired car at Hannah's Plain.

'One thing I want to do,' I said, 'is have a look at what was once Earwear mansion.'

Mona put her hand on my arm and said, 'Matt, don't spoil your dreams. I've been there and it's awful. One thing I wanted

216

to do was to find the lovely chapel window where Matt once found Grandma Mona praying with her rosary. I wanted to say a prayer there, too, but the vandalism broke my heart. I could have cried. I said my prayer, though, just the same. For the repose of the souls of all those who have prayed there in the past, and for those who could have allowed such a thing to happen.'

And so we left Woodreef. For neither of us had it been the homecoming of our dreams, but for both of us it had far surpassed anything from our wildest dreams. There was no question of either of us having the Roddas' second sight, yet it had all been foretold with uncanny accuracy by those who did have it.

When she dropped me off outside my hotel Mona declined to come in for a meal because she said the landlady of the small private hotel where she was staying in Haverfordwest would have a meal waiting for her. But I arranged to call for her the following morning and take her to see something of our 'native county.'

3

I telephoned Gad Skyrme that evening and he asked me how I had fared. I told him that even without the aid of his metal detector I had found a greater treasure than any silver buttons, and promised to let him know all about it later. For his part he had made enquiries on the local grape-vine, as he called it, and the word was that Woodreef and the Caban had recently been bought by people 'from off' who intended to rebuild the house and do something with the land. That was all he knew, but it was encouraging. If locals were not interested, then let somebody else have a go.

Although I had hardly known a good night's sleep ever since my Kiri had died so tragically, that night I slept the untroubled sleep of a newborn baby, and there was not the slightest hint of a vision of any sort. Not for me the second sight of the Roddas.

Mona's dear face was before me as I fell asleep, and it was still there when I woke. That was vision enough for me.

It was early breakfast again in the morning, but there was no need for any packed lunch. Mona was waiting for me on the pavement as I pulled up, and she looked even more breathtakingly beautiful than the previous day. There were people about, but I saw no reason why I should not take her in my arms and kiss her.

'Now that's enough of that,' she said. 'Let's go.'

'Where d'you want to go?'

'Get in the car and I'll tell you.'

Mona had been in the area for nearly a week and was due to leave the following day. She had already had a week in Ireland looking for family, where she had drawn a blank, but loved the magic of the Celtic atmosphere. There were, as I had already discovered, none of our family left in these parts, and now, before she left, she wanted to see something of what would have been the culture of Pembrokeshire in the years of long ago. For that reason we headed for St. David's and the beautiful Cathedral there. I will not write about it, because it is all there in the history books and the guide books for those who want to know. Suffice it to say that Mona was spellbound, whilst I was deliriously happy just to be with her.

Later in the day we drove south above the beautiful sea-girt cliffs, stopped for a meal at a wayside inn and eventually, as the sun was sinking in the west, in a wide, wide sunset beyond the far horizon, came by way of narrow lanes and flower-bestrewed, high-banked hedges, to the remote creek of St. Bride's where there was a lovingly maintained little church.

For all that we had been nurtured as children on stories of the family and the past, and descriptions of places, nothing had ever prepared me for coming upon antiquity such as this. Mona, too, looked and looked without saying anything, and I guessed that she would no doubt be thinking the same sort of thoughts. The little church was open, too, and the stillness and sense of peace were unbelievable. Then, at last, Mona began to enthuse about the windows.

'D'you know, Matt,' she said, 'you could bring children in here to teach them the Scriptures. There's Our Lady with Our Lord. There you have Prophet, Priest and King. That's the Holy Vine, and the Good Shepherd. And look! There are the three great Angels, Gabriel, Michael and Raphael. Oh, Matt, isn't it all just beautiful?'

A leaflet told something of the history, but no words could ever describe the overpowering feeling of antiquity, or the intense spirituality of such a remote sanctuary, where people had prayed, or so it seemed, since time began. Men and women of the soil they would have been, and no doubt many of them those who had gone down to the sea in ships. I noticed Mona put a five-pound note in the box and felt that I had to follow her good example.

When we were outside again we stood together and looked back at the old, old grey stonework, and the slated roof.

'I know those lovely windows are fairly recent,' Mona said, 'but the story is as old as the hills.'

'Not a Catholic Church, though,' I said, by way of teasing her.

'What!' she said, 'Twelfth century not Catholic? It would have been Catholic right enough in those days. That was all they knew. And you can say the same for that lovely Cathedral today.'

We sat on the green turf beyond the wall of the trim churchyard then, as the sea lapped gently on the sandy shore, and gulls above us made their leisurely way in the evening sunset towards the off-shore islands. Everywhere there was that same great sense of peace. Then Mona said, 'Matt, you're very shy and slow today compared with your rush of blood to the head yesterday.'

'How d'you mean?'

'Well, I'm going back to Canada tomorrow, and I want to know where I stand before I go. Aren't you going to ask me to marry you?'

'I asked you yesterday and you said you'd give me your answer today.'

'Nothing of the sort. I said to ask me again tomorrow.'

'Oh.'

'What's the matter? Changed your mind? Cold feet?'

'Do you mean you'll marry me?'

'No, I don't mean that. I just wanted to be sure you hadn't changed your mind.'

I took her hand, and she said, 'I'll tell you something. When I took that picture of you yesterday I was really shaken.'

She sensed my puzzlement, and said, 'I'll tell you. But don't laugh. Ever since my grandmother told me about coming over here to fetch Grandma Mona's rosary, and for years before that, I've had a picture of some man who would come into my life. And always I would push it into the background because I don't believe we should dabble in that sort of thing. Then yesterday when I saw your image isolated in the view-finder, I nearly dropped the camera.'

'Don't tell me you're another of them with this Rodda second sight.'

'I don't know what you call it. But whatever it is it shook me above a bit.'

4

So here I am in my hotel in Tenby, and tomorrow I shall be on my way. When Mona had returned her car I drove her to Carmarthen to catch the train for London, and by now she will be in the air and bound for Canada.

I learned enough from my talks with Gad Skyrme to know that the farming here is so strangled by officialdom that it would have nothing to teach us, but maybe I shall drive to Cardiff and go to see the famous Arms Park rugby ground. There will be no rugby there, but I would like to say I have been there. Then I shall drive to London to return the car and try to see at least one day's cricket at Lord's. After that I shall be on my way.

There is nothing to keep me here now. As Mona said after her fruitless search in Ireland and our own experiences during our couple of days together, there is no point in trying to go back. We are living in the here and now, and the future is ahead of us. There are business and farming matters to attend to as well, apart from the fact that Daniel, the springer spaniel, will be wondering where I am. He was Kiri's dog really, and ever something of a lady's man. He has pined for her terribly, and I reckon he will be giving Mona a really exciting welcome. For nothing can be more sure than that she will be coming back to me. She can have the rosary, and Sella's gold locket and chain, and anything else she wants. And I'll write to tell her she can even be married with Sella's wedding ring. That should tempt her if she still can't make up her mind.

Never have I felt more sure of anything. It's one of those crazy Rodda experiences all over again. There was no firm promise from her before we parted. No commitment. But her business with the camera was nothing to what has shaken me.

Lonely beyond words as her train pulled out of sight, I wandered round Carmarthen town without seeing anything. At last, when the afternoon was well advanced, I headed back for Tenby by the coast road from St Clears. I had a good map and identified all the places the names of which had long been familiar to me. Laugharne, Pendine, Marros. For how long had they been the happy hunting ground of so many of those whose names had come down to me over the years?

I had eaten nothing since breakfast, and at Laugharne I treated myself to an evening meal to remember. I drove on then through Pendine and eventually past Marros Church. As I drove slowly down Telpyn hill I came in sight of Caldey across the bay, and the sun was sinking in the west, just as how Mother had always sung about it.

Why, I do not know, but at Hannah's Plain I felt I had to stop for one last long look at a place which had figured so largely in the lives of forebears of mine beyond number. So I left the car and walked up the bank to the bluff of Dolman Head, and there I sat as the sun sank below the hill behind Saundersfoot.

Long after the sun had gone down did I sit, thinking of all the stories that had come down to me. How long I could not say, but the light was fading and the moon had risen over Gower Peninsula in the distance. How often had such a scene featured in the lives and stories of the Roddas, with the moon spreading a clear swath across the water?

Then I saw her. No more than a distant blur at first, the great ship began to take shape and her rigging became clear as she sailed on towards me. Towards Dolman Head, near where the Blackhorn caves had once been, and where Matt Rodda had come ashore three centuries ago. And if her rigging was not the rigging of the *Cornish Princess* then all the stories which had come down to us had been so much nonsense and meant nothing. At last the great ship was in so close I could see a figure standing on the fore-deck, and I could see it was Mona, because there was a beautiful light shining round her, and I knew with a certainty that no words of mine could describe that she was coming back to me.

I woke with a start, and my limbs were stiff with the cold of the summer night.

'Man proposes, but God disposes.' I came here in need of a good long holiday and intending to have one,

Half to forget the wandering and the pain,
Half to remember days that have gone by,
And dream and dream that I am home again.

No ship was there, but the sorrows of the past year were behind me and there was a great gladness in my heart. For I knew I was going Home.